GOOSEBERRY JAM

There was no help for it—he *had* to kiss her. He wondered briefly if he could be cruel so soon after her terrifying experience . . .

His arm tightened about her, and he brought his face down, watching closely for a sign of dismay or resistance. But Jenny remained motionless, gazing up at him with a surprised, almost trance-like expression. "Jenny?" he whispered softly.

"Yes?" It was the merest breath.

"Have you another jar of jam on your person?"

She blinked. "What a strange question. Why?"

"Because I'm afraid I must kiss you, and I want to be certain that I shan't be crowned with gooseberry jam for my pains . . ."

Berkley books by Elizabeth Mansfield

THE COUNTERFEIT HUSBAND
DUEL OF HEARTS
THE FIFTH KISS
THE FROST FAIR
HER HEART'S CAPTAIN
HER MAN OF AFFAIRS
MY LORD MURDERER
THE PHANTOM LOVER
A REGENCY CHARADE
A REGENCY MATCH
REGENCY STING
THE RELUCTANT FLIRT
A VERY DUTIFUL DAUGHTER

Elizabeth Mansfield

Her Heart's Captain

BERKLEY BOOKS, NEW YORK

HER HEART'S CAPTAIN

A Berkley Book / published by arrangement with
the author

PRINTING HISTORY
Berkley edition / January 1983

ISBN: 0-425-05501-9

A BERKLEY BOOK ® TM 757,375
Berkley Books are published by Berkley Publishing Corporation,
200 Madison Avenue, New York, New York 10016.
The name "BERKLEY" and the stylized "B" with design
are trademarks belonging to Berkley Publishing Corporation.
PRINTED IN THE UNITED STATES OF AMERICA

Her Heart's Captain

Chapter One

It simply never occurred to Jenny Garvin that her brother could be less than perfect. She had always—from the time the boy was born, when she was only six—accepted and concurred with her mother's evaluation of him. Robbie was the most brilliant, handsome and charming of boys—that was Lady Garvin's assessment of her son, and Jenny knew of nothing in Robbie's character, appearance or demeanor to give her the slightest doubt of the truth of that evaluation. It was that sublime confidence that both the Garvin ladies placed in the lad that caused them to accept without question the reports in his letters from his ship. And that unshakable belief in the accuracy of his words led directly to the misunderstanding which was so direly to threaten Jenny's own happiness.

For the fourteen years of his life, Robert Garvin had been the apple of his mother's eye and his sister's pride. The boy was affectionate, clever, fun-loving, generous and universally popular. There had never been a bad word said of him—not by a single member of the household at Willowrise, not by any of his many companions and not by the inhabitants of the village of Wyndham in Gloucester where they lived. And though the masters at Harrow (where Robbie had been spending the better part of the last two years) had sometimes written letters of complaint, Lady Garvin and her daughter did not pay them much heed. Schoolmasters were notoriously prissy, Lady Garvin was convinced, and they were not in the least capable of understanding the "special quality" of a boy of Robbie's high spirits and superior nature; she simply threw their letters of complaint into the wastebasket. The boy was a *paragon*; she would brook no argument on that score. And no one, least of all Jenny, saw fit to contradict her.

Except the old earl. Alistair Garvin, Earl of Wetherbrooke, though a bachelor, was the head of the family and the guardian of his late brother's two children. But only on matters of business did he intervene in their upbringing. Irascible and reclusive, the old earl left his Yorkshire castle as infrequently as possible and never entertained the family in his domicile. He met with his sister-in-law only when absolutely necessary to discuss financial problems or when they were forced to attend family funerals, but on those rare occasions, he never failed to comment disparagingly on Robbie's character. "Peacocky and spoilt," he would declare to Lady Garvin's face. "Your boy's peacocky and spoilt, and you'll never cure him 'til you recognize that fact."

"How *dare* you!" Lady Garvin would remonstrate violently. "You barely know the boy, not having seen him over half-a-dozen times in all these years. So how dare you take it upon yourself to criticize—?"

"Don't need to take more'n one bite of an apple to tell it's rotten," the earl would cut in. "I know the boy well enough. Anyone can see that you push him too much in the sun and your girl too much in the shade. I don't see why you view your daughter as second-best. You'll be the ruination of both of 'em, mark my words."

But Lady Garvin didn't mark his words at all. He only said those things to irritate her, because he was, by nature, a quarrelsome old nuisance. He'd never liked her, even when her husband had first brought her to meet him, twenty-three years ago. It had been just after she and William had been wed, and the earl had peered at her over the dinner table with such intensity that she'd felt as nervous as a mouse. She'd stammered, dropped her fork and giggled at everything the gentlemen had said. "Ninnyhammer," the earl had muttered in condemnation, and, as far as she knew, he'd never changed his mind about her since. If that was how he made his judgments of people—so abruptly and on so little evidence—how could anyone take such judgments seriously?

Lady Garvin always put the earl's words out of her mind as soon as she was out of his sight. His lordship might have control of the purse strings, but she ran her household as she saw fit. Since the earl was generous in matters of money and sought no control over her family, his insults merely slid from her mind as easily as droplets from the feathers of a duck. Her children were superior beings, both of them. Well, perhaps Jenny was a bit too retiring, but no one could tell her that Robbie wasn't a *nonpareil*.

Jenny herself had never been present during her mother's altercations with the old earl and so was unaware of any criticism of her brother from that quarter. As far as she knew, her Uncle Alistair gave little thought to her brother's existence and even less to her own.

Thus it came as a complete shock to both Jenny and her mother when the elderly earl appeared on their threshold one rainy forenoon in March, shouting from the doorway in a hoarse, irritable voice that they had better come down from wherever they were hiding and attend him in the library at once. They flew down the stairs in alarm to find him thrusting his hat and greatcoat into the arms of the openmouthed butler. "Alistair!" Lady Garvin gasped. "What *is* it?"

The earl glared at her, turned on his heel and strode down the hall to the library, not even casting a glance over his shoulder at the two flustered females who hurried after him. As soon as they'd all entered the room, he wheeled about abruptly. "Shut the door!" he ordered.

Jenny did his bidding while her mother gaped at her visitor in speechless apprehension.

"Do you know where I've been?" he demanded of his sister-in-law accusingly.

"Where you've *been*? How can I know—?"

"I've been to *Harrow*! Yes, Harrow! Three days in a draughty coach, three nights in uncomfortable, overpriced inns, and all because of your rapscallion son!"

"Robbie? You've been to see *Robbie*?" Lady Garvin paled, her hand flew to her breast, and she wavered on her feet. "Good God, the boy's *ill*!"

"No, Mama, that's not it," Jenny said quietly, slipping a supporting arm about her mother's waist while at the same time keeping her gaze fixed on her uncle's face. "Robbie's not ill. That's not what Uncle Alistair's come to tell us."

"Of course it ain't," the earl muttered, casting a quick, approving glance at his niece's face. "The girl seems to be the only one in this family with a dab o' sense. If the boy'd been ill, they wouldn't have notified *me*, would they? Not likely. It's his mother they'd have sent for. That's what you inferred, eh, lass?"

Jenny nodded. "That, and your calling Robbie a rapscallion." She led her agitated mother to the sofa. "Has he been involved in some mischief, Uncle? Is that what you've come to tell us?"

Lady Garvin sagged upon the cushions in relief. "Oh, is *that* all? Really, Alistair, it was most unkind of you to frighten me so badly over such a trifle."

His lordship stamped his foot in annoyance. "Trifle? Do you think I'd travel from Yorkshire to Harrow, and then to London and back to Harrow, and finally to Gloucester because of a *trifle*? You, woman, are a scatter-brained ninnyhammer. You were a ninnyhammer when my brother married you, and a ninnyhammer you remain!"

"And you, sir," Lady Garvin retorted with spirit, "were a curmudgeon from the first and will be to the last!"

"I think Uncle Alistair is merely showing signs of being travel-worn," Jenny put in soothingly. "Shall I order some hot tea for you, Uncle? Or a brandy, perhaps?"

"Thank you, girl," Alistair said in gruff appreciation, dropping into a wing chair, "a bit o' brandy would not be amiss."

As Jenny left to find the butler, Alistair looked after her with a softened expression. "Your girl, I must admit, has a touch o' rare sweetness," he murmured grudgingly. "Why ain't you married her off?"

"It's not *my* fault," Lady Garvin said, always on the defensive with her brother-in-law. "I offered her a come-out. I would have sent her to my friend, Millicent Hopgood, in London, who would have been quite happy to supervise the affair. But Jenny refused. Absolutely refused. She said she wouldn't have been comfortable going about in society under the protection of strangers."

"Then *you* should've taken her. You're her mother, ain't you?"

"You know my digestion is too delicate to endure the excitement of managing a London come-out. Besides, Jenny says she's quite happy in the country with me."

"Too shy, eh?"

"She's not shy, exactly. A little retiring, perhaps—"

"Too shy I say. I've always told you that you keep her too much in the shade. She'll wind up on the shelf if you don't push her forward a bit."

Lady Garvin drew herself up to her full height (which was two inches higher than the earl's) and, with her ample bosom heaving in annoyance, glared at him. "I don't see why you think *I'm* to blame for everything that goes wrong. After all, Jenny's nature is more like her father's than like mine. William was a quiet one, you know. Never liked to put himself forward. And Jenny has many of his qualities."

"Yes, modesty, good sense, and a pair o' speakin' eyes. Don't see that any of those qualities should keep her from findin' a husband."

"See here, Alistair, there's no need to behave as if she were an ape-leader. After all, the girl's just past twenty. There's plenty of time—"

But Jenny came back at that moment and caused the disputants to drop the subject. She was followed by the butler, Cullum, who placed a decanter of brandy and a glass on a small table at the earl's elbow and immediately withdrew. Jenny took a seat beside her mother on the sofa and looked at her uncle expectantly. "Have you already told Mama why you've come?"

"No, girl. Waited for you." He poured himself a generous drink and took a swig before commencing. "I was informed, ma'am, that you've been ignorin' the communications from Harrow concernin' your son. Ain't you in the least concerned about his scholastic achievements?"

"Concerned?" Lady Garvin's brows rose pridefully. "Of course not. Robbie is a brilliant student. His tutors always described him so, did they not, Jenny?"

"Yes, Uncle Alistair, they did. Always."

"They did, eh?" the earl responded coldly. "Well, I'm sorry to report that his masters at Harrow ain't nearly so effusive. In fact, the boy stands on the verge of expulsion."

"Expulsion? I don't believe it!" his mother said flatly.

"Whether you choose to believe it or not, ma'am, makes very little difference to the facts. Not only have I had the dismal experience of listenin' to his masters disparage his laziness, but I spoke to the boy himself. He has no patience with studies. *Despises* them. Those were his very words."

"You can't have understood him," Lady Garvin insisted. "My Robbie would never say such a thing."

"He not only would, ma'am, he *did*! If you're goin' to sit there and contradict every one of my statements, I shan't be able to get to the point of my visit here 'til nightfall. And I warn you, ma'am, I've no intention of remainin' on these premises until nightfall. Won't remain over half-an-hour. I expect to be halfway to Yorkshire by nightfall."

"Then tell us, Uncle, what the point is," Jenny urged mildly.

"The point is, girl, that your brother ain't cut out for the scholarly life," Alistair declared bluntly.

"Not cut out—? But that's . . . that's ridiculous!" Lady Garvin sputtered.

"Damnation, ma'am, are you goin' to keep interruptin' me, or will you hear me out? I had a long talk with the boy, durin' which he admitted to me quite forthrightly that his talents don't lie in a bookish direction. Of course, I couldn't get an answer to my question about where his talents *do* lie, except for some blather about a yearnin' for 'adventure.' "

"Well, he's only fourteen, after all," Lady Garvin muttered in sullen defense of her beloved boy. "All young boys love adventure."

"Do you think I don't know that? I ain't a nincompoop. I ain't even blamin' him for makin' a mull of his schoolin'. At least he admits to his limitations, which is more than you do."

"Are you saying, Uncle," Jenny asked, leaning forward and studying the earl worriedly, "that you don't think Robbie should continue at Harrow?"

"I'm sayin' that he *won't* continue. He's comin' home at the end of this week."

"Coming *home*? In the middle of term?" Lady Garvin gasped.

"No point in wastin' any more time there," the earl responded. "I've arranged somethin' else for him. I've got the lad a berth on a naval vessel."

The two women stared at him, horror-struck. "A *naval vessel*?" Lady Garvin pulled herself to her feet, trembling in every limb. "Have you taken leave of your *senses*?"

"Don't enact me a Cheltenham tragedy, woman. What're you tremblin' for? A naval vessel ain't a prison, y'know. And with Boney beaten, we ain't even at *war*."

Lady Garvin began to pace about the room in agitation. "I won't permit you to do this! You may be the boy's guardian, but a mother must have *some* rights. Surely the authorities will not allow you to tear a fourteen-year-old child from the arms of his mother!"

"Will you *listen* to yourself, Margaret Garvin? You're speakin' the most confounded foolishness. A fourteen-year-old youth is not a *child*. Do you know that a young man who wants a career in the navy must set off to sea at the age of *twelve*? Instead of carryin' on like a demented shrew, you should be thankin' your stars that I was able to accomplish the feat of procurin' him a berth at his advanced age."

"Thank my stars? For having my son torn from me and forced to go to sea, to face the hazards of the elements and who knows what else? It's *you* who are demented, if you ask me. I don't see why he needs the Navy. After all, he'll inherit the title one day."

"Yes, and that's about all. I ain't rich, ma'am. There's precious little he'll inherit except the title. The Yorkshire property is becomin' more of a drain than an asset, y' know. He'll be hard pressed to keep even Willowrise up to its present standard. Besides, even if I *could* leave the lad rich, I wouldn't want him to spend his days as a useless wastrel, would you? You want the boy to amount to somethin', don't you?"

"Yes, of course, but—"

"But me no buts, ma'am. If you'll still your tongue for a minute, I'll explain what my influence with the Admiralty has accomplished for your son. I've got him an appointment as a *midshipman*! On His Majesty's Ship *Providential*." His thin lips stretched into a smile of triumph. "Yes, you may well stare. It's true. A *midshipman*, on my word."

"You really *must be* demented. Am I supposed to be *impressed* by that?" his sister-in-law said scornfully.

"But Mama," Jenny interjected gently, "it really *is* impressive, you know. It is my understanding that a boy must serve as a sort of errand boy for the ship's captain a long while before he's appointed midshipman."

"That's right," the earl said, getting to his feet. "It takes *years* of service. That's why the boys all start at eleven or twelve. Fortunately for your Robbie, my friends at the Admiralty found a vacancy for midshipman on Captain Allenby's ship and were able to prevail upon him to accept a lad of Robbie's age and lack of experience."

"But I don't *wish* my son to—"

"What have your wishes to do with anything?" the earl rasped. "Your *son* wishes it! He was beside himself with delight when I stopped back at Harrow to tell him the news."

Lady Garvin gaped again. "He *knows*? And he's *glad*?"

"Of course! It's a corkin' good opportunity for him. I tell you, ma'am, this will be the makin' of the lad. The discipline of shipboard life will be good for his character, and the trainin' will make an excellent foundation for his future career."

"His future career?" Lady Garvin echoed, blinking in confusion.

"Yes, his career. What else have I been speakin' of? It's plain that any scholarly career is out of the question. You didn't want the boy to become one of those wastrels who spends his life in gamin' and carousin', did you?" He shook a finger in her face. "That's where he'd have ended if I'd left his future up to you. Now there's no tellin' what sort of success he can make of himself."

"Success?" she murmured thoughtfully.

"Yes, success. With my influence, he may not have to serve the full six years before sittin' for the lieutenant's examination . . . and once he's a lieutenant, I'll see to it that his promotions come thick and fast. If he has any talent at all, he could end up an admiral."

"An . . . *admiral*!" the mother breathed, sinking down on the sofa, stunned.

"Why not? I've started the boy on a road that can lead to wealth and prestige. *Now* are you ready to thank your stars?"

Margaret, Lady Garvin, didn't thank her stars right away, but after Robbie had returned home, quite overjoyed at having been released from studies in mid-term and wildly eager to embark on the new course his uncle had arranged for him, she began to abandon her objections. Now that the war with France was over, she reasoned, perhaps the Navy *was* the best place for him. And after Robbie had explained—with eyes shining in excited expectation—that the berth was on the *Providential*, a real ship-of-the-line, carrying more than sixty guns, with a crew of over six-hundred men and a main deck that measured over one-hundred-and-seventy feet, and that he was already one of its midshipmen in spite of the fact that he'd never set foot on a ship in all his life, she became quite impressed with the entire arrangement.

Soon she began to boast about the plan as if it had been her own. She told everyone who came within earshot—Lord and Lady Clement, their neighbors; the vicar, Mr. Boyce and his wife; Jenny's bosom-bow, Andrea Clement; Mr. Jubb, the bailiff of their estate; Mrs. Elvin, the seamstress; and every tradesman, servant and passer-by—that her son was soon leaving to become "a commissioned officer on a magnificent vessel—His Majesty's Ship *Providential*, you know!" and that he was destined, one day soon, "to become the most famous admiral of the fleet."

"The *Providential*, you say?" asked Alfred, Lord Clement, his eyebrows raised with interest as soon as the news was imparted to him. Lord Clement was the highest peer in the neighborhood, the largest landowner for miles round and the possessor of the region's oldest title. Clement Hall was huge and impressive, making Lady Garvin's property, Willowrise, seem paltry in comparison. Willowrise was the second-finest house in the area, but in any other town the size of Wyndham it would have been considered the first. It sat high on a hill, with an avenue of willows leading up to it, designed in the elegant Palladian style and very grand. It filled Lady Garvin's breast with venom to have had, all these years, only the second-highest place in the community. But at least *she* had a son. Lord and Lady Clement had only Andrea. And when her son became a famous admiral, she would take second place to none!

"The *Providential*, eh?" his lordship repeated with excitement. "That's my nephew's ship, you know. My sister Dulcie's second son. Tristram Allenby's his name. Made his name and fortune during the late hostilities. A fine, courageous sailor. Your boy is indeed fortunate to sail with him."

"So I've been told," Lady Garvin responded with an obvious lack of enthusiasm. Even in *this* matter the Clements were trying to get the better of her. The captain of the vessel *had* to be their relation. She ground her teeth in irritation but quickly recovered her smile. "The whole enterprise promises to be fortunate," she told Lord Clement with charming if obvious emphasis. "I hope you will tell your sister to tell her son that *he* is fortunate to have *my boy* on his staff. Very fortunate indeed."

Jenny, although not given to effusion in her mother's style, was nevertheless equally optimistic about her brother's future. The boy was his sister's beloved, admired darling, and as she sat stitching his monogram on the new shirts they'd had made for his dress uniforms, she happily envisioned a future for him every bit as glorious as the one her mother dreamed of. She would miss him when he was away at sea, of course, but she was very proud of him.

Not in her wildest imaginings, however, could she have guessed that her brother's very promising future would directly endanger her own.

Chapter Two

As the day of Robbie's departure neared, both Lady Garvin and Jenny were beset with misgivings. Lady Garvin, not one to keep her feelings hidden, expressed to Jenny her fears and sense of desolation as they sat together in the sewing room, putting the finishing touches on the boy's new shirts. "What if something dreadful should happen to him?" she asked, her eyes clouded by inner visions of shipwreck and disaster.

Jenny shook her head. "Don't think of such things, Mama," she said in her low, soothing voice. "Such fears are very natural, of course, but we've both agreed, haven't we, that the Navy is the best place for Robbie? It's in his best interest—and ours, too—if we behave bravely and keep from troubling his mind with our own anxieties."

Lady Garvin was convinced of Jenny's good sense, and she bravely held her tongue, letting her tears fall only at night in the privacy of her bedroom. Meanwhile, the two ladies stitched his monograms, ordered fresh linens to be made for him, supervised his new, manly haircut (the sight of which caused Lady Garvin to drip a few sentimental tears in spite of herself), sewed the insignia on the coats of his uniforms, selected his hats and packed all his belongings tenderly into a new, highly polished wooden trunk with brass fittings. When Robbie objected that they were packing too many things, telling his mother and sister that he was certain that "we sailing men" carry only a few items of clothing in a small, canvas seabag, his mother insisted that he was mistaken. "Surely *officers* don't carry seabags," she declared firmly. However, before they were done with the packing, they had filled not only the trunk but a portmanteau, two hatboxes and a leather case filled with toilet articles.

When the time for departure neared, it suddenly occurred to Lady Garvin that she and Jenny could delay the separation by accompanying the boy to Portsmouth. "Oh Mama," Jenny exclaimed, "what a splendid idea! We can see him off right from the wharf!"

Robbie, who'd been struggling to control his own feelings of apprehenson, willingly agreed to their company. On the morning of the day before Robbie was due to sign on, the three Garvins—Jenny, Robbie and their mother—climbed into their carriage and set out from Willowrise for what would be a three-day journey for the ladies and the beginning of a six-month journey for the boy.

By the time the carriage arrived at the Grey Gull Inn at Portsmouth, it was long after dark. The inn had been recommended to them by their Gloucester neighbor, Lord Clement, but it was a small, disappointing hostelry with draughty windows and only one private dining room which was far from clean. Lady Garvin, whose stomach was delicate in the best of circumstances, was taken ill with a digestive upset during the night and by morning was in no condition to rise from her bed. Queasy, miserable and unable to hide her tears, she was forced to bid her son farewell from her bed. "I hope you don't mind, dearest," she explained weakly, "but I'm completely incapable of facing a trip to the wharf and standing about in the cold sea breeze just to watch your ship depart."

"I understand, Mama," the boy assured her, bending over and kissing her cheek. "It was good of you to come this far."

Lady Garvin, with a cry of anguish, clutched him around the neck. "Oh, my beloved child!" she wept. "You *will* take c-care of yourself, won't you?"

"Don't worry, Mama. And don't cry. Please don't cry. I'll be home in a few months, you know. It's just the same as if I were away at school."

"It's not at all the same," his mother whimpered, falling back against the pillows and dabbing at her eyes with the corner of her comforter. "But I mustn't dwell on . . . I promised Jenny I'd be brave." She tried courageously to get herself under control. "Goodbye, my love," she said, managing a pathetic little smile. "Write as often as you can."

Jenny (after being assured by her mother that the digestive disorder which had troubled her during the night would soon be brought under control by the avoidance of any of the inn's dreadful food, a few additional hours of rest and the ingestion of some strong, hot tea) decided that she needn't deny herself the opportunity to see her brother embark. Leaving her mother under the protection of their coachman and the ministrations of a solicitous chambermaid, she set off from the inn with her brother in a hired carriage.

As they drew close to the dock, Robbie's qualms seemed to fade away. His pulse began to race in eager anticipation of the adventures that lay just over the horizon. "Can you smell the ocean?" he crowed, throwing open his carriage window and sniffing the air. He bounced on the seat, grinning in delight. "Isn't that the most exciting smell in the world?"

Jenny nodded her agrement and pressed her nose to her window to take in all the colorful sights. The streets were narrow and crowded with carriages, carts, wheelbarrows and pedestrians. There was too much activity for the eye to catch or the mind to grasp all at once. Everyone seemed to be in a hurry. All sorts of persons—from stiff-collared, dapper gentlemen to scruffy, ill-clad children—were skirting and dodging anyone or anything that impeded their progress to what surely must have been urgent and important destinations. Jenny watched in amusement as a top-hatted but shabby fellow, carrying a large parcel tied with cord, leaped with one jump over a wheelbarrow and hurried on his way without a change of expression. She also noted a woman in a voluminous, plum-colored cloak wending her way calmly among the vehicles while carrying a child in her arms and holding two others by the hand. Jenny stared at the intrepid woman in admiration and would have continued to observe her progress all the way down the street if the carriage hadn't taken an abrupt turn at that moment. But the vehicle lurched sharply to the left and suddenly they were on the wharf.

Jenny had time for only one amazed look at the strange new world spread out on the bay before the coachman threw open the door of the carriage and let down the step. Robbie hopped down at once, but Jenny gave the coachman her hand and let him assist her to descend in proper, ladylike style.

"That'll be two shillin's, Miss," he informed her as soon as she'd alighted. "Where do y' wish me t' drop the baggage?"

She turned to Robbie for advice, but the boy was already absorbed in scanning the coastline to catch his first glimpse of his ship, not in the least concerned with the mundane matters of finance and logistics which were occupying his sister. Nervously, she searched about in her reticule for coins with which to pay the driver. "Just leave the baggage right here," she murmured helplessly as she pressed the coins into the man's palm.

"There she is!" Robbie shouted. "There! Out to your left. Do you see her? She's the large one with the black and yellow stripes on her side."

The carriage lumbered off, and Jenny blinked at the sight spread out before her. The bay was dotted with what seemed like hundreds of sailing ships, most with their sails furled but some, their sails spread out to the breeze, moving majestically out to sea. Crossing back and forth between the ships and the shore was an even greater number of small, barge-like vessels, their flat surfaces covered with boxes, crates and bundles of all sizes, propelled only by men with poles and oars. And circling among them all, in far greater numbers even than the barges, were rowboats, skiffs, wherries and longboats of all descriptions, making the traffic on the port waters as busy and crowded as that on the streets. "Well," Robbie prodded eagerly, "do you see her?"

Jenny shielded her eyes and peered intently in the direction in which he was pointing, but she was unable to single out the *Providential* from all the other vessels that lay at anchor in the bay. Besides, there was such a blur of color and movement that she could hardly distinguish *anything*. In all that confusion of sail and rigging, of motion and activity, of bright spring sunshine casting glints of dazzle from the water to her eyes, how could she possibly identify one particular ship? And then she saw it. "Oh, *my*!" she breathed, awestruck.

She couldn't imagine how she'd missed seeing the ship at once; it was indeed the most impressive vessel in the harbor. Even with the sails furled, the *Providential* looked tall. There seemed to be three decks visible above the water line, their size emphasized by the wide yellow stripes painted on the black hull. Even from the shore she could see the enormous number of gun-ports, the bewildering tangle of ropes and ladders that hung from the masts, and the golden gleam of the gilded carvings on the prow. Brother and sister, standing side by side in the midst of the bustle of the dock, both gaped at the sight with quite similar expressions of wonder.

But Robbie, too excited to stand motionless for very long,

soon shook himself into action. "You stay right here with the baggage until I find out how I get to the ship," he instructed and promptly ran off. Before Jenny could object, he'd disappeared into the crowd.

Jenny, somewhat disconcerted at being so abruptly deserted, sat down on the curved lid of the trunk, drew the other boxes protectively close and looked about her. People and vehicles milled about the area in a seemingly endless parade. There were sailors of all ages in a wide variety of styles of dress, men and women of all classes, carriages, carts and wagons of every kind, and even a mongrel dog sniffing around a pile of sacks looking for a tear or opening. She watched in some amusement as the animal found a tiny hole, put his tongue inside, tasted the contents and then trotted off in disdain. Whatever the sacks contained, they were beneath the dog's standard fare.

After many minutes of observing the passers-by, she became aware of being observed herself. A tall, well-dressed gentleman, standing some distance from her and leaning negligently against a huge stack of crates, seemed to be studying her with a rather rude intensity. Catching his eye, she felt her cheeks flush hotly, and she turned away at once. How awkward, she felt, to be unchaperoned in such a public place. She wished Robbie would return at once. Her eyes searched through the crowd in the direction in which he'd gone, but there was no sign of him. Nervously, she glanced back toward the stranger. Yes, he was still watching her. Again their eyes met, and again she looked away in keen embarrassment. Why on earth was he staring at her so?

The only proper response to such boldness, she decided, was to ignore its existence, and so, by sheer exercise of will, she kept herself from glancing at him again, although the desire to do so was surprisingly strong. But after a few moments, something occurred to drive the stranger from her mind. There was a sudden shouting to her right, and a dirty little urchin of eight or nine came running by. When he'd gone no more than six paces past her, he tripped and fell. A woman in a garish dress and unruly hair trotted up after him, grabbed him by the neck and hauled him to his feet. "Y' rotten li'l filcher," she shouted, beating him about the shoulders with a rickety umbrella, "I whiddled the 'ole scrap!"

"Ow! *Stop*!" the boy yowled. "I din't mean nuffin'."

"Gammon! 'Ow many times do I 'ave t' tell yer not t' go

liftin' wut ain't yours?" And she kept at him with her umbrella despite his cries.

Jenny couldn't bear it. She jumped up from her perch and ran up to the woman, catching her arm in a strong grip. "Don't, ma'am," she ordered firmily. "You'll do the child an injury if you're not careful."

The woman blinked at Jenny, her anger seeming to crumble. " 'E stoled a sweet right from under the baker's nose," she said, breaking into sniffles. " 'E's me very own brat, but 'e ain't no good. Beatin's too good fer 'im, m' lady, take me word on 't."

"Oh, no, ma'am," Jenny said earnestly. "I'm certain he'd listen to you if only you'd speak to him gently." She released the woman's arm, knelt down and lifted the boy's chin so that the blue eyes in that grimy face were almost level with her own. "You're a good boy at heart, aren't you, my lad? You wouldn't have stolen anything if you'd understood that it's a very bad thing to have done, would you?"

"No, m' lady," the boy mumbled.

"Of course you wouldn't. You'd like to be a good boy, wouldn't you? Especially if you knew how happy it would make your mother?"

"Yes, 'm."

"I knew it." Jenny smiled and patted the child's head. "There's a good lad. Now, tell your mother how sorry you are for what you've done, and promise her that you'll never again—"

"*Gawd*!" the mother muttered suddenly. Jenny looked up to see that the woman wasn't watching her at all but was staring off at something behind Jenny's back, all motherly concern wiped out of her face. "Gawd," she said again, snatching the boy's arm with a warning yank, "let's 'op it. I think 'e's cotched it."

"*Blimey*!" the boy swore in a tone of shockingly mature disgust, and the two of them dashed off into the crowd.

Jenny got to her feet and stared after them in confusion. Their behavior made no sense at all. The mother's tears and the boy's pathetic expression had dropped from their faces like those of actors when the curtain falls. Had they been acting a little scene for her benefit? But *why*? What did they hope to gain by—?

With a blinding awareness, Jenny gasped and wheeled round to where she'd left the baggage. Of the five pieces—the trunk, the portmanteau, the toilet case and the two hatboxes—only one hatbox remained. Everything else was gone!

Chapter Three

Jenny clapped her hand to her mouth in chagrin, but not before a cry of frustration and self-disgust escaped her. How could she have been so *stupid*? She'd let herself be duped by what must be the most obvious trick in all Christendom.

Her eyes searched the crowd for a sign of the baggage or a glimpse of the woman and the miscreant boy, but there was none. Her baggage, the person who'd stolen it, the woman and the child who'd distracted her—they'd all melted away into the throng which milled about on the dock. And of all the people surrounding her, none seemed to have noticed her distress or her predicament, so intent were they all on their own concerns. She could think of nothing to do, no one to call on for help. There she stood in the midst of the indifferent throng, transfixed, immobilized, helpless. How could she have let this happen? How would she ever be able to explain to Robbie what she'd done? How was he to begin his new career with only the clothes he wore on his back? There would be no time in which to order new clothing, and Robbie had told her that promotions in the Navy could hinge on an officer's dress and appearance. In one thoughtless moment she'd blighted his prospects for the future.

In abject misery, compounded by her humiliation at her shameful naivete, she picked up the hatbox and began to move through the crowd in the direction in which Robbie had gone. She'd not walked very far, however, when someone tapped her shoulder. With a frightened little gasp, she turned to find herself face-to-face with the stranger who'd been eyeing her a little while before. He was even taller than he'd seemed from a distance, his face lined and weatherbeaten, and his dark eyes disconcertingly piercing. He looked down at her with an air of unconcealed disapproval. "I beg your pardon, 'ma'am," he said as, unsmilingly civil, he removed his hat, "but I believe these belong to you."

She gaped at him in bewilderment until she noticed that he was followed by a sailor trundling a wheelbarrow into which Robbie's trunk, portmanteau, toilet case and missing hatbox had been piled. "Oh, my *baggage*!" she cried in delighted relief. "However did you—?"

"I saw the fellow steal it," the gentleman explained curtly and turned to help the sailor unload the barrow. *Of course he'd seen the fellow steal it,* she said to herself in sudden comprehension. *He'd been staring at me all that time*. She felt herself flush again. He *had* been watching her, and with quite blatant impropriety. Therefore, he must have witnessed the entire incident. He'd stood there and observed her foolish behavior in every humiliating detail. For a fleeting moment she felt a flash of anger at his rudeness in having stared at her and thus having been witness to her stupidity. But the feeling passed in a wave of gratitude. If he hadn't been watching her, he wouldn't have seen the thief, and he wouldn't have been able to save her from a most difficult fix. "How did you manage to recover it?" she asked, unable to mask her admiration.

The gentleman shrugged, tossed a gold coin to the sailor and dismissed him with a wave of his hand. "It wasn't a difficult feat, ma'am. The thief was not aware that he'd been observed, and since he was burdened by the baggage, he was easy game."

"It doesn't sound at all easy to me," Jenny said, trying to find a graceful way to express her gratitude.

"You may take my word on it, ma'am. I simply blocked his path, knocked him down (which took very little effort, since his arms were burdened with his loot), and sent for the warehouse guards. At least he won't be free to play his games any more—not for a long time. I wish I could say the same for the woman and the boy who assisted him in his chicanery. Even though I gave the guards their descriptions, I very much doubt they'll be caught."

"I hope they aren't," Jenny murmured, half to herself.

His eyebrows rose in surprised disdain. "You hope they aren't caught?"

"Yes," she admitted. "I know that what they did was very

dreadful, but since you so very courageously restored my things to me, I find I can't wish them harm."

"I think, ma'am—if you permit me to be blunt—that you're much too tenderhearted," he said coldly. "These docks are infested with thieves—so much so that they are creating serious losses for the shipping companies. If many of them escape punishment, the problem will be exacerbated beyond repair."

"Nevertheless," Jenny said shyly, "I wouldn't like to think of a poor woman and a little child languishing in prison because of me."

"It would *not* be because of you." He frowned at her in disgust. "It would be because of their own moral turpitude. Don't you realize, ma'am, that if society is to function smoothly, the law must be upheld? Criminals, if judged guilty, must be made to face the full weight of retribution which the law specifies. Otherwise, society will be overwhelmed with undiscipline and disorder."

Something in his tone made Jenny glance up at him with interest. She noted that his square jaw was set in firm, forbidding lines and that his eyes glinted with a cold implacability. She was sure he could not be more than five-and-thirty, but his voice and expression bespoke such authority and self-possession that he seemed older. He was not a man who would easily be crossed, she realized, or who would readily forgive a transgression. He seemed very sure of himself, as if he were accustomed to having his own way. Even in this instance, he was looking down at her as if he expected instant agreement. "In theory, sir," she said in her quiet way, "I'm sure you're quite correct, but I, myself, would find it very difficult to sentence anyone to prison after I'd looked into his eyes."

"Fustian, ma'am. Pure fustian. You're expressing the most blatant sentimentality."

"Yes, I'm afraid I *am* given to sentimentality at times," she admitted with a small sigh.

He stared down at her for a moment as if he were about to scold her, but suddenly his expression softened. "Then I'm very glad, ma'am," he said, a smile appearing on his hitherto forbidding face, "that you aren't a judge or a magistrate. We'd find ourselves in a pretty pickle if you were."

The smile so transformed his appearance that Jenny couldn't

help but respond. "Yes, we would, wouldn't we?" she agreed with a giggle. "Our entire social structure might crumble away."

She threw a quick, amused glance up at his face to see his reaction, and for a moment their eyes held, a little spark of attraction igniting between them. She felt it with a shock and immediately dropped her eyes.

An awkward silence followed, during which Jenny couldn't find the courage either to look at him or to speak. Finally, her eyes falling on her baggage, she remembered that she hadn't properly thanked him. "I . . . er . . . hope you won't think it mere sentimentality, sir," she said softly, her eyes fixed on the ground, "when I tell you how grateful to you I am. You saved me from a great deal of anguish."

"Don't mention it, ma'am. It was no trouble." He hesitated for a moment and then made a little bow, put on his hat and walked away.

Jenny looked after him, feeling quite sorry to see him go. Then she abruptly recalled seeing him give the sailor who'd brought the baggage a gold coin. Should she not have recompensed him for the expense? She started to follow him but remembered the baggage. She mustn't leave it unguarded —not again. "Oh!" she cried in a dither of indecision and put out a hand as if to beckon him back.

He was much too far away to have heard her cry, but at that moment he stopped and looked back over his shoulder. Her expression and her pose gave an unmistakable message. He turned and strode back to her. "Is something wrong, ma'am? Did you wish me to do something for you?"

"No, thank you. It was only that . . ." She felt herself coloring up once more. If only her feelings didn't always reveal themselves in the flush of her cheeks.

"Yes?"

". . . that I remembered . . . that is, I would very much like you to let me recompense you for what you gave the sailor." She began to rummage hurriedly through her reticule. "Please . . ."

With a forbidding frown, he took the reticule from her grasp and pulled its cords taut. "I hope, ma'am, that you will not insult me by making such a suggestion again," he said, thrusting the reticule back into her hands.

"Oh! I'm . . . sorry. I meant no offense," she said, her

cheeks hot with embarrassment. "I only wanted to . . . to . . ."

"I know. To show your gratitude."

"Yes."

He studied her intently. "If you're truly grateful," he said after a long pause, "perhaps you'll reward me instead with the answer to a question that's been puzzling me since I first set eyes on you. A question of a somewhat personal nature."

Her eyes flew to his face. "Personal?" She felt her heart begin to pound in nervous agitation. "Wh-what is it you wish to know?"

"I can't help wondering what a young woman of quality is doing in such a place without escort of any kind."

"But I *do* have escort," she said, feeling both relieved and disappointed. She had hoped (and feared) that he would ask her name. She would have liked him to be interested enough to ask, but she wouldn't have known how to answer. Her mother would certainly not approve of her giving her name to a strange man. But this question was safe enough. "My brother is with me. He's only gone off on a brief errand."

"Brief? It's been over half-an-hour since I began observing you, you know."

"Is it?" Jenny's brow wrinkled worriedly. "Yes, he *does* seem to have been gone a long while. I wonder if he's forgotten where he left me."

The gentleman shook his head, the look of disapproval again in his eyes. "I must say, ma'am, I can't approve of his behavior. I'd offer to go and search for the fellow, but it would be a rather pointless exercise, since I don't know what he looks like. And *you* certainly can't wander about looking for him, not all alone, even if I remained to watch over your baggage."

"You needn't worry," Jenny said confidently. "Robbie will reappear at any moment, I'm certain."

"Hmmmm." The gentleman was obviously unconvinced. "If you've no objection, ma'am, I'll keep you company until your brother returns."

Jenny felt herself coloring again. It was probably quite improper for her to accept the companionship of a stranger, but every instinct told her that he was a man who could be trusted. Besides, if she refused, he'd probably go back to his post near those packing-crates and watch over her from there. (That was probably why he'd been watching her in the first place—to keep a protective eye on an unescorted female.) "I've no objection at all," she told him with shy frankness. "In fact, I'd be even more grateful to you than I am already."

He removed his hat and made an acknowledging bow. "You may as well resume your seat on the trunk here," he said, his tone making the suggestion sound more like an order.

She did as he bid. "You're very kind, sir, to wait here with me," she offered, peeping up at him from the corner of her eye and noting with a twinge of discomfort how he glowered as he searched the face of each passerby. "I hope I'm not keeping you from your business."

"I've nothing so pressing to do at the moment that would justify my abandoning an innocent girl to the dangers inherent in sitting alone on this dock in the midst of this press of rag-tails and cut-purses."

"I'm sure you exaggerate, sir. After all, it *is* broad daylight, and—"

He expelled his breath in disgust. "It was broad daylight when your baggage was stolen, wasn't it? Yet that didn't prevent the crime. And it didn't inspire any one of this mob surrounding you to help you, either."

Jenny couldn't help feeling that, kind as the gentleman had been to her, he was much too disparaging of his fellow man. "But someone *did* help me," she pointed out gently. "You."

"So I did," he admitted, a smile reluctantly making an appearance at the corners of his lips. "You were most fortunate."

"I know."

He turned to stare at her with knit brows and an arrested expression. "You, ma'am, are a very unusual young woman. I think, in your quiet way, you've just cut me down."

"Cut you down? Why do you say that?"

"You are trying to say that, if I hadn't come to your rescue, somebody else might have, is that it?"

"Nobody else did, though."

"But I've been a coxcomb to assume that I'm the only one in this crowd with an impulse to decent behavior—that's what you're trying to tell me, isn't it?"

Her eyes twinkled. "I'm much too beholden to you, sir, to tell you any such thing."

He laughed. "Yet you made me see it without saying it. It

was deftly done. Never have I been put in my place with more ladylike delicacy."

"I had no wish to put you in your place. Perhaps I *do* believe that you are a bit too harsh in your judgments of your fellow man, but I'm quite sensible of the fact that you've been unusually protective of me from the first. That was why you were staring at me earlier, wasn't it? You saw me sitting here all alone and were afraid I'd come to harm."

"Is *that* what you think, ma'am?" His smile widened. "How little you know of men, my dear."

"Why, what do you mean?" she asked innocently. "Are you trying to deny your kindness in—?"

"*Jenny*! What on *earth*—?" came a voice behind them.

"Oh, Robbie!" Jenny jumped up, startled. "*There* you are. Where have you been for so long?"

But her brother was glaring at the gentleman with obvious pugnacity. "Is this man bothering you?" he demanded, his fingers curling into fists.

"No, of course not. If it weren't for him—"

The gentleman held up a restraining hand. "So this tadpole is your brother, eh? He's a bit younger than I'd expected but not so young that he shouldn't have known better than to leave you unprotected. Have you no sense, fellow?"

Robbie's mouth dropped open, and he stared from the stranger to his sister and back again. "Are you acquainted with this man, Jenny?" he asked bewilderedly.

"Well . . . er . . . not exactly, but—"

"Then I fail to see," Robbie said, glowering at the stranger, "what he's doing here and why he should be ringing a peal over me."

"Robbie!" Jenny was appalled at his rudeness. "You don't understand. We owe this gentleman a great debt of gratitude. Why, he—"

"Excuse me, ma'am," the stranger interrupted, "but it's not necessary to go into that now. I just want this puppy to know that his behavior was utterly reprehensible. One doesn't leave a young woman unprotected in such a place, boy. It's a place where she is vulnerable to all manner of molestation. Remember that in future."

"Hang it," Robbie burst out, "I don't see what concern it is of *yours* what I—"

"Hush, Robbie," his sister said quietly. She put a hand on

her brother's arm and turned to her scowling protector. "You mustn't think ill of my brother, sir. He is about to embark on a naval vessel for a long voyage, and since it's his first, he's understandably distracted—"

"A naval vessel?" The stranger looked at Robbie with interest. "You don't mean the *Providential*?"

"Yes, that's what she means," Robbie said rudely. "Not that it's any business of yours."

"So you're sailing on the *Providential*. How very interesting." His scowling expression had changed to one of ill-concealed amusement. "I wish you good fortune in your travels." He turned to Jenny, took her hand and bowed over it. "Good day to you, ma'am. Thank you for this most enjoyable and enlightening encounter."

"Thank *you*, sir," Jenny said, blushing shyly, "for *everything*. I shan't forget—"

The gentleman grinned down at her. "Don't thank me for too much. What I began to say before your brother interrupted us was that I was not watching you because I thought you'd need protection."

"No? Then why—?"

"Because, ma'am, you were the prettiest creature within range of my eye. It was a purely selfish act, and quite rude. So you have a great deal less to be grateful to me for than you thought." With that, he tipped his hat and strode off, completely indifferent to the fact that both Jenny and Robbie stared after him, agog, until he disappeared from sight.

Chapter Four

For weeks afterward, Jenny wondered if the strange gentleman had really meant what he'd said about her being pretty. "He was probably only teasing, so that I wouldn't feel beholden to him," she told her friend, Andrea, when they discussed the matter.

"Not necessarily," Andrea said, considering the question seriously from her perch on the chaise in Jenny's bedroom where they often hid away to discuss matters of life and love. "You *are* rather pretty, you know . . . or you would be if you'd curl your hair and rub a bit of color on your cheeks."

Jenny studied her face in her dressing-table mirror with critical detachment. The face looking back at her from the glass was really quite unexceptional. Her eyes, large and dark-brown, were her best feature, and her skin was smooth and clear of blemishes, but there was nothing else particularly admirable about her. Her cheeks, as Andrea had pointed out, were lacking in color, her nose was too wide and her hair was a drab brown and pulled back from her face in severe simplicity, plaited at the moment in a single braid which hung carelessly down her back. "Not nearly pretty enough to cause a man to stop and stare," she muttered dejectedly. "He cannot have been sincere."

"I don't see why the matter should concern you anyway," Andrea remarked, putting her legs up on the chaise and stretching languidly. "You'll never see or hear of him again, so what difference does it make if he meant it or not?"

Andrea Clement was, like Jenny, twenty years of age, but their personalities were not alike. While Jenny was considered to be above average only in understanding, Andrea was above average in everything else—things like height, beauty and self-confidence. Those were the things, Jenny's mother often pointed out, that really counted. Andrea had silky blonde hair, wide hazel eyes and two large front teeth which protruded slightly from under a deliciously shaped upper lip and bit charmingly upon the full lower one. Her reputation as the prettiest girl in the district had been won when she was just a child, and it gave her character and movements an assurance that Jenny's mother described as "an air." Lady Garvin would often remark on it. "If you could put on an *air* like Andrea Clement's," she would say at the slightest provocation, "people would find you almost as pretty as she. Beauty, you know, is largely an illusion. If you would only carry yourself like a beauty—instead of like a shy little mouse—then someone might take you for one."

But Jenny had never been made to feel like a beauty and had no idea of how to carry herself with "an air." Andrea's remarkable self-confidence filled Jenny (who had so little of it herself) with admiration bordering on awe. Accustomed to feeling second best in her own home, she slipped quite easily into feeling second best in relation to her friend. Andrea, an only child—indulged and spoiled by a doting father and an ineffectual mother—was completely happy in the relationship. So long as everyone acknowledged her superior position, she was perfectly willing to admit that Jenny was generously supplied with good sense, good humor and one other quality which only a few people noticed and hardly anyone appreciated—sweetness.

At the moment, however, Jenny's normal good sense and good humor seemed to have deserted her. *Andrea is right,* she thought, rising from the dressing table and crossing listlessly to the window seat. *The whole matter shouldn't be of the least concern to me. The man doesn't know my name nor I his. I shall never see him again.*

But it did matter. In the weeks since she and her mother had returned from Portsmouth, Jenny had reviewed the incident repeatedly in her mind although, fearful of a scold, she'd never told her mother a word about it. After all, she'd behaved foolishly from first to last, and listening to her mother belittle her conduct would not soothe her feelings of humiliation. But she'd felt an overpowering urge to confide in *someone*, and she'd related the entire incident in explicit detail to her dearest friend.

Andrea had listened to the tale with the most fascinated attention and had declared it to be a marvelous adventure. But what she couldn't understand was why Jenny seemed so depressed by it. After all, everything had turned out well, hadn't it? Robbie's baggage had been recovered, he'd gone happily off to sea, and Jenny had returned home unscathed. Why was she harping on the matter? "What I don't understand, my dear," she remarked, "is why you're staring out of that window looking as low as a loaf of sad bread."

Jenny smiled weakly. "*Distressful* bread, if it's Shakespeare you're quoting. I'm not low, exactly, but I *am* disturbed at having made such an idiot of myself."

"I don't think you were so idiotic. After all, *anyone* might have been fooled by those thieves."

"Perhaps, but that wasn't the full extent of my stupidity. Not only was I a dupe of those knaves, but in the company of that . . . impressive gentleman I behaved like a veritable wet-goose. Didn't I?"

"It doesn't seem so to me," Andrea said, shrugging.

"Doesn't it? Don't you think I was . . . oh, too girlishly grateful, too trusting, too obviously eager for his companionship?" She pressed her palms to her cheeks. "Heavens, I *still* blush whenever I think of it."

"I think you're making too much of it. Even if you *did* act a bit goosish, who will ever know? Even if the gentleman related the story to his friends, he can't identify you by name. He doesn't know it."

Jenny sighed. "That's true enough. But I hate to have him remember me as a silly little *naif*."

"My dear child," Andrea said with her "air," swinging her legs over the edge of the chaise and rising impressively to her feet, "the chances are that the gentleman doesn't remember you at all."

"Yes," Jenny agreed sadly, "that's the most lowering thought of all. Especially since I remember him so well."

"Do you, Jenny?" Andrea looked over at her friend curiously. "He *must* have been impressive."

"He was." She drew her legs up on the seat, wrapped her arms around them and leaned her chin on her knees. "I remember everything about him, from the way the wind whipped at his dark hair to the way his boots gleamed when he strode off into the crowd."

"Was he very handsome?" Andrea felt that an affirmative answer to *that* question might explain her friend's unusual obsession.

"No, not in the way you mean. His face was too dark and lined to be considered handsome, exactly. But he was . . . sinewy, you know . . . and rather steely. Very forceful in manner and appearance. One would have to say he was good to look at. Impressive, as I've said, and . . . and . . ."

"And memorable," Andrea supplied drily.

Jenny smiled ruefully. "Yes, quite memorable."

"Of course you must realize, Jenny, that your only course is to forget him, in spite of his being so memorable."

"Yes, I realize that quite well," Jenny said dejectedly. "In the first place, I acted like a ninny."

"Yes, it seems so."

"So he certainly didn't find me nearly as impressive as I found him. Which is probably why he didn't ask for my name or direction."

"And which, even if he did, you couldn't properly have given him."

"Quite true. And I don't know *his* name, either."

"So that, memorable as he may be, he's not likely ever to cross your path again, is he?"

"Not likely at all."

"Then you're in full agreement with me that the only course for you to take is to—"

"—to put him out of my mind."

Andrea sauntered to the door. "Exactly. Forget him. And the sooner the better."

But after Andrea had gone and Jenny's chin had sunk on her knees again, she gave a sad little snort. Forget him indeed. She'd been trying to do just that ever since her return from Portsmouth. Easier said than done.

Robbie had been gone for almost two months before the first word from him arrived at Wyndham, but then three letters arrived at once. They were delivered one May morning before Lady Garvin had come downstairs, and Cullum, the butler, knowing how eagerly his mistress had been watching for them, brought them upstairs to her abigail, who woke her at once.

A short while later, Jenny, who was lingering at the breakfast table wondering whether it would disturb her mother if she sat down so early at the pianoforte to practice the sonata by Haydn she'd purchased the day before, was startled by a noise in the hallway. The door of the morning room burst open, and her mother (in a shocking state of *dishabille*, wearing only her nightdress) stormed in. She was waving a sheaf of papers and sputtering incoherently about Jenny's underhanded secrecy, flagrant immorality and treachery. "You've nipped your brother's career in the *bud*!" she declaimed. "And before it's even had a chance to bloom!"

"If I've nipped it in the bud, of course it hasn't had a chance to bloom," Jenny said, laughing. "Whatever are you talking about, Mama?"

"Go ahead, laugh! It's all of a piece with your shameless conduct in Portsmouth. Jenny, how *could* you—?"

Jenny's smile faded. "But who—? How—?" Though utterly confused, Jenny could nevertheless feel herself coloring to the ears.

"Your brother has written about it." She sank into a chair. "To think that a daughter of mine would comport herself like a common lightskirt!"

"*Lightskirt*? Really, Mama, I may have behaved unwisely, but surely Robbie doesn't say that I—"

"He says very little, but I can read between the lines. Taking up with a perfect stranger in a public place? How else can I interpret such conduct?"

"I should think you could find a less opprobrious interpretation if you tried," her daughter said with a tinge of sarcasm. "But what has my conduct to do with Robbie's career?"

"Here. Read his account for yourself." And she threw one of the letters across the table to Jenny's place.

Jenny smoothed the sheets and began to read. *Dear Mama and Jenny,* the boy had written, *I have been aboard the* Providential *for three days now and at Sea for two, and thus far I am finding it quite Disappointing. The work is very Difficult and Tiring, as I must stand Watch every four hours and never seem to get enough Sleep. On Duty, I must dash from Stem to Stern with messages, assist the Signalmen, help with the Guns during Gunnery Practice and assist the Lieutenants with Anything else they wish me to do. To make Matters worse, the Captain has taken a great Dislike to me, and that, Jenny, is all your Fault.*

My dealings with the Captain commenced in a most surpris-

ing Manner which I will relate to you in Detail since I have almost an hour until eight Bells when I have the Watch again. I had not been aboard Ship for more than an hour and was unpacking my Gear in the midshipmen's Berth (which by the way was the subject of much Mirth, for it should all have been packed in a sea chest) and becoming acquainted with the other Fellows, when a steward came in with a message that the Captain requested my Company for Dinner. This caused a great Stir among the other Middies, since none of Them had been asked. As you can well Imagine, I was quite Proud and dressed Myself in all my best for the Ocassion.

When I presented Myself at the Captain's Cabin, I found that I was the lowliest Person there, the others being the first and second Lieutenants, and a Captain of Marines—not even a third Lieutenant in Evidence. No one paid any Attention to me at all, making me feel quite Awkward, as you can well Imagine.

Then they all got to their Feet and Captain Allenby came in. You can well Imagine my Feelings of Shock when I saw that the Captain was None Other than the Fellow to whom Jenny had attached herself on the Dock!

As you can well Imagine, I was rendered almost Speechless by the Sight of him, but he didn't make any acknowledgment of my Presence other than to introduce me to the others. How he learned my Name I can't Imagine, for Jenny did not introduce us on the Dock and specifically told me later that they hadn't introduced Themselves. She had called me Robbie, of course, and he could have guessed I was a Middy, but since there is another Robert in my Berth, how did he know which one I was? Of course, the Captain is very Shrewd, and I can well Imagine that it was not very Difficult for him to identify me.

That Night, however, while we ate Dinner, I assumed that I had been chosen at Random (believing that he might ask one Middy to dine each evening) but I soon learned that that was not the Case. During Dinner no one said a Word to me, and you can well Imagine how Small I felt. But after Dinner was over and we had all drunk our Port (which I will admit was the only part of the Evening that I enjoyed, for I felt quite full grown when the steward filled my glass just like the others and you, Mama, were not there to tell me I'm not Old enough to drink strong Spirits) and the Others took their Leave, the Captain indicated that I was to remain behind.

You can well Imagine my Feelings. I had not the slightest Idea what he wanted with me. But he soon made his Intention clear—it was to give me a Thundering Scold! He said very coldly that the Officers aboard his Ship were all Gentlemen, and my Neglect of my Sister on the Dock was not the Act of a Gentleman, that it was Inexcusable even in the most Callow Youth, and that if I did not prove to him in Short Order that I could act like a Gentleman of Character and Sense, I would not long remain an Officer aboard his Ship. You can well Imagine my State when I at last was excused from his Presence.

On my return to my Berth I found the other Fellows had already dubbed me Tris's Toy (Tristram being the Captain's given Name), implying that I was a Favorite. What Humbug! I've encountered the Captain three Times since the Fatal Dinner, and each Time he had a Fault to find. Once it was my improper Dress, once my Clumsiness and once my Inactivity. He never pays the least heed to any of the other Middies —Midshipmen are usually beneath the notice of Captains of Vessels as large as this one. If Jenny hadn't been so forward as to take up with Captain Allenby, he would never have even been aware of my Existence or cast so much as a Look in my Direction. I only wish she'd never laid Eyes on him. As you can well Imagine, my Chances for Promotion are non-existent and my Hopes for the Future very Dim.

Jenny put down the sheets with hands that shook. Her emotions were in a state of upheaval. She was aware, first, of feelings of elation in having learned the identity of her stranger. (He was a Navy captain! She should have guessed it; everything about him had suggested strength and the ability to command.) She was excited by the realization that he now knew *her* identity, too. But with her mother glaring at her from the other side of the table and with Robbie's pathetic prospects spread on the papers before her, her excitement was overwhelmed by sensations of shame and guilt. "Oh, Mama," she murmured, raising her eyes to her mother's face, "you don't think Robbie's prospects are as bleak as he says, do you?"

"Of course I do! My beloved boy, blighted in his prime! Jenny, how *could* you have done it?"

"But I didn't do anything so very dreadful. I only tried to show my gratitude. How could I have guessed it was Robbie's captain? The man was not in uniform but dressed as any proper gentleman would be."

"That's no excuse. No female who calls herself a lady engages in conversation with a stranger, no matter what his garb. And you know that as well as I."

"But it seemed, at the time, quite natural. And even necessary. I did have to thank him, didn't I? It would have been *beastly* of me to ignore his kindness."

"Thank him? For what?"

Jenny briefly recounted to her mother exactly what had happened on the docks, but her mother, aware of the aftermath of the encounter, felt little sympathy for Jenny's plight. "You could have handled matters a great deal better than you did. You could have *cried out* when you realized you'd been robbed. That would have attracted a crowd around you. In a crowd, your lack of escort wouldn't have been so obvious."

"But I wouldn't have felt comfortable making a scene, you know—"

"There, you see? Thinking of your own comfort instead of your brother's future. Your shyness is nothing but selfishness —I've always felt it."

Jenny lowered her eyes miserably. "I'm sorry, Mama."

"What good is being sorry? It will not bring back Robbie's prospects." She heaved herself to her feet. "Not that I find you *completely* to blame," she muttered grudgingly, turning to the door. "That dreadful captain is quite as much at fault. Taking it out on Robbie just because you behaved so foolishly as to let yourself be robbed—"

"Don't blame the captain, Mama. He was only being gallant."

"Gallant? You *are* a goose. Read the other letters and see what a monster your uncle has foisted upon my poor son!" With that, she swept out of the room and slammed the door behind her.

Jenny reached across the table for the other letters and read them avidly. Then, her heart sinking in her chest, she read them again. Captain Tristram Allenby was the subject of all her brother's letters, and in all of them the captain was indeed monstrous. He was icy in his remarks, cold in his demeanor, exacting in his demands, aloof to his subordinates and heartless in every way. Robbie was miserably unhappy, homesick and hopeless. Jenny's heart bled for him. She had to conclude that Uncle Alistair had done the boy a disservice by urging him to join the Navy, her mother had been misguided in agreeing to the plan and Jenny had, albeit unknowingly, added the *coup de grace* by permitting herself to be robbed. By the time she left the morning room that day, her eyes were red with weeping.

There was only one hope: time. Time could heal wounds, could help one to adjust to new surroundings, could make one forget injuries to one's pride or prejudices against strangers. Time could change bad first impressions to more favorable second ones. So Jenny and her mother awaited the next batch of letters with that single ray of hope.

But the next group of letters dealt that hope a killing blow. They were devastating. Robbie's words were bleak, and he described his life as one of unrelieved agony. He was always cold and damp, the food was becoming more unpalatable with each passing day, and he'd contracted a fever but had not been permitted to miss a watch. Worse than all the rest, he'd been blisteringly reprimanded by his lieutenant on two separate occasions for infractions which were too insignificant to have warranted attention—indicating to him that the captain's prejudice against him had infected the other officers. He'd been warned that, should there be a third act of misconduct, he would be hauled before the captain. That threat obviously filled the poor boy with terror.

If, after all that, Jenny still nourished in her bosom the slightest vestige of warmth for the man on the dock, one of Robbie's letters obliterated that glow completely. It described his first observance of the practice of ship's discipline known as the Flogging. *This morning,* he wrote, *the entire Crew was assembled on the quarter Deck, with the Marines lined up on the Poop. The Master- at-arms paraded in a Prisoner while we all watched. Then we stood waiting while the Surgeon prepared his Medications. After about half-an-hour, Captain Allenby came on Deck and gave the order to rig the Gratings. The Master-at-arms then read a Statement telling that this poor Devil had stolen some Rum from the Ship's Stores and then had taken a swing at the Officer who'd come upon him. The Prisoner was asked if he had any reasonable Excuse. He shook his Head. The Captain then ordered three dozen Lashes.*

We all had to stand there and Watch. You call well Imagine my Feelings as I watched the Boatswain's man carry out the Sentence with a Cat-o'-nine-tails. With each Blow, I imagined it might one day be me. I could hardly keep from Shuddering. After nine or ten Blows, the skin broke and the man began to Bleed. It was Horrible. After they took him down, the Surgeon gave him medical Treatment, and we were dismissed. I went Below and was Sick.

Jenny felt sick herself. How had she ever believed that Captain Allenby was a kind and admirable gentleman? He was an inhuman beast. It was terrifying beyond measure to realize that her beloved brother had to live—especially in his tender years—under the governance of such a monster.

Jenny and Lady Garvin were inconsolable. Robbie's plight was never far from their minds. They waited with painful anxiety for the day they would see the boy again. When the ship returned to England, they would do everything they could to extricate the poor lad from his commitment to Captain Allenby's service. Until then, however, there was nothing they could do but pray for his health and safety.

Jenny offered her mother what little consolation she could, but Lady Garvin was disconsolate. For Jenny, the only consolation came from imagining herself in her brother's straits. On some illogical level of consciousness, she permitted herself to believe that by suffering with him she was expiating her own guilt. Meanwhile, her former feelings of warmth for Captain Tristram Allenby darkened, festered and transformed themselves to a deep, implacable loathing.

Chapter Five

More than six months passed before the *Providential* returned to Portsmouth, and it was November before Robbie was given leave. But he arrived home with the glad news that, since the ship was going into drydock at Buckler's Hard, a shipyard near Southhampton, for repairs, it would be two months before he was due to ship out again.

"Ship out again?" his mother exclaimed, embracing him for the third time. "You'll do no such thing."

"What are you talking about, Mama?" The boy squirmed out of her embrace. "I *must* ship out again. I'm in naval service now, you know, and have no choice."

"I don't care. Your uncle must do something. I won't have you going back to serve under that monster."

"Oh, is *that* what's troubling you? No need to raise a dust," Robbie said. "Allenby's a beast, of course, but I'm quite used to him. One learns to deal with that sort of thing, you know, in the Navy."

Jenny and her mother exchanged looks of relief as they accompanied the boy to the dining room. Taller and thinner than before, he seemed to have been starved on shipboard. He'd already informed them that he yearned for "a good landlubber's dinner, with green vegetables, Cook's rich mushroom soup, a thick slice of rare beef and every sort of cream and pastry you can find in the larder." They watched him as he ate voraciously everything that Cullum laid before him. The boy talked all the while. He had a thousand adventures to relate. He told them about the friends he'd made, the fight with another midshipman who'd taken to bullying the others (which, he bragged, he'd won without half trying), the ports they'd called at and the sights he'd seen. He kept them enthralled for hours on end, and they didn't even think of bed until well past midnight.

When at last she retired for the night, Jenny had much to think about. Whatever her brother's experiences on shipboard might have been, they didn't seem to have done him any damage. He was brown as a berry, and although much thinner, was taller and stronger than he'd been before he'd left. And much matured. He carried himself straighter, took a longer stride and seemed to look at the world with the assurance that comes with the knowledge that one has faced obstacles and conquered them. So sailing with Captain Allenby had not seriously harmed him after all.

Nevertheless, the boy had had only the most unkind words for his captain. There was no doubt at all, he'd reported, that Allenby was a curel, inhuman monster. But Robbie had grown almost philosophical about sailing under him. "One must learn to deal with cruelty in the Navy," he'd declared grandly. "I'm not a child any longer. I can take care of myself."

Jenny could only marvel that Robbie had become mature enough to keep from buckling under the stress. The captain's name had come up again and again, always as a sinister, frightening presence looming over the boy's days, yet he'd managed to adjust to it, to find friends, a measure of contentment and a new growth of self-assurance. She was more proud of her brother than ever before. She and her mother would not need to worry about him in future; as he'd said, he was quite capable of dealing with the world on his own.

But she gave the captain no credit for Robbie's apparent well-being. The tales she'd heard of Captain Allenby gave her no reason to soften her feelings of antipathy. He was a man distorted and brutalized by power, the absolute power that a sea captain wields over everyone on his ship. Even her recollections of their meeting now seemed changed in her mind. *"Criminals, if judged guilty, must be made to face the full weight of retribution . . . ."* She remembered those words of his. They had been icy, she now remembered, and she'd seen even then the cold implacability of his eyes. *Then* she'd chosen to disregard it. *Now* the memory came back with different, more ominous reverberations. If ever she met him again, she would not be misled. She'd know him now for what he was.

She was to have that meeting sooner than she thought. Robbie had not been home a week when the Clement carriage rumbled up the drive and Andrea jumped out. She ran up the walk with unladylike haste. "Jenny," she shouted up the stairs as soon as Cullum had admitted her, "come down at once! You'll never *credit* what startling news I have for you."

She made Jenny sit down on the sofa of the sitting room before she broke the news. "We're to have a guest," she announced with barely contained excitement. "A cousin of mine, whom I've never met, but who's quite well known to you. Can you guess?"

"No, I haven't the vaguest idea. A cousin of yours? What's her name?"

"*His* name, if you please. We are speaking of a gentleman. Papa invited him, but he never dreamed the fellow would accept. He never has before."

"Really, Andrea, you're being very mysterious. How can I have met a cousin of yours that you haven't? I've never gone anywhere without you except to Bath two years ago. Was that where—? No, for Mama contracted one of her digestive complaints right after we arrived, and we hardly ever left our rooms."

"It was not at Bath," Andrea said gleefully. "*Think*!"

"Well, the only other time I traveled anywhere without you was—Good *God*! You don't mean—? It *isn't*—?"

Andrea nodded eagerly. "It *is*! Your *Captain*!"

Jenny turned quite pale. "Captain Allenby? He's coming *here*?"

"Yes, at the end of the month. He and his mother, my Aunt Dulcie, are to stay until the New Year. Papa is completely puffed up about it, for Cousin Tris has never before condescended to pay us a visit—that is, not since he was a boy, and that, of course, was before I was born."

"Captain *Allenby*? Your cousin Tris is Robbie's Captain Allenby?"

"Yes, *truly*! Captain Tristram Allenby of His Majesty's Ship *Providential*. Papa has been speaking of nothing else all morning."

"Well, really, Andrea," Jenny said with a small sigh of annoyance, "you could have warned me before. Why didn't you inform me, when I first told you I'd discovered his identity, that he was your cousin?"

"I didn't realize it until today. I've never met my cousin, you know, and Aunt Dulcie uses her title—Lady Rowcliffe. I forgot about her surname. My uncle, Lord Rowcliffe, was Arthur Allenby, but he died years ago. His eldest son, Viscount Rowcliffe, lives in Scotland, and no one ever sees *him*. I've met Aunt Dulcie once or twice—when we've gone to visit at their Derbyshire estates—but the family is really almost unknown to me and never on my mind. When Papa proses on about them, I never pay attention. So when you first discovered your mysterious gentleman's identity, the name didn't sound familiar. It just didn't occur to me that your Captain Allenby and my Cousin Tris were one and the same."

"Please, Andrea, I wish you would stop calling him *my* Captain Allenby. I've only met him once in my life, and that was for no more than half-an-hour. He probably doesn't even remember me." She rose from the sofa and began to pace about the room uneasily. "It *is* the most amazing coincidence. And you say he's to stay with you for a whole month?"

"So it seems. Aunt Dulcie wrote that he's bored with London, in spite of the fact that she's arranged all sorts of amusements for him, and to her surprise he seemed receptive to her suggestion that they rusticate here at Wyndham for a few weeks. So they're coming for a prolonged stay. Papa is overjoyed at the prospect of having a man about the house—especially one with whom he can discuss military matters and politics and trade and such things. And Mama is beside herself with excitement, for Aunt Dulcie is a veritable doyen of the most fashionable circle in London and has never before deigned to spend more than two nights under our roof. Mama is planning all sorts of dinners and routs and balls." She jumped up, grasped Jenny round the waist and spun her around. "Oh, Jenny, isn't it the most thrilling happenstance?"

"Thrilling?" Jenny echoed in repugnance, withdrawing from her friend's embrace. "It can't be so to me. Think how awkward it will be if we meet—"

"*If* you meet? Of *course* you'll meet. Mama is already writing an invitation to your mother for the welcoming dinner."

"Your mother is most kind, but really, Andrea, you haven't permitted her to believe we'd *come*!"

"But you *must* come. Why shouldn't you?"

Jenny stared at her friend in disbelief. "Haven't you been listening to me for all these months? Your cousin, my dear, has been the terror of our lives. Mama and I have had *nightmares* about him. Robbie has lived under his tyrannical domination for half a year. Surely you don't expect us to sit at the same table with him as if nothing had happened?"

"Well, I *did* think, at first, that you wouldn't like it, but when I mentioned it to Papa, he only laughed. He says all seamen say their captains are monstrous. It's the way of sailors to complain about discipline at sea. He says Robbie will be glad to have this opportunity to gain greater intimacy with his captain."

"I hope, Andrea, that you're not implying that my brother is a scheming toady, eager to butter up his captain—"

"I'm not implying that at all," Andrea declared, drawing herself up in offense. "I don't know what's come over you this afternoon, Jenny, but this belligerence is not at all like you. One would think I'd come to announce that we were being invaded by an army of Huns instead of the very delightful prospect of a month of parties and balls at which we can dance and flirt to our hearts' content."

"*You* may dance and flirt to your heart's content, but I certainly shall not," Jenny declared firmly.

"You may please yourself, of course," Andrea said coldly, sweeping to the door with her nose out of joint. "I shall be perfectly content to keep all the young men for myself. Good day, Miss Friday Face. I hope, when I come to collect you tomorrow for our shopping trip, that I find you in a better mood."

Margaret Garvin's reaction to the news of Captain Allenby's imminent arrival was almost as strong as her daughter's, although she was sorry that, in having to refuse the invitations to the many festivities at Clement Hall, she would be unable to make the acquaintance of the famous Lady Rowcliffe. "It's really too bad that the odious Captain Allenby is her son," she sighed, "for Lady Rowcliffe knows everyone in London who counts. It would have been so pleasant to be able to gossip with her."

"Mama," Jenny exclaimed in disapproval, "surely you're

not sorry to avoid the acquaintance of the mother of that monster!"

Lady Garvin shrugged. "Well, there's no use in discussing it, for we shall not have the opportunity. Naturally I shan't accept an invitation which requires us to sit at the same table with that man."

But the matter was not so easily settled. Robbie, when he heard the news, indicated that he was positively eager to meet his captain socially.

"Robbie, you must be joking!" his sister cried, aghast. "You *can't* wish to be in his company. It's bad enough that you must come face to face with him aboard ship, but now you're on holiday."

"That's just it, Jenny. On holiday, on a social occasion, I can meet him on a more equal footing and make a better impression."

"But that's . . . that's *toadying*!"

Robbie threw her a look of scorn. "Not at all," he denied vehemently. "Is it toadying, Mama, to wish to be better myself in his eyes? After all, without his commendation, I may not even sit for the lieutenant's examinations when I've become qualified. My whole career depends on his favor."

Lady Garvin studied her beloved boy with a brow wrinkled in concern. "Is it as bad as that? Can't we ask Uncle Alistair to arrange for you to be transferred or some such thing?"

"No, it can't be done, Mama. I'm in the Navy, you know, not in some trumpery boys' school. Besides, I don't wish to be transferred. I've become accustomed to the ship. I have friends . . . and a standing with the other Middies. And now I've stumbled into this amazing opportunity—I find myself a mere two miles down the road from where the captain will be staying! The other fellows will be livid with envy when they hear of my luck—"

"*Luck*?" Jenny could scarcely believe her ears.

"Yes, luck. At a social occasion like a dinner party, the captain will not behave as he does on shipboard, you know. He's not the captain of the Clement household but only a guest. He can't issue orders or take command."

"But—" his mother began.

"I think," Robbie cut her off, excitement building in his breast, "that it will be the greatest lark to be able to talk with him familiarly."

Lady Garvin exchanged alarmed glances with her daughter. "But what if he shouldn't care to speak familiarly with a member of his crew?" she asked her son.

"Oh, I shan't be so foolish as to force myself into his notice. But if he gives me the opportunity to converse with him—"

"Robbie, love," Jenny said gently, "I think that, for many reasons, it would be much better *not* to try to stand on terms of familiarity with him. It seems to me to be most advisable to remain completely apart from the festivities at Clement Hall."

"That's not to be thought of," Robbie responded emphatically. "It's a real opportunity for me. I'd be a fool to miss it. Besides, if he learns that I was invited and didn't attend, he might very well take offense. It wouldn't stand me in good stead to arouse his ire."

"That's as good as admitting you're afraid of him," Jenny said bluntly. "I've never heard you speak this way before. It sounds to me, love, as if you are succumbing to cowardice."

"You may call it what you wish," Robbie retorted, "but now that I've seen something of real life, Jenny, I realize you're rather unworldly. An innocent idealist. I've learned to live as a realist, and I see that it will do me no good if the captain learns from the Clements that I've been complaining so bitterly about him that my family refuses to sit down to table with him!"

"Good heavens, I never thought of *that*!" his mother said worriedly.

"Then you'd better think of it. If he made my life miserable before, just because I left Jenny alone on the dock for half-an-hour, only think what he'd do if he learned I'd spoken ill of him to my relations and to his own!"

"Oh, *dear*," Lady Garvin murmured, "I *have* been telling the Clements how we feel about Captain Allenby. And all the while I *knew* they were related."

"You knew?" Jenny asked in considerable surprise. "Why did you never mention it to me?"

"I don't know. It didn't seem very important. He's never come to visit in all these years, so it didn't seem as if the man was any closer to them than to strangers. Now, however, it's clear that I should have been more discreet."

Robbie looked perturbed. "Are you saying you told the Clements what I'd written in my *letters*? Good God, you don't think they'd *repeat* any of that, do you?"

"No, I don't. But I shall go to see Sally Clement first thing tomorrow and tell her we shall be delighted to come to her welcome dinner. I'm certain that, if I drop a word in her ear, she'll caution her family not to repeat any of the things we've been saying about Allenby all these months."

"I hope so, Mama," Robbie said, "for if she spills the beans, I *shall* be in the soup. And as for you, Jenny, I hope you can be discreet as well. If you show the captain the slightest dislike, he'll undoubtedly blame me for it. So be sure to be polite to him, if my future means anything to you."

Jenny stared at her brother and her mother in dismay. They were both behaving in a way that Jenny could not admire. At *best* they could be called self-serving, and at worst hypocritical. And they seemed to expect her to fall right in with their machinations. She opened her mouth to remonstrate but on reflection closed it again. She couldn't impose her standards on them. Besides, she adored her brother. Suppose he was right about the captain's ability to determine his future? She couldn't take it upon herself to endanger that future because of her own —how had Robbie put it?—unworldly idealism.

Thus she made no objection when her mother and brother decided that the family was to take part in the festivities at Clement Hall after all. As soon as the decision was made, Jenny excused herself and went up to her room. Her stomach churned in agitation. She would have to face Captain Allenby, offer him her hand and even talk to him. She wasn't at all sure she could manage to endure it.

She sank down on her bed, her mind swimming with images of the forthcoming scene at the Clements' dinner, when she would face the captain for the first time. Would he smile at her in intimate recollection of their earlier meeting, or would he have forgotten her completely? If he remembered her, would he try to kiss her hand? She shuddered in repugnance. When she looked at him again, she would no longer see that kind gentleman of her former imaginings—the one who'd recovered her baggage and whose eyes had gleamed in a flash of attraction. No, that gentleman had been nothing but a fiction —the figment of an innocent girl's dreams. When she looked at him now, she would be able to see only the beast who'd ordered a man to be whipped until he bled.

She loved her brother, and for his sake she would have to hide her revulsion toward his captain. For the sake of Robbie's future, she would have to be polite, expedient, hypocritical. In a word, civil.

But to act such a role was very much against her grain. She *was* idealistic and didn't enjoy having to join her family in playing toady. Only for Robbie would she restrain her natural instincts and be civil; but even for Robbie she would do no more. She couldn't. She would be completely incapable of showing the captain a smile, a glance or the slightest expression of warmth. Toward the horrid Captain Allenby mere civility was all anyone could expect of her.

Chapter Six

Despite the fact that Lady Garvin awoke next morning with a digestive upset and a severe attack of the megrims, she rose from her bed, dressed and, refusing to swallow any breakfast, sent for the carriage. As she explained to Jenny, she intended to correct her indiscretions of the last few months (during which she'd poured into Sally Clement's ear every complaint Robbie had written about his captain and a few more of her own devising) by going to see Sally without delay. To avoid further damage to Robbie's career, it was necessary to secure Sally's promise never to repeat those confidences to a soul.

She returned home several hours later in a strange mood. Although her megrims were gone and her stomach had settled itself well enough to permit her to order Cullum to serve an early and proper tea that afternoon (she'd already partaken of a luncheon in Sally's company, but it had been light and quite inadequate), she couldn't say whether she felt relieved or annoyed as a result of her visit. "Though why I should feel so annoyed I don't understand," she said to Jenny as she joined her in the music room and sank down upon a chair.

Jenny, who'd been playing the piano energetically in an attempt to lose herself in the music, stopped playing and looked at her mother curiously. "Annoyed, Mama? Why?"

"Because Sally behaved as if we'd never uttered a word about Captain Allenby's reprehensible character. I believe that she's so delighted at the prospect of entertaining her distinguished guests that she's wiped from her mind all of my disparagements of the fellow."

"Then I think you should be delighted. You need no longer concern yourself about the problem of your remarks being repeated."

"I *am* delighted," her mother said, her frown so pronounced that it belied her words, "but doesn't it strike you as irritating that my earlier remarks should have made so shallow an impression on her?"

"Not so very irritating. I've noticed that one's troubles rarely make as deep an impression on others as they do on one's self. Lady Clement, not being Robbie's mother, can't be expected to feel as deeply about his problems as you do."

"You're right. She has no sons and therefore can't be expected to understand my feelings. And it's just as well that she doesn't remember all my complaints. The less the Clements remember, the smaller the chance of anything being repeated to cause us embarrassment."

"Or to cause difficulty for Robbie," Jenny added.

"Yes. I shall force myself to look upon the bright side. No matter how revolting it will be to associate with that man, we shall at least have the pleasure of meeting Lady Rowcliffe and of attending all the festivities." She leaned back in her chair, closing her eyes reflectively. "I think, Jenny, that I shall need a couple of new gowns. I've worn the purple ducapes too often, and the turquoise crape is sadly out of date. And as for you, my girl, I won't have you wearing that dove-colored poplin one more time. It makes you look a positive dowd. I've been saving five yards of the most beautiful apricot-colored silk which I shall have Mrs. Elvin make up for you."

"Just as you wish, Mama," Jenny murmured, turning back to her music.

Lady Garvin rose to leave. "I hope you don't intend to hammer away at the piano very much longer, Jenny," she said from the doorway. "I'm quite famished, as you may surmise (not having had any breakfast and only having taken the lightest of luncheons), and I've told Cullum to serve tea as soon as possible. I shall be ready for it in ten minutes. Don't keep me waiting for you forever."

Jenny resumed her playing, but though her fingers flew over the keys as busily as before, her heart and mind were no longer engrossed in the act. She was aware of a painful lowering of her spirits, and the few minutes left to her to lose herself in the music seemed an inadequate amount of time to lift those spirits to their usual, cheerful level. She'd always considered herself a lighthearted sort, finding contentment in many aspects of her daily life despite her mother's carping. (Even in childhood she'd been able to slough off the barbs that her mother shot at her, realizing that they were unwitting and not really intended to cut away at Jenny's self-esteem.) She'd always been optimistic, waking each morning with an eagerness to explore the coming day. It was only in the last few months that she'd begun to notice that her usual cheerfulness was harder to maintain.

Just now, for example, she'd found herself unable to ignore (as she'd always managed to do before) her mother's remark about her "hammering away" at her music. Jenny was quite proficient at the pianoforte; in truth she believed she possessed some little talent for it. Yet her mother rarely sat down to listen and never offered a word of praise. Ordinarily, Jenny would not be disturbed by this. After all, her mother had little knowledge of or interest in music of any sort; *Clementi himself* might play for her without receiving a nod of approbation. But today, Jenny had felt a little catch of tears in her throat when her mother had said those words. Why, after all these years of indifference to her mother's disdain, was she all at once so hurt by it? Why was she suddenly so vulnerable and so filled with unwonted sensibilities? Why after all these years had she become so painfully aware of being second in her mother's affections?

But it was not only her mother who could lower her spirits. Everything, of late, seemed to depress her. It was as if she'd moved abruptly from a sunny world to one of shadow. The people she met seemed, somehow, *darker* than they were before. They now seemed to hold within them the possibility of evil. An innocent-seeming little boy could be, in reality, a decoy for a thief; a gentleman who appeared kindly could really be a cruel, power-maddened tyrant. Things and people that had once seemed pleasant and friendly now might possess ugly, hidden secrets.

Probably that had always been so, but she hadn't seen it before. Something had changed within *her*. Some innocence that had made things seem light had died, and nothing was the same.

Perhaps her earlier cheerfulness had merely been childishness. Perhaps this new awareness of the darkness underneath the smiling surface of things was a symptom of adulthood. Was *this* what was happening to her—was she growing up at last? If that was so, it was really too bad. Life had been more pleasant before.

Two tears that had managed to rise from her throat trickled down her cheeks. With a quick brush of the back of her hand she rubbed them away. How foolishly she was behaving! Such maudlin self-pitying thoughts were quire unlike her and wouldn't do at all. She would simply not indulge in them. This was merely a mood, an attack of the vapors, a slight aberration. She would not make too much of it. With a spurt of energetic determination, she jumped to her feet, put on a pleasant smile and went out to join her mother for tea.

Dulcie Allenby, Lady Rowcliffe, pacing about the sitting room of her lavish London townhouse, was also ready for her tea, but her son had not yet made his appearance. She'd been waiting for him for fully a quarter-hour and was growing impatient. Lady Rowcliffe was not a woman to suffer impatience for very long. With a grunt of decision she turned on her heel, strode to the door, marched down the long hallway to the library and burst in without knocking. There, reclining on the sofa—his booted feet callously resting on the striped satin cushion—was her negligent son, engrossed in one of the dozens of newspapers that were piled in stacks on the floor beside him. "Must you put your boots up on my loveliest sofa?" she asked in mock annoyance.

"Sorry, Mama," Captain Allenby said with a sheepish grin, swinging his legs to the floor and sitting upright. "I'm so accustomed to reading in a bunk bed that I forget myself."

"And did you also forget about tea? I've been waiting for you for an age."

"Have you? I *am* a beast." He put the paper down and got to his feet. "Are you completely put out with me?"

"I should be," his mother muttered.

He strolled over to her, leaned down and planted a kiss on her cheek. "You're wishing me back on shipboard, I shouldn't wonder. It's better having me at sea than lounging about in your library, upsetting the schedules and muddying up the upholstery, isn't it?"

"Rubbish!" She thumped him affectionately on the chest. Only a bit over five feet tall, she barely came up to his shoulder. "I *love* having you home, and you know it. You're probably put out with *me* for interrupting your perusal of the news."

"No, as a matter of fact, I'm not," he admitted, stretching out his arms and yawning. "There's devilish little news worth reading in these sheets. Much too much debate about your eccentric Lord Byron's self-exile, and too much fuss about the Regent's desire to erect a monument to the Stuarts in Rome. I'm more interested in plans for the new docks, about which I can find nothing, and in what Parliament is doing about repealing the Corn Laws, about which there is precious little. Why don't the papers stir up some concern about the general distress of the population over the price of grain? There's very little printed in these tittle-tattle pages about *that*."

His mother frowned at him, all the while adjusting his neckcloth and smoothing his hair (which was just beginning to show a touch of grey at the sides) by standing on tiptoe and reaching up as high as she could. "You sound like a reformist Whig, my love, interested only in the plight of the poor. We rich have our heartaches, too, you know. And 'my' Lord Byron is as worthy of your sympathy as any indigent farm worker."

Having made her son presentable, she pushed him to the door. He obediently started down the hall, his brow wrinkled thoughtfully over the dubious logic of her last remark. "I can't agree with you, Mama. Lord Byron has a flock of soft-hearted, sentimental admirers to weep over his plight, but only a handful—those few you call reformist Whigs—show any concern over the indigent farm workers. Must a man be beautiful, romantical and poetical before you women will weep for him?"

Lady Rowcliffe shook her head in wry amusement. "I suppose so. It's quite difficult for me to become emotional about some theoretical 'common man' whom I've never met, whereas I feel quite keenly for someone like Byron, whom I've known for years. He *is* quite beautiful, you know, and much of his poetry is marvelous. I'm completely put out that all this dreadful gossip has driven him out of his own country."

"Nevertheless," her son said, settling himself on an easy chair before the sitting-room fire and stretching out his legs on the hearth, "I find it irritating to read the details over and over in the papers."

"Well, you *did* ask me to save them for you while you were

gone, so you have only yourself to blame," his mother muttered, pouring the tea.

"I suppose I do. But one must catch up with the world's happenings when one returns from a voyage. We hear nothing of the rest of the world when we're at sea. The world over the horizon shrinks away, and our little vessel takes on the semblance of a whole world in itself. It's quite appalling, really. I have to read the old papers on my return just to readjust myself to the larger reality."

His mother brought him a brimming cup. Then, pouring one for herself, she perched on a chair beside him. "Are you happy at sea, Tris? *Really* happy?" she asked, looking at him closely from beneath lowered lids.

"I suppose so. I can't imagine myself spending my days in any other way. Why do you ask?"

"Because I'm your mother, you great oaf. I worry over you. I would prefer to see you settled down in one place, with a wife at your side and little children at your feet. Dash it, Tris, I'm sixty years old and have not *one grandchild*! Your brother in Scotland is too reclusive ever to marry, I fear, so you are my only hope."

Tris stirred his tea silently for a moment. "My being a sailor needn't dash your hopes, Mama. There are many of us who have wives and families. It may not always be an easy life for a woman, but I know of several who are quite content."

"Then why haven't you married?"

"I've been occupied with other matters. There was a war, you know. But I am thinking about marriage now."

"Are you?" She put down her cup and leaned forward. "You've given no sign of it to me. I've thrust at least three perfectly suitable females at you since you've been home without noting a spark of interest in your eyes."

"If you're speaking of that creature with the orange hair—"

"Yes, she's one of them. Miss Hazelton. And her hair is *not* orange, it's Titian. Most gentlemen fall into transports over it."

Tris snorted. "That must be very pleasant for Miss Hazelton. If she has so many admirers, she will not be crushed by my indifference."

"Indifference is exactly what you showed her, you cawker. I'll admit that Miss Hazelton's appearance is somewhat . . . er . . ."

"Garish?" her son supplied.

Lady Rowcliffe tried to hide her grin. "Very well, garish. But one couldn't call Miss Daubney garish, yet you showed the same indifference toward her."

"Is Miss Daubney the young lady with the startled eyes? Good God, Mama, I've never met anyone so nervous. The sound of the dinner gong startled her, the music startled her, a raucous laugh from behind us startled her. Can you picture her on board a ship? The first strong wind would overset her for the rest of the voyage."

"Very well, I'll grant that Miss Daubney's sensibilities are too tender—"

Tris grinned at his mother appreciatively. "What a very nice way to put it, Mama," he taunted.

She ignored the interruption. "—but Miss Kingsbury is neither garish nor nervous. What about Miss Kingsbury?"

"The dark one? She's a very pretty girl."

Her eyebrows rose with a barely perceptible touch of eagerness. "Do you think so? I do, too. And quite a sensible sort, as you would learn for yourself if you would take her riding tomorrow."

Tris pulled himself to his feet and walked over to the tea table. "Let be, Mama," he said, his voice softly firm. "I'm thirty-five years old and don't need wet-nursing." He refilled his cup and turned back to his mother, fixing her with an unsmiling, pointed look. "I'm quite capable of pursuing a female without motherly guidance."

"You don't say," his mother muttered, putting up her chin defiantly. "Is that how you reprimand your crew? With that cold stare and threatening voice? But you can't terrorize *me* with that trick. I knew you as a child. Having in the past often wiped your runny nose and swaddled your naked bottom, I find it difficult, now, to feel awestruck."

A reluctant laugh burst out of him. "I can't be formidable to my mother, eh? How disappointing. Then I'm quite defenseless." He returned to his chair. "Nevertheless, ma'am, I can do without your motherly matchmaking."

"No, you can't. You may be thirty-five, but you don't know the *first thing* about finding a wife. If you did, you'd realize that the search requires time and effort. You've spent more than a week dawdling about the house reading your newspapers. The only times you've left the premises were those few afternoons you visited with your cronies at the admiralty and the three occasions when I dragged you out with me. And on *those* occasions you were cool and indifferent toward every female who passed by. I know because I watched you."

"Serves you right. You shouldn't have watched."

"But my dear, how can you pretend to be interested in marriage when you are unwilling to *do* anything about it? You've wasted all this time already, and in a little more than a fortnight you want to go off to the country—heaven knows why!—where the females are bound to be far less presentable than the ones I can introduce to you here in London."

"Are you sure of that, Mama?"

"What?" She'd been warming up to her thesis concerning the proper manner of pursuing a female, and she was distracted by his interruption. She'd been about to suggest that they write to her brother to cancel their plans to spend the month of December at Wyndham. She couldn't see the sense of it. Instead of burying themselves in a rural backwater for weeks, she was ready to urge Tris to remain with her in town, where they could concentrate on finding a lady suitable for him to wed. But he'd broken into her train of thought with this strange question. "What do you mean, am I sure?" she asked, blinking.

"Are you sure that country girls are less presentable than those in town? Isn't that a rather prejudiced view?"

"It's a view formed by years of experience and observation," his mother stated unequivocally. "I suppose that beauty and charm *can* appear occasionally in the wilds, but they can best be bred and schooled right here in town. It is only here that you'll find your cultivated, perfected, refined beauties."

He took a sip of tea. "I'd prefer someone *un*schooled, I think. Someone whose charm is more natural and . . . unspoiled."

"Hmmmph! his mother grunted in disgust. "All you men dream about is unspoiled beauties. They don't *exist*."

"I hope you're mistaken about that, Mama."

"Even if I am, you'll not find your unspoiled beauty at your uncle's place. Your cousin Andrea is considered to be the reigning belle of Wyndham, and she couldn't hold a candle to Miss Kingsbury."

"My cousin Andrea?" Tris stared at his mother in considerable surprise. "The belle of the whole district? Are you sure?"

"Well, that's what I've been given to understand. Why does that surprise you so?"

"It's just that I would have supposed . . ." His voice died, and he shook his head. "The bumpkins of Wyndham probably haven't sufficiently discriminating eyes."

"What *are* you babbling about, Tris?"

"Nothing, Mama. Pay me no mind."

She stared at him with dawning comprehension. "Good God!" she gasped suddenly. "There's a young lady in *Wyndham* who's caught your eye! That's *it*, isn't it? I should have guessed. For what other reason would you wish to rusticate at Clement Hall for an entire month?" She jumped up from her chair in girlish eagerness. "Who *is* she, Tris? Where did you meet her? Shall I like her? What a silly question . . . of *course* I shall! Oh, I am quite beside myself! This news has completely altered my mood." She ran to the door and shouted into the corridor, "Lockhurst! Lockhurst, bring a bottle of champagne. The Pinot Chardonnay, I think."

Tris raised an amused eyebrow. "Mama, really! Champagne?"

"Of course champagne. One can't celebrate such news by drinking *tea*!"

"But there really isn't any news to celebrate," he cautioned, frowning. "You're getting a bit ahead of yourself, my dear."

"Nonsense. You've no idea how long I've waited to hear you say something like that. I *must* celebrate. You know, I wasn't looking forward to leaving London, but now I can't *wait* to start for the country."

Tris started to make an objection to his mother's effusions, but Lockhurst, the butler, came in with the wine and a pair of glasses on a tray. Conversation was halted while he opened the bottle with expert precision and poured. As soon as he withdrew, however, Tris took the glass from his mother's hand. "Your wish to celebrate, Mama, is much too premature. You're leaping to a great number of conclusions without any substantiating facts. It seems to me that you ought to haul sail and slacken speed, or you'll find yourself on the shoals."

Lady Rowcliffe laughed. "Very well, Captain, I'll slow down. But let me have my wine and give me what 'substantiating facts' there are. I'm not mistaken about my basic premise, am I? There *is* a girl in Wyndham, I take it."

"Yes, there is. But I've only met her once, so it wouldn't be advisable for you to begin counting your grandchildren just yet," he said, handing the glass back to her.

"But this is too exciting for words!" she exclaimed delightedly, sinking down on the hearth and sipping her drink. "Tell me all about it. Where did you meet her? It couldn't have been at Wyndham, for you haven't visited there since childhood."

"I met her on the dock at Portsmouth."

Lady Rowcliffe's smile faded. "On the *dock* . . . ?"

Tris laughed. "You needn't look so stricken, Mama. She's no lightskirt. She'd come to see her brother off. He's a middy on my ship."

"Oh, I see." She leaned back in some relief. "She must be dazzling if you were so taken with her in one meeting. I don't know why I haven't heard Alfred or Sally speak of her."

"I don't think you can call her 'dazzling' at all. That's not the right word. She's a rather shy sort, I believe. The kind who hesitates to put herself forward and who colors up at the slightest provocation. 'Reticent,' I'd say."

"Are you attracted to *reticence*?" his mother asked in amazement.

"I was to *hers*."

Lady Rowcliffe studied him dubiously. "But her shyness may only have been a response to the situation. You are, after all, the awesome Captain Allenby of her brother's ship."

"Yes, but she didn't know it then. Our meeting was quite accidental. We've not *yet* been introduced."

"I don't think I understand. Are you saying that you struck up an acquaintance with a young woman who was absolutely unknown to you . . . and you to her?"

"Yes, that's about the size of it."

"Really, my love, such an encounter doesn't sound at all seemly. A young woman who would permit herself to indulge in such a *rencontre* can *not* be a proper sort."

"You don't know the circumstances, so you can't judge," her son retorted flatly.

Lady Rowcliffe could see that her son had not the slightest intention of enlightening her about those circumstances. "Tris, my dear, you can't be serious about this," she said, troubled. "How can you, after one brief meeting with a young woman whose identity you didn't know and who didn't know yours, propose to go to the country for a month just to seek her out? It seems quite shatterbrained to me."

"It probably is. But if she's at all as I remember her, I want to marry her."

"*Tris!*"

"Is that very shocking?" he asked naively.

"Of course it is. Good heavens, can she have made so strong an impression on you as *that*?"

"I must admit she did."

"But, my dear, suppose you find, when you meet her again, that she's not at all as you remember her. What then?"

He shrugged. "I have no idea. That's why I didn't wish to speak of this at all. I was certain you'd think I was behaving like a moonling."

"And you are," she said bluntly.

"I suppose I am. Sometimes I think she can't possibly be as lovely as I remember her. But I must find out. You see, Mama, I've been able to think of very little else since the day I met her."

"Oh, dear, that *does* sound serious. In the circumstances, I suppose we'd better not cancel our journey to Wyndham after all."

"Cancel it? Certainly not. Whatever gave you the idea that we should?"

"I was convinced that you'd find the sojourn dull beyond belief. And I was positive *I* would. Now, however, I'm beginning to believe that a stay in the country may turn out to be a great deal more interesting than I thought."

"It will certainly be that," Tris murmured a bit ruefully. "You do realize, Mama, that we should prepare for the possibility of complete disaster."

"You mean if you should find that you don't care for her after all?"

"I mean if I find she doesn't care for *me*."

"Oh, pooh! She can't be such a ninny as that."

Tris shook his head. "Don't be so fondly blind, Mama. I'm years older than she, not at all the comely youth of whom a girl dreams, and a sailor to boot. I've given myself a month in which to win her over, but I might soon learn that she won't have me."

His mother hooted and got nimbly to her feet. "What is much *more* likely, you gudgeon, is that you'll have one brief meeting with her, find her conversation innocuous or her manners revolting, and wonder whatever made you think for a moment that she was the woman for you. Then I shall have to invent some sort of excuse for your uncle Alfred to explain why we are packing up so abruptly and returning to London."

But Tris was not listening. He was staring into the fire with a most uncharacteristic half-smile on his face, as if he were envisioning the most beatific reunion the world had ever seen. His mother sighed, half in amusement and half in dismay. She hoped her son was not embarking on a path that would lead to a crushing disappointment.

But Lady Rowcliffe was a woman of action, not of contemplation. She immediately roused herself from the mire of useless speculation. "Will you be wanting the rest of this champagne?" she asked her son.

He seemed not to have heard. With another amused shake of her head, she picked up the bottle and her glass and went briskly to the door. "I'm not going to let this expensive champagne go to waste, whether I have something to celebrate or not," she announced gaily to no one in particular. Then, on the threshold, she paused. "I wonder," she murmured thoughtfully, "what one must pack for a whole month in the country."

But realizing that she would get no response from her oblivious son, she went out and closed the door behind her without waiting for an answer.

Chapter Seven

Everyone in the district knew that Lady Rowcliffe and her famous son had arrived at Clement Hall, for as soon as the news had leaked abroad that one of the doyens of the *haut ton* and one of the heroes of Trafalgar were to pay a visit to their region, the populace had kept watch for them. The nine-year-old son of the owner of the livery stable had seen a line of carriages approaching and had actually run down the road shouting, "They're coming! They're coming!"

Never before had the inhabitants of Wyndham seen such an entourage. Lady Rowcliffe, in a black-and-bronze coach drawn by six horses, had led the parade, followed by two other carriages—a phaeton painted a shocking lapis-lazuli blue, carrying her ladyship's abigail and her special "dresser," and a barouch-landau piled high with trunks, parcels, bandboxes and dressing cases. Captain Allenby himself, who'd brought up the rear, was to the onlookers a decided anticlimax, for he'd not worn his naval uniform but merely modest civilian dress, he'd been unaccompanied by a single servant ("Not even a valet!" Mrs. Jubb later exclaimed to the vicar's wife who'd been too conscious of her family's dignity to run out to the road to watch) and he'd been driving his own curricle with not even a tiger standing up behind.

Lady Clement's welcoming dinner was to be held on the very night of her guests' arrival, and the event was anticipated by all those who'd been invited with the most avid excitement. Even the worldly wise Lady Rowcliffe found herself somewhat anxiously expectant, for she'd managed to learn from her unsuspecting sister-in-law that Tris's Miss Jenny Garvin was on the guest list.

Lady Rowcliffe hadn't had the least difficulty in worming

out the information from Sally without giving Tris's secret away. She'd simply waited until everyone in the household had retired to their dressing rooms to dress for dinner, she'd removed a bottle from a large wooden crate which she'd brought with her and, in her elegant dressing gown trimmed with gold cord, the bottle tucked under her arm and two stemmed goblets in her hand, she'd walked down the hall to her sister-in-law's bedroom. "May I come in for a moment, Sally?" she'd asked guilelessly from the doorway. "I've brought you a dozen bottles of the Carcavellos wine you so much admired when you visited me last, and I thought you might enjoy sampling it before dinner."

"Oh, come in," Sally said with a welcoming smile to cover her surprise. Waving her abigail out of the room, she added, "Although I don't remember admiring any wine. Not that I didn't admire *everything* you served. You are *such* a connoisseur."

"Rubbish," Lady Rowcliffe said, closing the door carefully behind her.

Sally, Lady Clement, peered up at her stylish sister-in-law from her place at her dressing table with vaguely troubled eyes. Pale-haired and plump, Sally Clement was always vaguely troubled. Having won for herself a husband much grander than anyone had ever expected, she'd thought when she'd married that all her earthly troubles were at an end. But happiness always seemed to elude her. Her husband was devoted but not intimate, her daughter was beautiful but quite spoiled, her life was always just short of expectation. She was sensitive enough to realize that things in her life were awry but not clever or strong enough to set them right. *If only,* she thought with a sigh, *I could be as clever and purposeful as this diminutive, dynamic sister-in-law of mine.*

"I remember quite distinctly," Lady Rowcliffe insisted, setting up the glasses and opening the bottle, "that you admired it because it's both sweet and pungent." She poured the golden liquid into the glasses and handed one to her sister-in-law.

Sally took the glass and sipped the wine gingerly. "Mmm. It *is* sweet and pungent, isn't it? This is so kind of you, Dulcie, dear. Imagine your remembering to bring it for me when I don't even remember asking—"

"Doesn't the taste remind you? Drink it up, my dear, and it will all come back to you," Dulcie urged. "You will not find a wine like this anywhere outside of Portugal. I have a special source of supply, you see."

"You mean smugglers, don't you?" Sally began to drink with more relish. "Oh, it is lovely. I do thank you."

"Have some more," Lady Rowcliffe murmured, refilling her sister-in-law's glass and seating herself on the chaise with casual nonchalance. "You've gone to so much trouble to make our first evening here festive that I'm glad I have something tangible with which to show my appreciation."

"That wasn't at all necessary. It's the greatest pleasure to me to be able to present you to my friends and neighbors."

"Oh, dear," Dulcie said with exaggerated alarm, "I hope you're not going to have a great crowd."

"No, not tonight. Only my very closest friends, and the vicar, of course. And some of their offspring. Only eighteen guests in all. I mean to have a musicale afterwards, and some card games." She looked at her sister-in-law in sudden apprehension. "I didn't overdo it, did I, for your first evening?"

"No, not at all. It sounds utterly delightful."

"But will Tristram like it, do you think?" Sally persisted worriedly, reaching for the bottle and refilling her glass.

Lady Rowcliffe shrugged. "How can I tell what Tris will like? He rarely deigns to socialize with me, you know."

"I'm so eager to arrange our social events to please him," Sally confided, taking a large swig of her wine. "We shall have a few young ladies who're unattached, and Toby Boyce, of course, but he's only barely in his twenties. Perhaps Tristram will find them all too young for him. And all our friends are, naturally, much too old—"

"I wouldn't concern myself about Tris, if I were you. He's very resourceful and will be able to make his own amusements. He enjoys good conversation with people of any age, and as for unattached young ladies, do you know of any gentleman who's not susceptible to them?"

"Yes, you must be right," Sally said with a hiccough. "I've been overanxious. Our young ladies are bound to please. Why, there's Andrea right here at hand, and I needn't tell you what a diamond *she* is, and then there's Jenny Garvin, who is rather retiring but quite capable of witty conversation when she's drawn out."

"Garvin?" Lady Rowcliffe casually picked a piece of lint from the sleeve of her gown. "I've heard that name, I think."

"You may have heard it from Tristram, for the young Garvin boy sailed with him on this last voyage."

"Ah, yes. Tris did mention that one of his 'middies' resides in Wyndham. What a coincidence that the family should be known to you."

"Oh, very well known to us, I as . . . assure you," Sally said, waving her glass in the air unsteadily. "They were the very first I invited for this evening. Lady Garvin is very well connected—the Earl of Wetherbrooke is her brother-in-law. She's a widow like yourself, and I'm convinced you will take to her. Her son, Robbie, is quite the most popular young man in the district, despite the fact that he's not quite fifteen." She giggled whoozily and then covered her mouth in surprise. "He's frightfully good-looking, as you will see."

"And Lady Garvin has a daughter, too, you say?" Lady Rowcliffe persisted, although she exhibited no more than a casual, polite interest.

"Jenny. A lovely girl, lovely." She poured the last of the wine into her glass. "She and Andrea have been bosom-bows since childhood." She smiled dizzily. "Bosom-bows."

"How nice. I don't suppose, however, that it's possible she can be as charming as your Andrea, for a country village like Wyndham can hardly be expected to have *two* such diamonds."

Sally's eyes wavered from Dulcie's face. She'd had too much wine and she knew it. She hoped she wouldn't say anything foolish while her head was so dizzy and her tongue so thick. Her sharp-eyed sister-in-law would discover soon enough, she supposed, that Andrea had a hidden flaw. The girl could sometimes exhibit unexpected signs of being spoiled. If only she could keep her daughter from having a tantrum while Dulcie and Tris remained in residence.

Her head was swimming. She mustn't let herself take anything else to drink tonight. It wouldn't do for her to reveal her secret dream . . . the hope that Tris would develop a *tendre* for her daughter. Alfred always said that he didn't approve of marriages between cousins, despite their legality, but she would be overjoyed to see her daughter so well settled. If only Andrea . . .

But she was too dizzy to follow the thought. She had to concentrate on what her sister-in-law had just said. Something about Wyndham having two diamonds . . .

"Well," she said, smiling a little too brightly and focussing her eyes on her sister-in-law's face a little too intently, "I don't like to be the one to ex . . . toll the virtues of m' own daughter, but I'll admit that she's con . . . sidered to be Wyndham's gem." Her speech was just a trifle thick, and she went bravely on. "Don't want to give you th' idea that Jenny is not a pretty li'l thing. Very pretty li'l thing. Speaking eyes, you know . . . even if she hasn't Andrea's air. But she's very clever . . . very clever in her quiet way." She gave another unexpected giggle. "Y'know, Dulcie, I do b'lieve I'm just the sli . . . slightest bit foxed . . ."

Lady Rowcliffe had heard enough to give her cause for an attack of nervous anxiety. She soon excused herself and returned to her room, her brow creased with worry. Had Tris fallen top-over-tail for a dull, colorless little country mouse? All the signs were unpropitious. If Andrea (whom Lady Rowcliffe found to be a rather average, provincial, overly forward sort of girl) could put Jenny Garvin in the shade, then Miss Jenny Garvin didn't promise to be very impressive.

She went into her room and sank onto the bed with a sigh. She'd often tried to imagine what Tris's wife would be like. Her fondest dream was that the girl would be someone with whom she could feel congenial. She yearned for someone with whom she could share intimacies and on whom she could lavish affection—someone who could be the daughter she'd never had. What a joy it would be to be able to help the girl set up a home, to buy her gifts, to exchange gossip, to share to some extent in the upbringing of her grandchildren. With the right wife for Tris, life would be richer not only for him but for her, too. The wife and the mother-in-law could care for each other, advise each other, console each other and, when Tris was away on long voyages, ease the other's loneliness. But a shy little dab of a country girl, without personality or spirit, would not be at all what Lady Rowcliffe had in mind.

She was quite certain that Tris had been hasty. How could he, a man of sophistication and intelligence, have made such a mistake? She knew that there was no accounting for taste—especially in matters of the heart—but she'd hoped her son had better sense than to lose his heart to a nonentity.

But wait, she cautioned herself, *I haven't even laid eyes on the girl as yet*! How ludicrous to make a judgment on the basis of the scraps of information she'd gleaned from a dizzy, befuddled Sally. (She felt not a shred of guilt for having plied poor Sally with wine; she'd probably be a livelier, more spirited hostess than she'd ever been in her life.) Dulcie Allenby was not the sort of woman who would let other people make judgments for her. She would see the girl for herself, and until then, she would keep an open mind.

She jumped up from the bed and rang for her maid. She had better begin to dress for dinner. As she paced about the room waiting for her abigail to answer her summons, she felt time passing too slowly. She could hardly wait for dinner time to take a look at the girl for herself.

Lady Rowcliffe was not the only one who awaited the appointed hour with anxiety. Lady Garvin and Jenny, both ill-at-ease at the prospect of facing the detestable captain, had spent the afternoon discussing the situation. They'd agreed that it would be a most difficult evening. Lady Garvin had declared that, for Robbie's sake, she would not reveal her dislike, but she would avoid outright hypocrisy when in the company of "that inhuman monster" by speaking of nothing but her son in his presence. She would merely extol her son's virtues and avoid participation in any discussion of the captain, his voyages, his career or his character. Jenny, however, had made up her mind to avoid any discussion at all. She didn't say this to her mother, but she was determined that, while the captain was at hand, she would utter absolutely nothing but polite monosyllables.

Lady Garvin insisted that they begin preparing for the occasion in mid-afternoon, and Jenny dutifully retired to her room to dress. But she accomplished all the preliminaries in short order, having had to spend very little time dressing her hair. All the other ladies she knew—her mother, Andrea, Lady Clement, everyone—sat at their dressing tables for hours while their hairdressers crimped, teased, and curled their hair into elaborate coiffures. Jenny, however, didn't like crimping. She merely plaited her long locks into one tight braid and twisted it into a knot at the back of her head. In recognition of the formality of this occasion (and to avoid hearing her mother describe her again as a dowd), she made one concession to fashion—she left the lower half of her tail of hair unbraided and let it fall from the knot and lie curled over one shoulder. It was, for her, a daring departure from her usual restraint, and it was quite good enough, she decided, for the likes of Captain Allenby and his *haut-monde* mother.

With her undergarments on and her hair dressed, she had only to slip into the new apricot-silk evening dress which her mother had had made for her. There was still plenty of time before the family was due to depart for the Hall—two hours, in fact. Rather than pace about the room in all her finery while waiting for the appointed time, she postponed putting on the dress. She wrapped herself in a dressing gown and sat down on her window seat with a copy of Scott's *Guy Mannering*, which she'd just purchased. But the agitation of her spirit was so great that the novel failed to grasp her attention.

After a while, she put the book aside and took out her new gown. She shook the tissue paper from the sleeves and slipped it on, but a glance at herself in the mirror appalled her. The dress was *dreadful*. With its tiny sleeves and low-cut bosom all one could see was *flesh*! The revealing *décolletage* and the high waist accented her breasts and made her entire form seem shockingly seductive. At the fitting, when she'd suggested to her mother that the dress was a bit too daring, her mother had merely shrugged. "That's how young ladies are *noticed*, my love. You may as well accustom yourself to it, for you cannot spend your life hiding away from people's stares," she'd declared and had complimented Mrs. Elvin, the dressmaker, on her handiwork.

But Jenny *couldn't* appear in public in this vulgar creation. She would die of embarrassment. Good Lord, in such a dress she'd appear to be trying to *catch* Captain Allenby's eye instead of trying to avoid it! Desperately, she ransacked her drawers until she found a square of lace. With trembling fingers, she folded it into a triangle and pinned it, pointed end down, into the center of the *décolletage*. She studied herself critically in the mirror. The lace, while not quite blending with the trim of the gown, nevertheless managed to cover the cleavage of her breasts—a small salve to her sense of modesty. But even when wearing her longest gloves, her upper arms would be uncomfortably bare, and her neck and shoulders would remain much too daringly exposed. While wearing this dress she would not be able to feel a moment's comfort or relaxation, and, in an abrupt act of determination, she pulled it off.

She stood, hesitant, in the center of the room, trying to

decide what to do. Her mother would be furious with her, she knew, if she made an appearance in her old dove-grey poplin. But the poplin was her best gown and the one most appropriate for formal occasions. It had a ruche at the neck trimmed with the finest Alençon lace and a deep flounce at the bottom which moved gracefully when she walked. The sleeves were long and the neck high, and she was always comfortable when wearing it. Purposefully, she pulled it out of the wardrobe and put it on.

But this act of defiance would be quite useless, she knew, as soon as her mother looked at her. She would surely be sent back to her room to change. There was only one thing to do. She would hide here in her room until the very last minute, when it would be too late for her mother to send her back upstairs. This decided, she packed away the apricot silk, returned to the window seat, picked up *Guy Mannering* and waited.

Lady Garvin, having changed her own gown twice (her indecision having been caused by a desire to make a good impression on the famous Lady Rowcliffe, whose gown would undoubtedly put all the Wyndham ladies' finery in the shade), was late, herself, in coming downstairs. After she'd looked Robbie over carefully (uttering exclamations of approval over his pale yellow breeches, his well-cut coat of deep blue superfine and the impressive chapeau bras he carried under his arm), she realized that Jenny had not yet come down. In considerable irritation, she sent a housemaid to fetch the girl at once. "I shall never be able to look Lady Rowcliffe in the eye if we're so *gauche* as to keep them all waiting," she said to Robbie impatiently.

Jenny appeared at the top of the stairway, but Lady Garvin, being helped into her cloak by the butler, was facing the other way. Robbie, however, blinked up at her. "I thought," he said in surprise, "that you'd gotten a new—"

Jenny put a finger to her lips and shook her head at him warningly as she ran down the stairs. She snatched up her own cloak, threw it quickly over her shoulders and said, "I'm quite ready, Mama."

"At last," her mother said, scarcely glancing over her shoulder. "Come along, then. This evening shall be ordeal enough without our being the very last to make an appearance." And, herding her offspring out the door before her, she hurried to the waiting carriage.

Chapter Eight

They *were* the last to arrive. But the *faux pas* was not noticed in the crush of people in the entryway, for the vicar's family had arrived just before them. Mr. and Mrs. Boyce were accompanied by their son Tobias and their two daughters; and, with the butler, two footmen, the host and Andrea's noisy little lap dog milling about, the Garvins' entrance only added to the general gaiety. While the butler and footmen took the wraps, Lord Clement greeted the last arrivals.

Jenny hung back, hoping that Lord Clement would lead her mother away before a footman reached for her cloak and revealed to her mother what she'd done. But Toby Boyce came up behind her to do the service for her. "I like your new way with your hair," he murmured into her ear.

Jenny tried to cling to her cloak. "Go along, Toby," she whispered. "No need to play the gallant with me. You don't wish to keep the notable Captain Allenby waiting to meet you, do you?"

Tobias Boyce, the vicar's eldest son, was a friend of long standing. He was a snub-nosed, blond, freckled youth with a pair of broad shoulders, an easy disposition and a talent for drawing. Despite his ready smile and appealingly open face, he was a disappointment to almost everyone: to his father because he could settle on nothing for a career; to his mother because he was incredibly lazy; and to himself because he couldn't win the one prize he wanted more than anything else in the world—Andrea. But he and Jenny had always been comfortable with each other, for each one gave to the other words of admiration which they heard from no one else. Tonight, preferring Jenny's company to that of his parents' or his sisters', he intended to escort his friend into the drawing room. "Trying to hide away, my girl?" he asked, *sotto voce*, tugging at her cloak. "Don't you want to meet the so-admirable Allenby either?"

"Don't you?" she asked in surprise.

"Not particularly," he confided. "Andrea is so overjoyed at his presence in this house that it's put me completely off. She's so captivated she's even neglecting her precious Lumpkin." He bent down and picked up the little dog and tucked him under his arm.

"Come now, Toby, you're not jealous, are—? *Oh*!"

The exclamation was caused by the abrupt removal of her cloak. A footman had come up beside her while she'd been looking at Toby as he tried to calm the yapping dog, and he'd whipped the cloak off with such expertise that she'd been unable to clutch it. Her cry made everyone look round.

"Good God!" her mother gasped, seeing for the first time that her daughter was garbed in the dove-grey dress. "Jenny, you goosecap! Why haven't you put on—?"

But Robbie, eager to make his way to the drawing room to meet his captain, put a hand on his mother's arm. In belated realization that this was neither the time nor the place to discuss matters of attire, Lady Garvin clamped her mouth shut. She threw the daughter a scathing look—a look that promised retribution later—and went off on Lord Clement's arm, all the others but Toby following.

"*What* haven't you put on?" Toby asked rudely, handing the wildly barking Lumpkin to the footman and offering Jenny an arm.

"None of your business, you clunch," she muttered, reluctantly permitting him to lead her down the hall.

Toby leered down at her. "If you've forgotten to wear your petticoat, young lady, I shall refuse to escort you further."

She gave him a rather shaky grin. "Don't try to distract me with nonsense, Toby. The evening is bound to be an ordeal for me and shall require my full concentration."

His eyebrows rose. "Really? Why is that?"

She could already hear the babble of voices from the drawing room, her mother's high-pitched laugh above the rest. "Captain Allenby," Lady Garvin was gushing, "this is *indeed* a great and long-anticipated honor . . ."

So much for my mother's avoidance of hypocrisy, Jenny said to herself as her stomach did a flip-flop in disgust and nervousness.

Toby looked down at her curiously. "Why is tonight such an ordeal?" he persisted.

But she couldn't answer, for they'd arrived at the doorway. She looked away from his questioning gaze and into the room. Her first impression was of a confusing array of color and movement, for the room, though large, seemed crowded to capacity. Almost all the faces were familiar, but Jenny had never seen them draped in such festive elegance. They were all in their finest clothes, carefully coiffed and dazzlingly bejeweled. A good number of Lady Clement's domestic staff was moving among them, offering glasses of sherry or trays of little pastry shells filled with savory-smelling fish pastes. But before she could take in all the details, she became aware that she was being closely observed by a tall man standing in the center of the room.

Those piercing eyes were instantly recognizable. She felt herself color up, and she had to fight a cowardly urge to run and hide. Instinctively, she grasped Toby's arm for support. Toby, who'd been looking at her quizzically, now followed the direction of her gaze.

Captain Allenby, surrounded by a large number of other guests, was staring directly at Jenny. It seemed to Toby that the fellow had been watching the doorway for her arrival. Had Jenny met the captain before? One would almost think something had passed between them. He looked down at Jenny and then back at the captain. To his sudden discomfort, he found the captain now staring at *him* with a dark, rather glowering frown. Toby blinked back uncomfortably, feeling a sudden admiration for Robbie; *he* certainly wouldn't care to find himself under that fellow's command.

Jenny, too, had the feeling that Captain Allenby had been watching for her, but the idea was too ridiculous. He was completely surrounded by fawning women. Even Andrea seemed to be hanging on him, looking up at him admiringly. Jenny could see why the women were drawn to him. He was imposingly tall, and although in the light of the chandelier he looked darker and more weathered than he had in the sunshine of the dock at Portsmouth, he was nevertheless devilishly attractive. His evening clothes set off his dark skin and eyes to advantage, and the lines of his face and the touch of grey at his temples only gave his face a stronger character and made him seem more appealing. There was no sign in that face of the monstrous cruelty she now knew was a part of his character. No one else could notice the stoniness she now could detect in his jaw or the glitter of coldness she could see in his eyes. She couldn't expect the others to see it. All they could recognize was the aura of drama and excitement he exuded, the sense of adventure, the aroma of courage, the smell of command. It was like an essence that surrounded him, a vapor that could tickle one's nostrils and dizzy one's senses, like a whiff of the sea itself, and it could easily mask the true character of the man beneath.

Yes, she could see why the others were so taken with him. She'd once been taken with him herself. *But why, with all that adoration surrounding him,* she wondered in considerable agitation, *is he staring so fixedly at me?*

Toby nudged her gently and began to guide her into the room, but before they'd gone three steps, Lord Clement stepped forward and claimed her arm. "Come with me, Jenny. My sister wishes to meet you," he said jovially and drew her away.

Lady Rowcliffe was sitting on a sofa near the window, surrounded by a circle of admirers of her own, one of whom was Lady Garvin. But when Lord Clement came up to her with Jenny on his arm, Lady Rowcliffe turned away from the circle and looked up at once. Mrs. Boyce, who was about to engage her in conversation, looked very disappointed.

"So you are Jenny Garvin," Lady Rowcliffe murmured, staring up at the girl intently.

"How do you do, your ladyship?" Jenny said with a little bob, discomfitted by the intensity of Lady Rowcliffe's scrutiny. There was little about the diminutive, grey-haired lady to suggest she was Captain Allenby's mother except for that disconcerting gleam of the eyes.

"I've been looking forward to making your acquaintance, my dear," the older woman said with a small smile.

"M-Mine?"

"Yes, my dear, yours. Are you surprised?"

"Well, I . . . I didn't suppose you'd even *heard* of me . . ." the embarrassed girl responded awkwardly.

Lady Garvin glowered at her daughter, annoyed at her *gaucherie* and still seething over Jenny's replacement of the apricot-silk gown. "My daughter," she remarked with a look of unmistakable disparagement, "is not at her best at social gatherings."

Lady Rowcliffe turned to peer at Lady Garvin for a moment, her shrewd eyes unreadable. "Isn't she?"

Jenny colored painfully. "It's been an . . . an honor to meet you, ma'am. If you'll excuse me, I won't any longer interrupt your conversation." She took a step backward and started to turn away.

"No, child, please don't go," Lady Rowcliffe urged. There was something about the girl that touched her—some clear, undaunted look in the eye. Shy and sensitive to insults, the young woman seemed nevertheless to have a streak of independence under the demure exterior. "Do sit down and chat with me a moment." She moved over on the sofa to make room. "I've heard so much about you from . . . from my sister-in-law that I wish to become better acquainted."

There was nothing for Jenny to do but acquiesce. She sat down beside the older woman, clenched her hands in her lap and murmured, "It was kind of Lady Clement to mention me."

"She told me you were very pretty, but she didn't say that you are quite out of the common way."

Jenny's eyes flew up to Lady Rowcliffe's face. "Am I, ma'am?" She was not at all sure what the woman had meant by that remark, and she quickly turned her eyes down to her hands again. "That's the sort of thing one says to console a girl for *not* being pretty, isn't it?"

"*Jenny*!" Lady Garvin exclaimed in sharp disapproval.

Lady Rowcliffe put up a restraining hand toward Lady Garvin but otherwise ignored the interruption. "I suppose some might do so, but in this case it was not what I meant. It was intended as a compliment. Your look *is* unusual, you know." She cocked her head and studied Jenny's face with surprising directness. "There's something more in you of beauty than mere prettiness, I think. The sort of face an artist would seek. Has no one ever told you that?"

"No, your ladyship. Never," Jenny said, looking at Lady Rowcliffe in wonder.

"In fact, you put me in mind of a Renaissance painting I saw in Italy. Not that you look like the girl in the painting, exactly, but you have the same quality of . . . of clear-eyed sweetness."

"Oh, Lady *Rowcliffe*!" Jenny breathed, quite overwhelmed.

Lady Rowcliffe smiled. "It was by Antonello da Messina, called *The Annunciation*. Have you ever seen it?"

"No, ma'am. I've never been to Italy."

"Well, you'll go one day. When you do, and you see the painting, you'll remember my words and feel very pleased."

"I feel very pleased now," Jenny said quietly, throwing Lady Rowcliffe a quick, if tremulous smile. Then, looking down at her hands again, she added, "And I'll remember your words whether or not I ever see the painting."

Not accustomed to compliments, Lady Rowcliffe thought as she leaned over and patted the girl's clenched hands. This sweet child was not without spirit, and she was indeed beautiful, in an odd, understated way. Leave it to her son to find himself an unusual creature like this. *I like her*, she thought in surprise. If she was any judge, the girl was sensitive and complicated. It would take some patience to draw her out. But Lady Rowcliffe felt exhilarated at the prospect. This was not some innocuous country mouse but a creature of value and depth. Lady Rowcliffe could see it even if the chit's own *mother* didn't have the sense to realize it. She couldn't help but wonder what damage the mother had done to the girl's development.

But her speculations were interrupted by the approach of her brother. He was returning, this time with Tris in tow.

Lord Clement stopped before Jenny and cleared his throat. "My nephew has asked me to present him to you, Jenny, my dear. It seems that, in all the commotion of your arrival, I somehow neglected to introduce you. Miss Garvin, Captain Allenby."

Lady Rowcliffe could feel the girl stiffen as Tris bowed over her hand. She could feel a sudden and alarming tension pervade the girl's entire body. What was wrong with her?

Tris, however, was grinning down at her warmly. "You may remember that we've met before, Miss Garvin," he said, "but since we hadn't introduced ourselves on that occasion, I thought that it might be wise to convince my uncle to make up the omission."

There was no answering warmth in the girl's face. "How do you do, Captain Allenby?" she said, unmistakably cold.

That the iciness of her reply was a blow to her son may not have been obvious to anyone else, but to Lady Rowcliffe it was unmistakable. He looked as if cold water had been dashed into his face. Lady Rowcliffe felt her breath catch in her chest.

"You do remember me, don't you, Miss Garvin?" he asked, bewildered.

"Yes, of course, Captain."

"She's told us all how you rescued her from her own stupidity," Lady Garvin put in, sensing a certain awkwardness in the air. "You must let me express my gratitude, Captain Allenby, even though belatedly."

The captain, nonplussed by Jenny's lack of response, turned to her mother. "Thank you, ma'am," he said with a bow, "but you must not believe that I was reminding your daughter of the incident because I wish to be thanked. I had only hoped—"

But his hope was not to be expressed. The butler threw open the dining-room doors at that moment, and Andrea pranced up to Tris and boldly took hold of his arm. "Papa says that he will escort Aunt Dulcie in to dinner first and that you are to follow with me." She tossed her head with her most confident "air" and gave him an enticing smile. "Are you ready, Cousin Tris?"

He took a deep breath and forced a smile. "I'm not at all certain that I'm ready for *you*, Cousin Andrea," he said, teasing, "but I'm quite ready for dinner."

He let her lead him off, throwing back only one look over his shoulder at the girl he'd come so far and so eagerly to see, but her eyes were resolutely fixed on the hands in her lap. Instead, he met his mother's eyes. *What's gone wrong?* she seemed to ask.

He flashed back an answer: *I only wish I knew.*

Chapter Nine

The three Garvins were silent on their ride home from the dinner party. While their heads teemed with impressions of the evening which, normally, they would have been eager to share with the others, they each found, tonight, that they needed to think before they spoke. Robbie, for one, was preoccupied with speculations about his relationship with his captain. The evening had been most interesting. He'd had only one real opportunity to converse with Allenby—at the table after the women had withdrawn. He'd found the captain surprisingly cordial. Allenby had shown interest in his comments and had not been patronizing in the slightest way. There had been no sign of the cold, indifferent commander he'd been aboard ship. If he still held Robbie in dislike (or even remembered that he had, on two occasions, given him a most severe scold), there was no sign of it. They'd conversed without strain, and even reminisced about a couple of events which had occurred on the voyage—and all without awkwardness.*Could it be*, Robbie wondered as the carriage rolled through the blackness of the night, *that I can still find favor in the captain's eyes?* His hopes for a successful naval career began to soar again.

Lady Garvin, too, was lost in thought. For her it had been a strange sort of evening. She'd found Captain Allenby not at all detestable, and this had confused her. Her son had given her the distinct impression that the man was a beast. It was possible, of course, that Allenby could be hateful on shipboard and quite the opposite on land; there were *women* on land, and men often benefited from the company of women. The truth was that she'd found him a charming, approachable gentleman, and she busily made plans in her mind about how to take advantage of that approachability. She intended to seek out his company whenever possible and slowly convince him of her son's many merits. She was certain that he would be receptive to her suggestions.

She had expected to dislike Allenby and admire his mother, but she'd found that her response had been quite the reverse. Captain Allenby had been very likeable, but, to her, Lady Rowcliffe was formidable and cold. The London matron had obviously taken her, Lady Garvin, in dislike, although she couldn't imagine why. She reviewed her behavior from the time of her arrival to the time of departure but could fix on nothing that she'd said or done to cause Lady Rowcliffe to despise her.

More confusing still was her ladyship's delight in Jenny. Lady Garvin was Jenny's mother and would yield to no one in her devotion to her child, but she couldn't imagine why Lady Rowcliffe found the girl so interesting. *Beautiful*, she'd said. What nonsense! In that colorless poplin gown the girl had chosen to wear even she, Jenny's own mother, had to admit the girl looked nondescript. And in conversation she'd shown herself graceless and flat. In contrast, there had been Andrea, glowing in a gown of turquoise lustring, laughing, flirting, singing and holding everyone's attention with her air of self-assurance. Yet Lady Rowcliffe had not paid her own niece half the attention she'd showered on Jenny. What did it mean?

Lady Garvin glanced at Jenny, sitting opposite her in the carriage. The girl's eyes were fixed on the window as if she could see something in the blackness beyond. She really ought to give the girl a proper scold for what she'd done tonight. After all, hadn't she given Jenny her very best silk to have the apricot gown made? Why had the ungrateful girl spurned it? She deserved to be chastised with a severe tongue-lashing. But Lady Rowcliffe, who was reputed to have exquisite taste, had found Jenny beautiful. Even in the dove-grey gown! It gave one pause. Perhaps she'd better think of it further before she gave Jenny a reprimand. It was all quite puzzling.

Jenny, staring unseeing into the dark, had found the evening alternately thrilling and terrifying. Never in her life had she been subjected to so much attention, nor had she ever suffered such extremes of emotion. It would take hours of cogitation, she imagined, before she could understand all that had occurred. But one thing was already quite clear: it would take all her will to keep in mind the fact that Captain Allenby was a beast. He had certainly made himself very likeable this evening.

Everyone at the Clements' had found him likeable. The men had hung on his stories of sea adventures, and the women had doted on his half-smile, his quips and his magnetism. She, of course, had been able to withstand the attraction, keeping in her mind the remnants of Robbie's letters and that vision of a man being beaten on board his ship by his order. But tonight there had been that moment . . .

She couldn't help but dwell on it, for it had been so moving and so unexpected. Dinner had ended, the gentlemen had rejoined the ladies, and they'd all gone to the music room, where Jenny had been asked (as she always was) to accompany the ladies who'd volunteered to sing. Andrea had been the first, charming her listeners with her clear, confident soprano. Ellen Boyce had followed, and then Sylvia Vesey had volunteered, embarrassing everyone by going sharp on all her high notes, a failing which Jenny couldn't cover up no matter how loudly she played. Then, at the request of the assemblage, Andrea had sung again. When she'd finished, and Jenny had stood up to leave the piano, Lady Rowcliffe had insisted that she play a selection for them.

Jenny had been taken completely by surprise, for never before had anyone shown an interest in hearing her play solo. All the singers in Wyndham knew her as a competent accompanist, but nobody had thought, before, of asking her to take the spotlight. Even if they had, she would probably have resisted. She was not comfortable with everyone looking at her. Tonight, too, she'd wanted to excuse herself. But Lady Rowcliffe had asked so eagerly that Jenny would have felt surly to refuse.

She'd sat down at the piano again, flexed her fingers and launched into one of her favorite Haydn sonatas. She chose it because it was light, short and so familiar to her that she knew she could get through it no matter how nervous she became. At first she played almost automatically, aware that several in the audience hadn't bothered to cease their chatter to listen to her —her mother's babble quite recognizable among the rest of the voices. But the intricacies of Haydn's design required her attention, and if the allegro was to be performed *con brio* as required, she had to concentrate. Before she realized it, she'd lost herself in the music, just as if she were at home, and by the time she reached the adagio she was feeling her usual delight in chasing the theme through its various plunges and reappearances among the ripples of the harmonics. It was not until she played the last chord that she realized the room had become silent. Before she looked up, there was a burst of applause —*enthusiastic* applause. They'd *liked* it! She felt her heart begin to pound and her cheeks redden in pleased surprise, and when she lifted her eyes she found herself looking right into Captain Allenby's.

There was no mistaking his look. It glowed with delight and an astonished pride, like that of a father who'd only this moment discovered in his child a marvelous talent which he'd never dreamed existed. Yes, like a father . . . or a lover. The look caught her breath and froze her blood. For a timeless instant she couldn't look away.

But Lady Rowcliffe jumped up from her chair and came up to her. "That was exquisite, my dear. A really *splendid* rendition," she said, planting a kiss on Jenny's cheek. "You've given me the evening's most delightful moments."

Before she could respond to this very satisfactory praise from the guest of honor, she was surrounded by several others, all eager to express their pleasure in her performance. Several minutes were occupied with the effort of graciously accepting their effusions while gently-but-firmly refusing to play an encore, and when at last she was able to turn away to make her escape from the room, she blundered right into the captain.

She was so startled that she almost lost her balance. He grasped her arms to support her. "Don't run off, Miss Garvin," he pleaded, his voice low and intimately warm. "Can't you bear to hear one more compliment from an admirer of your music?"

It took all of her resolve to remind herself that this was the same man who'd given her brother all those months of torture. If she hadn't known the truth, she would have found him irresistible. *But these are only his party manners,* she told herself. She had to remember the real man underneath, to keep foremost in her mind the horror of his shipboard behavior. "I . . . I must go," she said breathlessly. "Please excuse me."

His smile faded instantly, and he dropped his hold on her. Faultlessly polite, he made a stiff bow and stepped aside. But his eyes showed that she'd hurt him.

She felt a sharp sting of regret as she noted his look and the tightening of his jaw. If only he were someone else, what a delightful evening this could have been. *Blast you, Captain Allenby,* she'd thought, fighting an urge to say the words aloud, *don't look at me with that pained stare! So you think that, just by being kind to me (devastatingly kind, I admit) I can forget how cruel you really are? Do you expect me to forget about my brother? Well, I won't. So, please, sir, don't be so charming to me. Don't bother to disguise yourself with these party manners. Stop trying to confuse me!*

But of course she'd said nothing. She'd merely lowered her head and, with heart beating rapidly, passed by him and run from the room.

Now, staring out of the coach window, she again felt those confused and conflicting emotions. The look in his eyes when she'd glanced up from the keyboard was one she would never forget. Why had it been Allenby who'd given her that look? All these years she'd felt inside her an arid place . . . a bit of dry soil that hungered for the water of recognition, praise, *love*. In that one instant, with one look, the captain had watered it. She could almost feel something flower inside her. Dash it all, why had it been *Allenby* who'd done it?

The carriage drew up to the doorway and, still silent, the three Garvins alighted. In the hallway, Robbie was the first to speak. "You played very well tonight, Jenny," he said, giving her an affectionate hug. "Captain Allenby and his mother were quite impressed. I was proud of you."

"Yes," Lady Garvin said thoughtfully as she mounted the stairs, "so was I."

In the Clement household, the last dinner guest had departed, and everyone, even the servants, had gone to bed. But Lady Rowcliffe still sat at her dressing table, wide awake and staring abstractedly into the mirror. Her abigail, too, was still up, fussing about with her ladyship's undergarments and casting quizzical looks at her mistress. She'd long since helped her into her nightdress, but her ladyship showed no inclination to go to bed.

The abigail dropped a pair of shoes into the wardrobe with a loud, obvious clatter. Lady Rowcliffe roused herself from her reverie. "Are you still bustling about, Cora? It must be past midnight."

"I was about t' say the same t' you, ma'am," the maid said reprovingly.

"I shall go to bed presently. But you go along at once."

"Yes, my lady."

Cora bobbed and started to the door. But her ladyship rose from her chair and followed her. "On your way to your room, Cora, will you tap lightly on my son's door? If he doesn't answer, don't wake him. But if he does, tell him to come to me for a moment, will you?"

Tris had evidently not been asleep, for he knocked at her door a short while later still clad in his breeches and shirt. "Haven't you even undressed yet?" his mother asked, tying the sash of her dressing gown around her.

"I've been sitting at the window, brooding," he responded glumly.

"I've been brooding, too. I've been wondering . . ." She hesitated, uncertain of how much to say. Keeping her eyes fixed on her son's face, she lowered herself onto the edge of the chaise.

"Wondering—?" he prodded, strolling to the fire.

"—wondering if perhaps you wouldn't like me to make our excuses to Alfred and Sally. I could say I'm not feeling up to snuff, and we could go home."

He threw her a quick look and then turned back to the fire. He picked up a poker and stirred the embers, saying not a word until a bright flame had sprung up. "Does this mean you don't like her?" he asked, his eyes on the blaze.

"Your Miss Garvin? I like her very much."

"Do you? I thought you would."

"Yes. She's a bit too reticent, perhaps, but there's spirit underneath. And intelligence and sensitivity. And above all, a pervading sort of . . . of . . ."

"Sweetness," he supplied, carefully replacing the poker.

She studied the back of his head worriedly. "Yes, exactly."

"So you do like her."

"Yes."

He looked round at her. "Yet you think we should return home?"

"I'm not sure there's any point in our staying," she said bluntly.

He turned back to stare at the flames. "In other words you don't think I have a chance with her."

His mother sighed. "I don't know *why* the chit dislikes you, but it seems to me she does."

"Yes, it seems so to me, too. That's why I haven't felt much like going to bed tonight."

"I don't understand why you insisted that we come in the first place, Tris. Couldn't you see . . . Well, why mince words? . . . Couldn't you see her *antipathy* at your first meeting?"

Tris shook his head. "There *was* no antipathy at our first meeting."

"Truly, my dear? I hate to cause you pain, but I may as well be frank. Are you sure that your infatuation didn't blind you?"

He wheeled around. "What sort of coxcomb do you take me for, Mama? I'm not some green-headed schoolboy. There was a definite attraction between us—on *both* our parts. You may take my word on it."

"All right, Tris, all right. Don't rip up at me! I didn't mean to indicate any real doubt of the soundness of your judgment. After all, you did recognize, tonight, that her feelings are not favorable, which shows you are capable of detached, objective evaluation."

"Thank you," he said with heavy irony. "Considering the stark obviousness of her—as you call it—antipathy, you can hardly be surprised at my ability to discern it."

Lady Rowcliffe ignored his sarcasm. If her son was correct in his first impression of the girl's reaction to him, the matter was most puzzling. "But Tris, my love, this makes no sense. If she liked you at first, how do you explain—?"

"I *can't* explain it. That's what's driving me distracted."

"It can't be anything you did tonight, for she seemed to reject you from the first moment that Alfred brought you over."

"You noticed that, did you? How?"

"I felt her stiffen."

"I see." He kicked at the fireplace fender with the toe of his boot. "But, of course, I really don't see. I don't see at all."

"I don't either, even though I am usually quite familiar with the vagaries of the female mind. Assuming you're right in your assessment of the attraction of your first meeting—"

"Yes, let's proceed on that assumption, if you please," he insisted.

"Then something must have happened to change her first

impression. Something that occurred between your meeting at Portsmouth and her arrival here tonight."

"But what possibly could have occurred? I haven't laid eyes on her from that day to this."

His mother shook her head hopelessly. "It's baffling. There's nothing I can imagine which could so alter a girl's mind—"

"Unless . . ."

She looked up quickly. "You've thought of something?"

"Suppose that in the interim she fell in love with someone else."

"Oh. Do you think she has?"

He shrugged. "I don't know. She came in this evening with that fair-haired lad, Boyce. They seemed thick as thieves."

"I suppose it's possible." She got up and paced thoughtfully about the room. "However, even *that* wouldn't explain her taking you in *dislike*."

He rubbed his chin thoughtfully. "That's what I decided, too. If she'd treated me with mere indifference, I could have made some sense of all this. But there seems to be something more. Something worse."

She came up beside him and put a hand on his arm. "Poor dear. I *am* sorry. But you mustn't feel that there's anything tragic in this incident. It's not as if you were really in *love*, you know. After one brief meeting, one can hardly call the affair any more than an infatuation. You'll get over it."

"Yes." He roused himself from his contemplation of the fire and gave his mother a quick grin. "But not yet."

"What?" she asked, bemused.

"I don't want to get over it yet."

"But, Tris, my love," she remonstrated gently, "there seems to be little point in our remaining—"

He started for the door. "For the mother of a sailor, my dear, you counsel surrender much too easily."

"Do you mean you intend to *pursue*—"

"Did Nelson flee at the first salvo? Of course I intend to pursue the matter. Good night, Mama. And sleep well, just as I intend to do. It's much too soon to despair. The battle has only begun."

Chapter Ten

So the celebrated visitors remained at Clement Hall, settling in for a month-long stay, just as originally planned. During that first week, Tris made no effort to seek out Jenny Garvin, thinking it wise to keep himself in the background to observe. Besides, his uncle, aunt and cousin made every effort to keep him and his mother fully occupied. Whenever the weather was favorable (and the first week of their stay proved to be pleasant and remarkably mild for December), they were taken on outings—trips to see the renowned Hailes Abbey and every other place of historic or artistic interest within an hour's drive. In addition, Lady Rowcliffe was invited to several afternoon card parties, while her son was taken twice on shooting parties with the local gentlemen. Captain Allenby even found himself short of time to take his daily ride on the mare he'd brought with him from his London stables.

Every evening, too, was fully engaged. Lady Rowcliffe, Captain Allenby and their hosts were inundated with invitations to receptions and fêtes of all sorts as every fashionable hostess of northern Gloucester sought her turn to entertain the famous visitors. Tris expected to see Jenny at each of these affairs, but the girl was present at only one. The occasion was a rout-party given by Mr. and Mrs. Vesey, for which all the gentry of the region for miles around had gathered. During the dancing, he noticed that Jenny was sitting on the sidelines, watching the dancers forming their sets, the broad-shouldered young Boyce standing beside her. He approached them and tried to convince her to stand up with him, but she gave him a frightened look and said she was spoken for.

"Spoken for, ma'am?" he asked, eyebrows raised.

Her hand flew up to her throat, where a deep flush was

spreading quickly from her chest (enticingly revealed by the *décolletage* of her pretty apricot-colored gown) to her cheeks. "M-Mr. Boyce has already asked me, haven't you, Toby?" she murmured awkwardly.

But Tris had caught sight of the slight movement of her foot as she'd stepped quite deliberately on the young man's toes.

The Boyce lad started in surprise, blinked at her stupidly and then said quickly, "Oh, yes. Yes, indeed," and the two of them went off together to the dance floor.

But Tris contained his chagrin. He refused to permit himself to be put off by her ridiculous little subterfuge or to become discouraged by the girl's withdrawal. For one thing, it had been quite plain that she'd had no intention of dancing with Boyce until he, Allenby, had come up to her. And Boyce had had no intention of asking her. Therefore they were probably not romantically involved. She'd gone off with Boyce only to avoid what was, to her, a less-pleasing alternative. Tris could see quite clearly that the girl had found a reason to wish to avoid him, and until he could discover what that reason was —and act on that knowledge—he couldn't expect her attitude to change. Meanwhile, he would keep his eyes and ears open . . . and bide his time.

For Jenny, that first week of Captain Allenby's visit had been a difficult one. In order to avoid attending social gatherings where she knew she'd encounter the captain, she'd had to resort almost daily to little falsehoods—she'd told her mother that she had headaches. By patient arguing, she'd managed to convince her mother to go to all the celebrations without her. (Since Jenny always appeared to be completely recovered by the next morning, she was able to keep her mother from feeling unduly troubled by the state of her daughter's health.) Only for the Vesey rout-party had Jenny been unable to win her mother's permission to remain behind, and *that* occasion, being such a squeeze, produced only one very small encounter with the captain she was so assiduously trying to avoid.

But even without having attended the dinners and parties, Jenny found that the presence of Captain Allenby and his mother in Wyndham was a troublesome distraction. She did her best to ignore their presence by proceeding with her life in her usual fashion. But Robbie and her mother talked of nothing else, which made mealtimes annoying. And even if she wished only to take a stroll, she restrained herself, for with Clement Hall a mere two miles away, who could tell when one might accidentally come upon the captain on the road?

Another distressing effect which the presence of the London visitors had upon her daily routine was the absence of her friend. Andrea had become infatuated with her awe-inspiring, swarthy, seafaring cousin and tried to be in his company as much as possible. And when it wasn't possible (as for example when her "Cousin Tris" was so uncharitable as to go off shooting with the men), she was too busy preparing her wardrobe or her hair for her next encounter with him to find time for Jenny.

Therefore it gave Jenny particular delight, one sunny morning at half-past ten (just one week to the day after the arrival of the London visitors), to learn from Cullum that Miss Andrea Clement had called and was awaiting her in the downstairs sitting room. Jenny dashed down and embraced her friend with such enthusiasm that one would have thought four months rather than four days had separated them. "Andrea, my dear, what a gratifying surprise! How did you manage to tear yourself away from your guests?"

"Well, you see, Cousin Tris has gone off to spend the day with a retired admiral under whom he once served, who's settled somewhere in this vicinity. And Aunt Dulcie's been invited to Mrs. Welker's for luncheon, as you know. So I have the day completely free."

"I'm *so* glad. It's been much too quiet and inactive here without your company."

"Then you'll be pleased to learn that I've come to shake you out of your inactivity," Andrea declared briskly. "Get out your warmest pelisse, for we are going to Cheltenham in Toby's phaeton."

"*Cheltenham*? That will take *hours*. Why do you want to go there?"

"I need a pair of gloves to wear with my orchid gown—for Mama's ball on Saturday, you know—and there's not a thing to be found here at Marsden's. And since Toby has been ordered to pay a call on his grandmother in Winchcombe (she's ailing, you know, since that injury to her hip), we've decided to join forces for the outing and agreed that you must come, too."

Jenny eyed her friend with amused suspicion. "And how did

you convince Toby to agree to *that*? He certainly can't wish for me to make a third when you've given him this rare opportunity for a *tête-à-tête*."

"I don't care what he wishes," Andrea retorted with a toss of her head. "If he wants my company, he must accept my terms. *Do* say you'll come, Jenny! If you don't, I shall have to listen to Toby declare himself again, and you know what a bore that can be. Every time I refuse him, he spends the whole day pouting. I can't bear him when he's in that state. Besides, I have a *thousand* things to tell you."

"Yes, I'm sure you do." Jenny, her smile fading, turned away. "And they are all about Captain Allenby, I've no doubt. I don't wish to sound rude about your relatives, Andrea, but you know my feelings on the subject of the captain, and you must understand that I don't wish to discuss him."

"Really, Jenny, must you poker up every time you hear his name? I'm convinced you're wrong about him. I've been with him every day for a week and find him invariably charming and agreeable."

"I know you do," Jenny said, biting her underlip to keep from making a sharp retort. "I've no wish to change your mind on the subject. I just don't want to talk about him."

"Very well, we won't. If I give you my word on it, will you come?"

"I'd love to, Andrea. I've not been anywhere all week, and the sun looks glorious. But I promised Mama I'd be here this afternoon when Mrs. Elvin comes to fit her new ballgown. She wants my advice about the trimming. And she's also insisting on having her old burgundy velvet cut down for me. If you're going all the way to Cheltenham, we would never return in time—"

"At what time is Mrs. Elvin expected?"

"No later than three, I believe."

Andrea pursed her pretty lips. She was not the sort who would easily permit anything to interfere with her plans. "Can't you ask your mother to excuse you this once?" she asked petulantly. "Must you always obey her every whim?"

"She might very well excuse me, if I could ask her. But she's already left for Mrs. Welker's, to—"

"To attend the luncheon for Aunt Dulcie," Andrea finished irritably. "I might have guessed."

She paced about the room thoughtfully for a moment while

Jenny tried to placate her with promises to join her "the very next time."

But Andrea would not abandon her plans without a struggle. "Wait," she said, brightening, "I have an idea. What if you came with us only as far as Winchcombe? I expect that old Mrs. Boyce will insist that we stay for a late luncheon (for you know that she doesn't permit visitors to leave her premises before she's filled their stomachs), so we shall have to remain at Winchcombe until two at the very least. That will give us three hours together, which is better than nothing. And then Toby and I can proceed to Cheltenham, while you return home in plenty of time."

"Oh? And how, pray, am I to get home? Eleven miles on shank's mare?"

"Tell Cullum to have your carriage sent to Winchcombe to pick you up at two o'clock sharp."

"But Stebbins has taken Mama in the barouche, and heaven only knows *when* they'll return."

Andrea, remarkably ingenious in finding the means to get her own way, was undaunted. "Then tell Robbie to come for you in the old laudalet."

"I don't know, Andrea," Jenny demurred. "It seems a great fuss for nothing—"

"Nothing?" Andrea drew herself up in offense. "Is my company *nothing* to you?"

"Oh, pooh! I was going to say nothing *urgent*. Don't raise a dust, love. You know I would go with you if I could."

"But you *could*, if you weren't such a mollycoddle." She put up her chin and stalked to the door. "Where is Robbie? Just leave this to me."

"Wait, Andrea. Where are you going? Don't disturb him. He hasn't come down yet."

"Hasn't come down? It's almost *eleven*! I'm going up. I don't see why that . . . that sluggard can't be made to do something useful." And she swept out the door.

"Andrea! You're not going to *wake* him, are you?" Jenny hurried out after her friend, half dismayed and half amused. It was just like Andrea to insist so doggedly on having her own way.

"Of course I'm going to wake him," Andrea said over her shoulder, marching up the stairs. "He's not the crown prince, after all. He can't have me *beheaded*, can he?"

"But Mama doesn't want him disturbed in the mornings. She says he needs all his rest after having endured such dreadful strain on board his ship."

Andrea refused even to slacken her stride. "What folderol! He's been home for weeks since then. Besides, Papa says your mother makes too much of that so-called 'strain' of shipboard life." She strode down the hall, arms swinging purposefully. "Papa says Robbie is healthy and strong and quite capable of dealing with the sailorly life."

Yes, Jenny thought, hurrying after her, *I'd quite agree with you if the sailorly life the boy had to endure was a normal one. But under that monster of a captain . . .*

But aloud she said nothing. There was no point in arguing the matter with Andrea. Her friend would not be receptive to disparaging remarks about the cousin to whom she'd suddenly become so attached.

Andrea had arrived at Robbie's door and was hammering at it. "Robbie," she clarioned loudly, "*do* get up! It's I, Andrea, and I want to talk to you."

There was a muffled reply, and after a few minutes the door opened. "Andrea?" he asked bewilderedly, peering out into the hallway. His thick curly hair was disheveled, his eyes bleary and his dressing gown inside-out. "What's the to-do?"

"I want you to promise to take out the laudalet this afternoon and drive to Winchcombe to call for Jenny. Will you do that, please? You're to be at old Mrs. Boyce's cottage at two o'clock. Two o'clock sharp. Is that clear?"

Robbie looked from Andrea to Jenny in utter confusion. "Why? Is somethin' amiss?" His voice was thick with sleep.

"No, but Jenny must be home at three, and this is the only way we can think of to get her back."

"Tha's why y' *woke* me?" He blinked at them in annoyance. "Can't do it. It'd take an hour to get there an' an hour back. Waste th' entire afternoon."

Andrea grasped his dressing gown and tried to shake him. "Have you anything better to do, you slugabed, than to look after your sister?"

"Andrea!" Jenny interjected, trying to restrain her friend.

"As a matter of fact," Robbie said more clearly (having been shaken awake), drawing himself up in a semblance of injured dignity, "I've an engagement for billiards with Timothy Vesey and some of the other fellows this afternoon."

"When this afternoon?" Andrea persisted.

"I don't know. Threeish."

"Then you'll be ready for it. If you have any consideration for your sister at all, you'll do it. You can be at Winchcombe *and back* by three."

Robbie made a face. "Do you really have to go to Winchcombe, Jenny?"

"I don't *have* to, exactly," she admitted, "but it's such a lovely day, and I haven't had an outing all week . . ."

He sighed in ungallant acquiescence. "Well, if I must, I suppose . . . Did you say I should meet you at old Mrs. Boyce's cottage?"

"Yes. You know where it is, don't you?" Jenny asked, smiling at him gratefully.

"I think so. But if I meet you there, Mrs. Boyce'll be bound to see me, and she'll insist that we stay for tea. And then I'll be too late for the billiards."

"I know what to do," Andrea suggested, ever able to override objections which threatened to block her plans. "We'll drop Jenny at the crossroad. You know the one I mean —where the Cheltenham road crosses Hailes Abbey Lane. She can meet you there."

Robbie cast Andrea a look of disgust before he nodded. "Very well. Two o'clock." And he shut the door in their faces.

Chapter Eleven

A triumphant Andrea hurried Jenny into her pelisse, snatched up her friend's bonnet and muff and pulled her out the door. Jenny, beset with guilty misgivings, nevertheless greeted the waiting Toby with a smile, tied the strings of her bonnet tightly and climbed into the phaeton. Toby tucked a warm lap-robe about the knees of his two passengers, jumped up on the driver's box and started off.

Once Toby's phaeton turned onto the road, Jenny's misgivings vanished. The day was lovely, crisply cold and golden. The wind smelled of sea, of frozen grass and the acrid spice of woodsmoke. The horses' breath was whitely visible in the sparkling air. Even the riders' high-pitched laughter seemed to turn to ice and tinkle in the cold like bits of glass. There was a great deal of laughter. Everything that was said seemed to elicit merriment—every little sally that Toby threw over his shoulder, every silly response that the girls returned, even the occasional neighing of the horses seemed full of wit.

They arrived at old Mrs. Boyce's cottage with their ears frozen, their cheeks red and their appetites sharp. The old lady was delighted to see them, and, her condition being much improved, set about preparing a luncheon for them. They sat at the table in her large, low-ceilinged kitchen as the old woman hobbled about with her cane, setting out cold sliced mutton, a wheel of Stilton, two loaves of fresh-baked bread and a variety of pickles and preserves, while a pot of barley soup bubbled on her prized Rumford stove and a kettle boiled for tea. She was a gifted cook, famous in the region for her jams and preserves, and she would permit none of them to give her any assistance. She took such obvious pleasure in their company and in the opportunity to serve her special dishes to her grandson and his friends that the effort seemed to cause her no physical discomfort.

Finally they prevailed upon her to sit down, and Toby, who always carried a sketch pad with him, took out his charcoals and drew a likeness of his grandmother that made them all exclaim in admiration.

It was a delicious and merry luncheon, and the three friends were contentedly sated when they rose, a little past 1:30, to take their leave. The elder Mrs. Boyce (or "Gammer" as she insisted they call her) pressed upon each of them a large jar of her much-praised red gooseberry jam as gifts for their mothers. Then, giving them each an embrace, she waved them on their way.

But during the short time they'd spent indoors, the sky had changed. Heavy clouds had gathered in the west, and the sunlight, though not quite obscured, was now markedly diminished in brightness. The wind, too, was not the same. It was no longer brisk and invigorating but cold and threatening. Toby looked up at the sky, frowning. "I think," he said, "that we ought to forget about Cheltenham and set out for home."

"Forget about *Cheltenham*?" Andrea cried in outrage, looking up from her muff into which she'd been attempting to stow the large jar of jam. "That is a *dastardly* suggestion! Now that we've helped you to accomplish *your* mission, you want to renege on *mine*. Well, I won't have it. My errand is every bit as important as yours."

"Ha!" sneered Toby. "Orchid gloves? I'd hardly call their procurement an earthshaking necessity."

"Never you mind! You promised to take me to Cheltenham, and to Cheltenham we shall go."

Toby shrugged and promptly gave in. He'd been looking forward to this opportunity to spend a few hours alone with her anyway. If he had to spend it in a snowstorm or downpour, so be it.

The crossroad where he was to deposit Jenny was three miles from his grandmother's cottage, but when they arrived there was no sign of Robbie or the Garvin carriage. "Are you certain you told him to meet you here?" Toby asked, peering down the road worriedly.

"Yes, positive," Jenny said confidently. "Don't look so dismayed, Toby. We're a bit early, you know. I'll just climb down and wait. You two go along."

"We'll do no such thing," Toby insisted. "We'll wait 'til he comes."

"Oh, Toby, don't be an ass," Andrea muttered. "Your behavior is overly scrupulous. I see no need for us to sit here wasting time. We gave Robbie the most precise instructions. He'll be along."

"Yes," Jenny agreed, "I know he will. And if we *are* to have snow, the sooner you go on your way the better."

Toby, despite a strong feeling of reluctance, surrendered. He was, after all, outnumbered. He watched with apprehension as Jenny slipped down from the phaeton, but after he'd gotten a prod from Andrea, he pushed his misgivings aside, gave Jenny a guilty wave and turned the carriage south onto the Cheltenham road.

Jenny watched until the carriage trundled out of sight. As soon as it disappeared, the sun, as if it had timed its movements to that of Toby's phaeton, ducked behind the clouds. Ten minutes later the sky had darkened to an oppressive and threatening grey, and still there was no sign of a carriage approaching from the north. Jenny, though beginning to shiver a little from the cold, was not uneasy. Robbie had said he would come; she could count on him.

There was a sound of hoofbeats from the south, and she turned to see if Toby and Andrea had changed their minds and were already returning. But it was not Toby's phaeton which approached. It was a smart little black curricle, drawn by two horses. She stepped back out of the way as the vehicle wheeled past. A flashing glimpse of the driver caused her to gasp. It was Captain Allenby.

At the same instant, he recognized her and drew his horses to with an abrupt pull on the reins, scraping to a stop a few yards beyond the place where she stood. "Miss *Garvin*!" he exclaimed, jumping down and striding back to her. "What a surprise to find you walking along the road so far from home. Surely you're not attempting to reach Wyndham on foot, are you? It must be more than ten miles."

"No, of course not, Captain. I'm merely awaiting my carriage."

There was no trace of warmth in her tone or in her face. Captain Allenby was nonplussed, not only by her coolness but by the strangeness of finding her, apparently unescorted, at the side of the road so far from home. There was not even a house nearby to give him a clue to her reason for being here. It was no business of his, of course, but he couldn't like seeing her on a public thoroughfare alone and unprotected. "May I take you up with me, ma'am? I am on my way back to Wyndham, as you've probably surmised. Your driver would have to pass us by, so we can watch for your carriage while we ride."

"Thank you, sir, but I expect my carriage at any moment," she answered, eyes lowered. "There's little point in joining you just to ride for a moment or two."

His brows knit in perplexity. Did the girl so dislike him that she preferred to remain alone in the cold wind rather than sit beside him for a brief ride? Whatever the answer, he could hardly ride off and leave her, could he? He looked down at her and offered her his most gracious smile. "Then I hope, ma'am, you'll not object to my keeping you company until your carriage arrives."

Without actually moving, she seemed to draw into herself and step back from him. She threw him a darting, dismayed look before lowering her eyes again. "There's not the least need to delay yourself, Captain Allenby. I assure you that I shan't be waiting long."

His smile died. Her rejection of his simple, friendly request was almost rude. He could no longer restrain himself. "Have I done something to offend you, Miss Garvin? Is that why you're so reluctant to endure even a few moments of my companionship?"

Another darting look showed how startled she was by his question. "No, of course not, captain," she answered awkwardly. "You've always been kind . . . to me . . ."

She kept her eyes resolutely lowered, and after a moment he realized she wouldn't say anything more. "But even though I've been 'kind,' you still prefer to remain alone in the cold rather than come up beside me in the curricle, or even permit me to remain here beside you, is that what you mean?"

The muff in which her hands were clenched seemed to tremble. "I only m-mean that I don't wish to . . . to delay you."

His jaw tightened. There was no question that she'd dismissed him. And without any explanation for her obvious repugnance for his company. A surge of anger welled up inside him. *If I'm so odious to her,* he told himself, *then I'll be damned if I'll force my presence on her for another moment. Let her stand out here and* freeze!

He made a curt little bow. "Very well, then, ma'am, I'll take my leave. Good day to you." He strode back to the curricle, leaped up on the seat and was off before she could catch her breath.

She watched the curricle bowl out of sight, her mind whirling with conflicting emotions. She'd offended him deeply, that much was clear. What was much less clear was why he should show such concern for her good opinion. Why should a man of Captain Allenby's importance take the slightest interest in a mere country miss's opinion of his character? But he obviously valued her feelings, just as his mother had seemed to do. But why? It was very puzzling.

At that moment her thoughts were interrupted by the sound of droplets on the hedgerow and a cold splash against her cheek. Sleet! It was coming down as heavily as it was sudden. *Good God,* she wondered, peering up the road, *what's happened to Robbie?*

There was still no sign of him. The sleet was sharply cold, and her toes were beginning to freeze in her thin half-boots. She couldn't possibly walk all the way home, and if she turned back to Gammer Boyce's house, she might miss Robbie altogether. In an agony of indecision, she heard another sound that drove everything else from her mind. It was a sharp crack of a branch. Someone was hiding in the hedgerow! "Wh-Who's there?" she asked, panic-stricken.

"On'y me, pet, on'y me," came a thick voice, and a man pushed his way through the brush. "Alone, are ye?"

The man, shabbily dressed in a wool cap, thick sweater and heavy workboots, was obviously under the influence of strong spirits. His step was unsteady and his eyes bloodshot. A knitted muffler was twice wound about his neck and covered his chin, but his mouth was uncovered and revealed a wide and terrifying leer. "I'm *not* alone," Jenny said bravely, nevertheless taking a step backward. "My brother is . . . er . . . with me."

The man hooted. "Is 'e now? An' where'd 'e be 'iding'? Under the 'edge?"

"He's just down the road," Jenny said, fixing her eyes on him firmly. "And he's very large. Very large indeed. So heed my advice and take yourself off before he gets here, or he'll land you a facer you won't forget."

The man laughed again and came toward her. "I ain't sayin' as 'ow I disbelieve ye, m'lass. Not a-tall. So let's you an' me take off afore 'e gets 'ere, eh? Jus' down th' road to th' Red Bull."

Jenny backed away again. "Please leave me alone. I *warn* you—!"

"Now, don' take on so, li'l poppet. I don' mean ye no 'arm. I on'y want ye t' come out o' this sleet. It's nice an' warm at th' Red Bull. I'll buy ye some jackey first, and then warm ye right an' proper in one o' th' upstairs rooms—"

Jenny, more terrified than she'd ever been in her life, took two slow steps backward and then turned and began to run. The man, lushy as he was, lumbered after her. "Now 'old on there," he shouted drunkenly and reached out for her.

He managed to grasp her arm just below the shoulder and, with a tug that caused her to scream in pain, whirled her around. The road, badly rutted, caused her to trip and fall heavily against him. He tottered from the unexpected weight of her but kept his balance and locked his arms about her. "There!" he said, grinning down at her, "ain't that better?"

His breath was fetid with drink and decay, and his leer revealed a row of blackened, misshapen teeth. She struggled wildly, managing to free one arm, but succeeded only in pulling off his cap before he pinioned her again. She pulled her head back away from him as far as possible. "Let me go!" she begged as her own bonnet fell off.

His eyes widened with pleasure at the sight of her clearly revealed face. "Ain't ye th' prime 'un! This *is* me lucky day. Gi' us a kiss, eh, so's we cin 'ave a taste o' wut's comin'?"

"No, *don't*!" she protested in horror, but he put a huge hand on the back of her head, drew it toward him and locked his mouth on hers.

She felt sick. Her stomach heaved in revulsion. She wished she would lose consciousness and never wake, but her mind remained sharply alert to all the hideous sensations. The repulsive embrace seemed to last for eons, and she felt powerless to end it. But she *had* to find a way to end it! If only she had a weapon of some kind . . . anything at all to help extricate herself from this horrible predicament . . .

But there *was* something. She could feel it even now,

pressing against her ribs right through the muff—her *jar of jam*. She moved the hand that had been pressing against his chest . . . down slowly toward the muff . . . wriggling her fingers to grasp the jar within . . .

He lifted his head and leered down at her. "Wut's this? Wut're ye doin', dearie? Tryin' t' tickle me—?'

He never finished, for she lifted the jar with a sudden jerk of her arm and brought it down in desperate violence upon his head.

There was a hideous, cracking sound, and the jar shattered. She saw his eyes go blank before his body went limp and slid to the ground.

He lay right upon her feet, on his side, unmoving. Shivering from head to toe, she stared down at him. "Oh, my *God*, what have I done?" she whispered.

She bent down to turn him over so that she might look at his face, but she couldn't bring herself to touch him. Finally, she slipped her feet out from beneath him and, with a light push of her boot against his hip, rolled the body over. He lay sprawled out on the road, face up. His eyes were shut and his mouth open and still leering. And from his head, slowly seeping over his forehead, into his ear and down his cheek was a red, sticky oozing mass of gooseberry jam.

Chapter Twelve

Tris Allenby's rage lasted only a few minutes. How could he maintain a feeling of anger against a girl whom he'd convinced himself he loved? During the six months of his last voyage—the only one in his life which had seemed unendurably long to him—he'd spent half his days dreaming of her, imagining their reunion, the whirlwind development of their mutual affection, his proposal of marriage, her acceptance, an almost-immediate wedding and a shipboard honeymoon. Now he felt a complete fool. How could he have fallen in love with a girl he hardly knew? How had he deluded himself into believing that she, too, had felt the attraction? What did he know about love anyway?

During all his adult years he'd known only a sailor's sort of intimacy with women—brief, unemotional alliances with the lightskirts and trulls one finds at seaports and anchorages the world round. But love itself was still very much a mystery to him. This ignorance in a man of thirty-five was probably a sign of serious emotional retardation, even though his mother would undoubtedly find excuses for him in the fact that, in the hectic activity of the wartime Navy, he'd never had an opportunity to develop long-standing relationships with the proper sort of women. But excuses notwithstanding, his ignorance was a real handicap to him now.

However, he was not so ignorant that he couldn't see that Jenny Garvin had no liking for him. She wanted nothing to do with him. She couldn't even bear to have him near. The realization was painful—more painful than he'd dreamed possible—but he'd not commanded warships in battle without learning how to face and deal with painful truths. She didn't want him; that was the beginning and the end of it. There was no point in prolonging his agony. He'd tell his mother, as soon as he returned to Clement Hall, that the time had come to take their departure.

He was so depressed at the disintegration of his dreams that it was several minutes before he became aware of the little pinpricks of ice which were stinging his face. Sleet was coming down heavily. Already the fields were pebbled with little white pellets. He shook himself out of his lethargy and clucked at the horses; the roads might well be covered with ice before he reached Wyndham.

But what about Jenny? he asked himself with a start. She must still be standing back at the crossroad. He hadn't noticed a single carriage pass him by. No one had come for her. Good Lord, she must be half frozen by this time!

For a moment, injured pride kept him from turning the curricle, but even while he hesitated he knew he would go back for her. She'd repulsed him, true, but he couldn't let her stand unsheltered in the sleet. He turned the horses, whipped them up to the fastest pace possible on the rutted road and hurried back.

His first glimpse of her gave him a shock. She was standing in the middle of the road, her back to him. She was bareheaded and her braid, which had been twisted into a bun at the nape of her neck when he'd seen her earlier, was now loose, tousled and hanging down her back. She seemed not even to have heard his approach, so engrossed was she in staring down at the bundle of rags which lay at her feet. He halted the horses and jumped down, but only after he came up beside her was he able to recognize that the bundle of rags was a man—a large, ill-clad man with a great, gaping wound in his head.

"Jenny! What—?"

She turned to him. Her face was white, and the look in her eyes, dilated with terror, made his blood freeze. "I've *killed* him," she whispered brokenly, blinking up at him without a sign of recognition in her eyes. "I've killed him . . . and I don't know w-what to *do*."

He threw a quick glance at the man sprawled on the road, but he could see at once that there was something decidedly strange about the wound. The blood was too red, too thick, too mottled with lumps. He knelt down and examined the man closely. He pulled off one of his gloves, felt for the pulse, lifted an eyelid and put a finger to the red mass. "Good heavens, what's *this*? *Jam*?"

Jenny nodded dully. "Gooseberry jam. I h-hit him with it."

He almost laughed aloud in relief. "Yes, now I see the pieces of the jar." He stood up, took her by the shoulders and gave her a little shake. "Don't look like that, Jenny. He isn't dead."

"He isn't—?"

"No. Only stunned." He gave her a comforting grin. "It's not at all easy to turn a jar of gooseberry jam into a lethal weapon, you know."

A light of hope sprang into her eyes. "Are you *sure*? Only stunned?"

"I'm certain. He may have a cut or two under that covering of preserves, but nothing more serious. I'll wake him up in a moment and prove it to you. But first, tell me what the wretch did to drive you to so unladylike an assault."

"He . . . He . . ." Jenny shut her eyes and shivered as the memory of the man's leer—those reddened, lustful eyes, the blackened teeth—flashed through her mind. She put a hand up to her mouth as if to wipe away the recollection of the pressure of that drunken mouth on hers. "I . . . *can't*—!" she whispered, covering her face with her hands.

But he'd seen enough. The repulsive lout on the ground had molested her—had laid hands on this, the sweetest, most gentle girl he'd ever known. He looked at the ruffian's huge hands—their thick, red fingers with their black-edged fingernails protruding from the fingerless knit gloves—and felt ill with revulsion. A murderous fury swept through him, a feeling so strong that it dilated his pupils and stopped his breath. It was a fury that demanded immediate release. He dropped his hold on Jenny's shoulders, whirled around and knelt beside the fallen miscreant. He slapped the fellow sharply, twice, across the face. "Get up, you piece of scum!" he hissed savagely. "Get up so that I can smash you properly!"

"*Captain*!" Jenny objected, appalled by his rough handling of the unconscious man.

But Tris barely heard her. He slapped the man again across both cheeks. "Get *up*, I say!"

The man whimpered and opened his eyes. He stared up at the captain stupidly but was soon able to read the menace in the face glowering down at him. "Wut . . . ? Who . . . ?" His eyes flickered to Jenny, and a look of recognition came into them. "Oh," he muttered, licking his lips in fright, "yer brother . . ."

Tris grabbed the muffler wound round the ruffian's neck. "So you're awake, eh? Get to your feet!"

"I din't mean nuthin'," the terrified fellow muttered, trying to edge himself away from the threat looming over him. "Nothin' real bad . . ." He lifted himself on his elbows to push himself out of reach.

Tris snorted, stood erect and hauled the man to his feet. "I'll show you what it means to molest an innocent female," he said, his voice icy with fury. And, still gripping the fellow by his muffler with his left hand, he drew back his right fist to swing.

To Jenny's perception, the scene now being enacted before her was worse than anything that had happened so far. Her attacker, now white-faced and helpless, gooseberry jam dripping from his head down the side of his face and onto his shoulders, was nothing more than a poor, pathetic creature, while Captain Allenby, with that murderous look in his eyes, was *fearsome*. She was horrified. *This* was the Tristram Allenby that Robbie had spoken of—cold, vengeful and terrifyingly brutal. His raised fist seemed to her like a sledgehammer, about to smash the poor beggar's skull to bits. "*Don't*!" she screamed.

The shrill cry made Tris freeze in mid-motion. Holding the wretch by the neck with one hand, and his other raised to strike, he looked over at the open-mouthed girl. The horror in her eyes was unmistakable. But it was directed *not at the miscreant he held by the throat but at himself!*

He stared at her in utter bafflement. Why was the girl looking at him as if he were a savage beast? *He* hadn't assaulted her—he was only defending her from someone who *had*. Yet she was looking at him as if he were a worse criminal than the blackguard he held. "What *is* it, Jenny?" he asked, stupified.

"Don't . . . *kill* him . . ." Her pleading voice was shaking.

He had a flash of recollection. They were standing together on the dock at Portsmouth. He'd just told her that the thieves—the child and the woman who'd plotted to steal her baggage—had probably escaped. *Good,* she'd said. *I wouldn't wish to have them languishing in prison because of me.* He'd answered that criminals deserved punishment, but she'd not agreed. Had this anything to do with her dislike of him? Had she found him then—and did she find him now—too vindictive? Was that it?

He lowered his fist and looked at the poor wretch sagging in his hold. "The lady doesn't want you killed," he muttered through clenched teeth, "so I'm going to let you go. Go home, and when you get there, go down on your knees and thank the Lord that the lady is so much more merciful than I would have been."

He shoved him away with such force that the fellow toppled over backward and fell on his rear. Using his hands and his seat, he pushed himself back along the road (keeping a wary eye on the gentleman who'd mauled him) until he judged it safe to get up. Then he got clumsily to his feet and scampered off with remarkable haste.

But neither Tris nor Jenny watched him go. They stood unmoving, staring at each other with breathless, puzzled intensity while the sleet pelted down, all unheeded, on their heads. *She thinks I'm some sort of beast,* Tris thought with despair. *There's nothing I can do, it seems, to win her good opinion.*

He didn't strike the poor man, Jenny was thinking, eyeing him in relieved gratitude. *He restrained himself . . . and all for my sake. Can it be that he's not such a brute as I thought?*

Tris, taking note of the ice forming on her uncovered hair, forced himself into action. He whipped off his greatcoat, threw it over her, lifted her into his arms without a word and carried her to the curricle. "No, please," she murmured as he placed her gently on the seat and pulled the coat snugly about her, "you'll catch your death. Please put your coat on again."

"I don't need it," he assured her, "and you're shivering."

He walked carefully round the carriage (for the thin glaze of ice forming over the ruts of the road was treacherous), spied his glove lying forgotten on the ground, picked it up and climbed up beside her. Holding the reins tightly to keep the horses from moving too quickly, he guided the animals into a turn and set off up the road. The girl beside him was still trembling, and he himself was too shaken to think clearly. "Are you all right? That blackguard didn't *harm* you, did he?"

"N-No," she said shakily. "He only . . . k-kissed me."

"Damned lout," Tris muttered under his breath.

She shivered again and held the greatcoat tightly at her neck. "I don't s-suppose it was important, since I did escape from him. One shouldn't r-refine on such matters in one's mind, should one?"

"No, I don't think one should," Tris said, throwing her a comforting smile. "A kiss is not an act of very great significance."

She didn't even notice his smile but stared out ahead of her, considering his statement with intent seriousness. "No, I don't suppose it is," she said, her tone distinctly relieved.

"Then you *are* feeling better?"

"Yes, I'm quite all right . . . now."

They rode along in silence. Tris would have liked to ask her why she'd stopped him from striking her attacker, for it seemed to him a completely justified punishment. Was the girl so foolishly tenderhearted that she'd instantly forgive even so vile a man as that? Did she have some sort of religious conviction on the subject? And did it have anything to do with her obvious aversion to *him*? He would have liked to ask her all of those questions and more. But they were both too shaken to deal with these matters sensibly now. It would be best to discuss only trivialities. "I wonder what's become of your carriage," he remarked, keeping his voice calm and impersonal.

"I don't know." There was a long pause. "I don't know what I should have done if you hadn't come back for me," she said quietly. "I . . . I must—"

"No, you must *not*," he cut in coldly. He was revolted at the prospect of receiving a token of reluctant gratitude from someone who abhored him.

She looked up at him in confusion. "What?"

"You must not bother to tell me how grateful you are. That's what you were trying to say, wasn't it?"

"Yes, it was. Why may I not say it?"

"I don't want to hear it, Miss Garvin." He could almost *feel* her eyes on his face, wide with surprise, but he kept his fixed on his horses.

"You called me Jenny back at the crossroad," she murmured. "Twice."

"Did I?" He couldn't resist stealing a quick look at her

before turning his attention back to the horses. "I shouldn't have thought you'd noticed. You were in quite a state."

"Yes, I was. But I *did* notice. It would seem an excess of formality to return to calling me Miss Garvin after all that's passed."

"I thought you *liked* an excess of formality."

"*I*?" The surprise in her tone clearly indicated that she'd become aware of a tinge of hostility in his manner. "Why do you say that?"

"Because it seems to me that you've been treating me with an excess of formality ever since I arrived here a week ago. I hadn't noticed that trait in you during our first meeting, I admit."

There was another pause. He wondered what she was thinking. Was she offended by his coldness? It gave him a touch of bitter satisfaction to think she might be. He'd been offended by hers often enough.

"Why don't you want my gratitude, Captain?" she asked after a long silence. "You've rescued me twice from the assaults of miscreants. I *must* be grateful for that, mustn't I?"

He took a deep, unhappy breath. "I'm sorry you feel you must, my dear. It's difficult, isn't it, to have to be grateful to someone you dislike so much?"

She didn't answer. The silence hung between them like something palpable. When it became insupportable to him, he turned to look at her. She was crying. Large tears were flowing unchecked down her cheeks and mingling with the droplets of icy rain. She was a pitiful sight, staring straight out before her, eyes filled with tears, lips trembling and hair glazed with ice and hanging in pathetic tendrils about her face. Even his greatcoat, which she clutched about her like a cloak, added to the pathos.

He was smitten with self-reproach as if from a blow. He should never have said what he did. She'd already been through a shattering experience and was only trying to thank him for having rescued her from it, and he'd turned on her with his accusation. He'd rejected her sweet and natural wish to express her gratitude and, instead, had flung his own resentments in her face. "Damnation," he muttered, putting an arm about her and pulling her to him, "I'm a stupid clod."

She turned her face into his shoulder, sobbing. "N-No . . . you're n-not . . ."

"I am! Forgive me, Jenny. I should never have said what I did."

"You d-don't *understand*," she wept. "I don't d-dislike you. I only w-wish I *did*."

He would have sworn he felt his heart take a leap inside his chest. Whatever it was, it was a completely new experience. "Now *that*," he said cautiously, "is a fascinating, if bewildering, statement. I hope you intend to elaborate on it."

"Well, I don't," came the muffled voice from his shoulder. "And I hope you won't p-press me."

"But you must explain—"

"I *can't*." Her sobs were more easily felt than heard. "Please . . ."

He sighed. "Very well, I won't press you. At least not now. I didn't intend to upset you, you know. I'd made up my mind to speak of nothing but trivialities. If only you'll stop crying, I promise to discuss nothing but the weather."

She gave a hiccoughing little sniff. "I've s-stopped." Her head came up, and a hand emerged from the folds of the greatcoat to wipe her cheeks. "So, you see, you may t-take your arm away now . . . quite safely . . ."

Her face looking up at him caused another tremor inside his chest. Her eyes were red-rimmed and her lips swollen from her weeping, yet she seemed to him more appealingly lovely than she'd ever been before. He wanted so much to kiss her that the need became a knot in his stomach. But of course such an act was unthinkable, especially after what she'd just been through. "I . . . er . . . What a lovely day we've been having, Miss Garvin," he said with a little grin, holding fast to the promise he'd just given her.

She didn't laugh but continued to gaze up at him, not even attempting to move from his encircling arm.

The knot in his stomach tightened. "One rarely expects to find such exceptionally pleasant days in December, wouldn't you say?" he tried again.

There was not even the suggestion of a smile in her widened eyes. She continued to look at him as if she'd never seen him before. There was no help for it—he *had* to kiss her. He wondered briefly if he was as despicable a creature as the wretch at the crossroad for wishing to kiss her so soon after the other incident. But he pushed the thought aside. He loved her. That had to make a difference.

His arm tightened about her, and he brought his face down within an inch of hers, watching closely for a sign of dismay in her eyes or a stiffening of resistance in her body. But she remained motionless, gazing up at him with a surprised, almost trance-like expression. He couldn't, if his life depended on it, stop himself now. "Jenny?" he whispered softly.

"Yes?" It was the merest breath.

"Have you another jar of jam on your person?"

She blinked. "What a strange question. Why?"

"Because I'm afraid I must kiss you, and I want to be certain that I shan't be crowned with gooseberry jam for my pains."

Chapter Thirteen

It was strange to ride in absolute silence through the deepening shadows in a shower of sleet with a lovely young woman whom one has just released from a stirring embrace. The only sounds were the brittle taps of the horses' hooves on the icy road and the crackle of pellets of sleet as they fell on the curricle's roof. He wanted very much to speak to her. He wanted to tell her that he loved her. But he restrained himself. The time was not yet right.

The words he'd said to her earlier echoed in his head with a mocking irony: *a kiss is not an act of very great significance*. After what had just occurred, the words sounded ridiculous. The very nature of his relationship with Jenny had been changed by the kiss. He'd held her in his arms and felt her respond, and he now knew there was no going back. He would not leave Wyndham until he'd won her.

He'd wanted to tell her as soon as he'd released her. But he knew that there was something about him that troubled her, and until he learned what it was, it would be unwise to force the issue. He had to hold his tongue. And, since it was difficult to think of anything trivial to say after having been so deeply stirred, he merely kept his eyes on his horses, his hands on the reins and said nothing.

Jenny was grateful for the silence. This had been the first time she'd been kissed by a man, if one didn't count the attack of the man at the crossroad, the occasional peck on the cheek from her brother, or the friendly buss from Toby on her last birthday. And if one compared those kisses with *this*, one certainly *shouldn't* count them. The other kisses had been ugly or paltry; this one had been profoundly moving—the sort of kiss a girl dreams of. She knew she was inexperienced in these matters, but it seemed to her that the embrace had been both passionate and tender . . . and certainly not the sort of kiss she would have expected from a man she believed to be a monstrous brute.

Even more surprising had been her response to the embrace. She'd felt no urge to resist. From the moment she'd glanced up at him, after her bout of weeping on his shoulder, she'd *wanted* him to kiss her. It had been the expression in his eyes that had moved her. He'd looked down at her with a glow in his eyes so gentle and loving that all her misgivings about him melted away. And when he'd actually kissed her, she'd had no desire to see it end. She'd quite forgotten where she was; she'd had no awareness of the sleet, the open carriage, even the time of day. She'd been aware only of the arousal of her senses, a pervading warmth and a heady and delicious dizziness. The after-effects of her dreadful experience at the crossroad which still lingered in her mind simply evaporated away, like a sliver of ice on a hot coal. Instead of being horrified (as any proper young lady should have been if she possessed a grain of sensibility) she'd felt completely, foolishly, wildly exhilarated.

It was only after he'd let her go that she'd remembered he was Robbie's Captain Allenby. It was as if this man had two identities: one the man who'd twice saved her life and twice charmed her, and the other Robbie's brutish commander. There had only been one instant in which the two had come together—the moment when he'd been about to strike her assailant. And even then he'd restrained himself. She'd not *quite* seen the bestial side. And now, after the kiss, it would be even more difficult to keep the brutal image of him foremost in her mind. The memory of the look on his face as he was about to kiss her would be an image very hard to supersede.

His voice, though low and hesitant, made her start. "I hope you're not angry with me, Jenny," he said sheepishly.

"I'm not angry, Captain. After all, we did agree earlier that a kiss has no special significance."

"Yes, we did, didn't we? What a very shortsighted view that was! But I wish you'd stop calling me Captain. You did ask me to call you Jenny, and you therefore must be equally informal with me."

"I'm afraid I don't know the informal mode of address for a sea captain, sir."

"It's the same as for anyone else—the given name. Mine is Tristram, but I prefer Tris."

The thought of calling the imposing Captain Allenby by a nickname made her flush. "Oh, I don't think I can be as informal as *that*," she told him.

"Why not? I quite insist on it. *All* the girls I've kissed call me Tris."

A laugh escaped her. "I'm sure they do, but perhaps it would be best to forget that I'm numbered among them. Since we did agree on the incident's insignificance, I'd be most grateful if you'd forget it ever happened."

"I very much doubt that I can. And you're not going to pretend that the embrace we've just shared is as insignificant as most such occurrences, are you?"

Jenny was saved the embarrassment of a reply because she noticed at that moment a large, dark object lying on the side of the road. "Good God!" she exclamed, pointing. "Look over there! It's our laudalet!"

He pulled the horses to and jumped down to examine the vehicle lying on its side in the ditch. "An axle's broken," he told her as he climbed back upon his seat. "Whoever was driving it realized he couldn't fix it and just walked off."

"Robbie," she muttered worriedly. "He was to have come for me. I hope he wasn't injured."

Tris looked at her for a moment with upraised brows. *He'd better have been injured,* he thought grimly, *or he'll hear a few choice words from me*. Had the boy no thought for his sister at all? Even though the carriage had been wrecked, the fellow still had had his horses. Why hadn't he ridden for her?

But Tris didn't express those thoughts aloud. He merely told her not to worry. "I'd not be concerned for his safety if I were you. Your brother impresses me as an ingenious lad. He can take care of himself."

She didn't notice the irony in his voice. "I'm so glad to hear you say that, Captain. Mama and I have always felt that he's a boy of remarkable self-sufficiency. It's good to know that his captain agrees."

Tris felt himself growling inside. If there was anything he disliked, it was doting relatives. He'd often been subjected to the effusions of fond parents about the characters of their sons who were sailing under him. Nonsense, most of it. Every fond relation believed that his particular kin was the most courageous, ingenious, clever, hard-working, upright, intrepid sailor on the ship and expected the captain to concur. If all the lads in question had half the ability their relations claimed, a captain's lot would be sheer bliss. Jenny's beloved brother was an excellent case in point. Remarkably self-sufficient indeed! The boy seemed to Tris to be remarkably lazy and self-indulgent. Midshipman Robert Garvin was nothing better than a selfish brat. And unless he'd been carried home unconscious from the wreck, Tris had every intention of telling him so to his face.

It was dark when the curricle pulled up to the door of the Garvin house. Tris lifted Jenny from the seat, set her on the ground and walked with her to the door. But as she lifted her hand to the knocker, he caught it in his own. "Before you go in, Jenny, I must have a promise from you," he said firmly.

"Yes?"

"I want an opportunity to talk to you. Soon. And alone. Will you let me?"

She lowered her eyes. "How can I refuse, after all you've done for me?"

"Then I have your word? Whatever happens?"

"Yes, of course."

"Good." He gave her a sudden grin. "And while you're still feeling this quite unnecessary gratitude, I'll push my advantage and make another request. Will you stand up with me at the ball on Saturday? For two dances? And a waltz, if my aunt is brave enough to permit waltzing?"

She smiled up at him shyly. "*Three* dances? I think you *are* pushing your advantage. I'm afraid you'll have to be satisfied with two. I don't know how to waltz. And now, sir, I think you'd better let me knock."

Cullum, on opening the door, couldn't prevent a look of unbutlerish surprise from crossing his face. "Miss *Jenny*! We thought—"

"Jenny, is that *you*?" came her mother's voice from the top of the stairs. "We thought you were spending the night at Winch—Good *heavens*!" The sight of her daughter's bedraggled appearance, as well as the glimpse of a sodden Captain Allenby looming behind, brought her running down the stairs. "What on earth's *happened* to you?"

"She's been making her way back from Winchcombe in an

open curricle," Tris informed her in a distinctly censorious tone, "because the carriage from home which she was awaiting failed to appear."

"Well, I *know* that, Captain. It broke down, you see. But naturally, when we saw the sleet, we assumed that Jenny would spend the night with old Mrs. Boyce. That's where you were, wasn't it, my love?"

"Not exactly, Mama. But we'll talk about this later. Cullum, will you take the Captain's greatcoat to the kitchen and dry it at the fire? And if you'll give him your coat as well, Captain, he'll have your things warm and dry before you've had time to drink your tea. I think we *should* offer Captain Allenby some tea, don't you, Mama? He's been riding through the sleet for hours without his greatcoat, and all because of me."

"Oh, dear! Yes! Yes, of course. I don't know *where* my head is. I'll see to it at once. *Do* give your coat to Cullum, Captain. I'll get you a blanket to wrap about your shoulders in the meantime. You must be chilled through."

"Thank you, ma'am," Tris said, "but I shan't be able to stay to tea." He took his wet greatcoat from the butler's arm and threw it carelessly over his shoulders. "I only came in to inquire about your son's condition."

"Robbie is quite well, thank you," Lady Garvin said complacently. "He sustained a bruise to his left arm when the carriage collapsed, but it's of small moment. But, Captain, you *must* stay to tea. You're soaked through and are bound to catch a chill if you don't warm yourself."

The captain's mouth was tight and a small muscle worked just under his left cheek. "You'd do better," he said coldly, "to concern yourself about Miss Garvin, ma'am. She suffered exposure to the elements for a much longer period than I."

Lady Garvin looked at Jenny with sudden alarm. "*Did* she? Oh, my poor dear child, you *do* look dreadfully bedraggled. Are you much chilled? Go along to the sitting room, love. There's a good fire there, and I'll have a tea tray sent to you directly."

"I'll see to it at once, my lady," Cullum said and went off.

Jenny, before obeying her mother's directive, turned first to the captain. "Please stay for tea," she urged shyly. "It would be much more sensible to give your clothes a chance to dry before setting out again into the weather."

His expression softened, and he smiled down at her, a look

of intimacy coming into his eyes which Lady Garvin did not miss. "But it's such a remarkably fine day for December, as I've pointed out to you before," he said with a glint in his eye.

This time Jenny did laugh. "Nevertheless, I wish you would stay."

"It's kind of you to concern yourself about me, my dear," he said in a voice meant only for her, "but I've only two more miles to go. My mother was expecting me to return by three, and I don't wish to cause her more anxiety than necessary."

Jenny nodded and offered him her hand. "Then I'll say goodnight, sir. I haven't properly expressed my thanks for all you've done, but I think you know how grateful I am to you."

He kept his eyes on her face as he lifted her hand to his lips. "I know," he said softly. "Good night, ma'am."

Lady Garvin looked speculatively from one to the other. Just *what* was going on here? A thrill of excitement coursed through her breast. Had her daughter caught the eye of the famous, wealthy, sought-after Captain Allenby? It was too good to be true. But if it *were* true, Sally Clement would be *livid*. It had been clear from the moment the Clements' London relatives had announced their intention to visit that Sally intended to match Allenby with her Andrea. If Jenny managed to steal Allenby from under Andrea's nose, it would give Lady Garvin the greatest satisfaction. But even better, if Jenny snared the captain, what a stroke of luck it would be for *Robbie*! The boy's career would be *made*.

As if on cue, Robbie appeared at the top of the stairs. "Did I hear Captain Allenby's voice?" he asked.

"Yes, you did," his mother clarioned. "Come down, Robbie, dearest. The captain has brought your sister home."

"Oh, that's famous!" Robbie said, running down. "However did you manage to—?" He stopped in his tracks as he caught sight of their drenched dishevelment. "Oh, I *say*! What's happened?"

"What's happened, you clodpole," Tris said, all softness disappearing from his face, "is that you left your sister unattended at the side of the road, exposed, defenseless and vulnerable to attack from man and nature. I've spoken to you once before on this very subject. I didn't think I'd have to do it again."

Robbie whitened about the mouth. "But I had an accident—"

"I know all about your accident. You weren't crippled by it, were you? You still had your horses . . . and your two healthy young legs. Why didn't you use them?"

"Well, I . . . you see, it started to sleet . . . and I'd bruised my arm and was a good deal shaken up . . . and I was certain that, when she saw the change in the weather, she'd spend the night with old Mrs. Boyce. Damnation, Jenny, why *didn't* you—?"

"Are you going to shift the blame to *her*?" Tris demanded, enraged.

Jenny interfered hastily. "I thought of going back to Mrs. Boyce's," she said to her brother, "but it was three miles from the crossroad, and I was afraid I'd miss you."

"Well, it was damned silly of you," Robbie said, now reddening as quickly as he'd paled. "Is it my fault if you didn't use your head?"

"Keep a civil tongue in your head when you speak to your sister!" Tris barked, his years of awesome authority ringing in his voice. "I had not intended to dress you down before your family, but your reluctance to face up to your callous behavior disgusts me. Whether your sister had decided to seek shelter at the home of her friend or to wait for you at the crossroad makes little difference. If you had a smidgeon of character you'd understand that it behooved you to make certain she was safe before you slunk home to your own warmth and comfort. Your behavior this afternoon was irresponsible, thoughtless and completely reprehensible."

"Now, *really*, Captain," Lady Garvin interjected, putting a protective arm about her son's shoulders, "aren't you being a bit hard on the boy? He only—"

"*Hard*, ma'am? This tongue-lashing is nothing! When I think of the torment to which his sister was subjected because of his neglect—and the even worse possibilities which might have come about had she not managed to protect herself and I not happened on the scene—I'd like to thrash the puppy within an inch of his life! However, I'm not captain here, nor do I have any familial rights to punish the boy, worse luck. I have no choice but to leave the resolution of this matter in your hands. But if you'll heed my advice, you'll give the boy as severe a punishment as you can contrive. Good night, ma'am." And he turned on his heel and stalked out.

"*Well*!" Lady Garvin exclaimed, staring at the door with eyebrows raised.

Robbie was trembling. "Damn you, Jenny, *now* see what you've done!" He turned and kicked helplessly at the balustrade of the stairway. "I'll never get on his right side now!" His voice was thick with tearful animosity, and he ran up the stairs, pausing at the top only to throw his sister a last, blistering look.

His mother and sister gazed up after him from the foot of the stairs until they heard his door slam. Then Lady Garvin heaved a deep, troubled sigh. "I must say, Jenny, you might have been a bit more discreet. Did you *have* to tell Captain Allenby that Robbie was supposed to come for you?"

"I don't see how I could have avoided it, Mama. How else could I have explained why I was standing at the side of the road all by myself?"

"You shouldn't have *been* standing there. I don't see why you went to Winchcombe in the first place. This entire matter could have been avoided if only you'd stayed at home as you were supposed to do."

Jenny hung her head. "Yes, it was foolish of me to have gone. I'm sorry."

"Sorry words won't fill a sack," her mother recited, unwilling to show even a touch of forgiveness. "And as for your Captain Allenby, I don't care if he's interested in you or not. The man's a perfect *brute*! If I had any doubts before, I've certainly lost them now. To speak to my Robbie in that frightening way—it was *monstrous*! I'd better go upstairs and see if I can console the poor dear."

Without waiting for a reply, Lady Garvin mounted the stairs, leaving Jenny, wet and shivering, to take care of herself. The girl remained motionless until her mother disappeared, and then she went slowly down the hall to the sitting room. The hem of her dress dragged soddenly along the floor, and the ice that had accumulated on her hair, now melting, dripped slowly down her face and the back of her neck. Her teeth chattered with the damp cold that seemed to have penetrated to her very bones. The deserted hallway and the quiet of the house only added to her feeling of aloneness.

Her mother had accused Tris Allenby—as her brother had accused *her*—of being at fault in this incident. Jenny didn't feel at fault, nor could she see anything particularly monstrous in Captain Allenby's behavior to Robbie this evening. As far as she was concerned, this time at least, the captain's harsh scolding had been absolutely justified.

In the sitting room, a fire was blazing and a tea-tray awaited her on the table near the window, but Jenny felt no inclination to take tea all by herself. Instead she huddled near the fire and waited for an onset of the depression which she was certain would come. During the last few months, that depression had often attacked her spirit whenever her mother had stung her with disapproval or neglect. *If ever an onslaught of depression can be justified,* she thought, *tonight should be the time*.

But no depression came. Quite the contrary. A feeling that was the opposite of depression seemed to be spreading, like the warmth of the flames, right through her. What *was* it? As the heat of the fire worked its way into her bones, the last vestiges of her self-pity vanished. Despite the shock of Robbie's resentment and the ring of her mother's scolding in her ears, she felt . . . she struggled for a word to describe it . . . *euphoric*!

She didn't have to look far to discover the source of her euphoria. It was really quite obvious. Tonight she'd had a champion. Yes, like a beseiged lady in a medieval romance, she'd had a champion—and one with the most awesome powers. He'd come riding, totally unexpectedly, from out of the south and had exercised his mighty powers for her protection and *hers alone*.

It was ridiculous, she knew, to imagine herself as a Guinevere or an Elayne of Astolat; there was not a jot of the romantic heroine in her nature. But in this instance—this one time in her life—she'd had a champion every bit as strong, as powerful, as unyielding as any Arthurian knight. And the recollection of all his deeds bubbled inside her with joyful satisfaction. For once, someone had taken her side in a struggle. For once she hadn't been second best. After a lifetime of taking second place, she'd been, for this one time at least, somebody's very first concern. And oh, how very satisfying being first had been!

Chapter Fourteen

Tris expected everyone at the Hall to fall on his neck in relief when he returned, but his arrival caused barely a ripple. Even his mother failed to greet him with the expected eagerness. "I'm delighted to see you safe, my dear, of course," she said, taking his arm and walking with him to the drawing-room fire, "but I wasn't worried about you. You've sailed across oceans in the most fearful storms, so I had no doubt you could maneuver safely through this shower of sleet. It's Andrea we're concerned about. She's not yet returned from her outing to Cheltenham. Sally and Alfred are quite beside themselves."

Despite their agitation, Lord and Lady Clement took pains to make Tris warm and comfortable. Lady Clement ordered a mulled brandy to be prepared for him, while his lordship urged him into a chair near the fire and made him put his feet up on the hearth. Andrea's little dog, Lumpkin, lying on the hearth, gave him a woeful glance. Even the dog appeared to be worried about the missing girl.

Tris tried to calm everyone with assurances that the roads were not impassable and that the downpour of sleet was letting up, but the pair was not comforted. They paced about the drawing room, their faces tight with apprehension. But when Tris rose and offered to go out and search for the carriage, they would not hear of it. He was already soaked through, they noted, and they insisted that he go upstairs and dress for dinner. It was finally agreed, after much debate, that they would all dress for dinner and carry on as usual until the meal was over. If the missing Andrea had not returned by then, a search party would be organized.

An hour later they reassembled in the drawing room, but Andrea had still not appeared. Dinner (which because of the weather was to be taken quietly at home for the first time in six days, with only the family and the two guests at the table) was put back an half-hour in the hope that Andrea might still arrive on time. Then it was put back another half-hour. When that, too, passed, Lady Clement, afraid that the cook would fall into an apoplexy, led the party into the dining room. But no one felt much inclined to eat.

The second course had just been laid when they heard a commotion in the hallway—the sound of voices, laughter and Lumpkin's joyous barking. They all rushed out to find that Andrea and Toby had finally arrived, hungry, cold, laden with parcels and perfectly safe.

The girl was greeted with not a word of rebuke. Her mother and father embraced her with effusive expressions of loving solicitude, and then both of the travelers, with Lumpkin leaping and racing wildly about their feet, were ushered into the drawing room and settled at the fire with comforters thrown about their shoulders. They were plied with tea, hot brandy, soup from the dining room and a dozen exclamations from the Clements of their relief and delight. The contrast between the reception which Andrea received from her parents and that which Jenny had received from her mother made Tris gnash his teeth.

It was decided that Toby (who, because he'd been riding all afternoon on the driver's box, had been too long exposed to the elements) was not to venture out again but was to spend the night at the Hall. One of the stable boys was dispatched to take word of these arrangements to the vicar and Mrs. Boyce. With that matter arranged and Toby supplied with a dry coat from Lord Clement's wardrobe, the entire party returned to the dining room and fell upon the repast with renewed appetite.

"Despite my pleasure in seeing you safe, Andrea," Lord Clement remarked while slicing the roast, his voice revealing mild disapproval, "I must admit that I cannot be completely sanguine about your conduct. It seems to me that you—and especially *you*, Toby—showed a want of sense. As soon as you saw the sky darken, you should have turned about and started for home."

Toby looked up from his plate. "I tried to convince your daughter to do so, right after we'd set Jenny down at the crossroad near Winchcombe, but you know your Andrea. She *would* have her orchid gloves."

Tris looked up, startled. He'd not inquired of Jenny how she'd come to be standing alone at the crossroad, so it had not occurred to him that her outing and Andrea's had been in any way connected.

"See here, Toby," Andrea was saying irritably, "I've heard enough on the subject of my gloves. You are becoming very vexing. Though I suppose one can't expect a man to understand the importance of such things."

"Do you mean to say," her aunt Dulcie inquired, "that you worried your parents and kept this young man on the box for hours in the sleet just to purchase a pair of *gloves*?"

"But it was not only gloves, Aunt Dulcie," Andrea responded with cheerful complacency. "I purchased an ell of swansdown for a scarf, and some French lace—you'll love it, Mama, for it will make a beautiful collar for my green lustring—and a new pair of slippers."

"You see?" Toby grinned at the gentlemen. "With such important errands to execute, what could we do but ignore the sleet and spend the entire afternoon parading through the Cheltenham shops?"

But Tris was staring at him with knit brows. "I beg your pardon, Boyce, but did I understand you to say that you'd set Jenny down at the crossroad? Jenny *Garvin*?"

"Yes, I did say that. She traveled with us as far as Winchcombe, you see, to visit my grandmother. But she couldn't go on with us to Cheltenham, so we put her down at the crossroad."

"You left her there all alone?" Tris persisted, a wave of anger flooding over him.

"Well, yes," Andrea said, a shade defensively. "Her brother was coming to take her home."

"Was he indeed?" Tris looked at his cousin with cold disdain. "Did you wait to *see* that he did?"

Toby began to feel uncomfortable. "Why are you asking these questions, Captain Allenby? *Didn't* he come?"

"No, he didn't, as a matter of fact."

Toby and Andrea exchanged looks of guilty alarm. "How do you know?" Toby inquired, his face falling. "Has something . . . happened to Jenny?"

"No. She's safe, no thanks to you. I happened along and took her home."

"Oh, good," Andrea breathed in relief. "Everything's all right, then."

"Is *that* what you think?" Tris threw down his fork and leaned forward, his jaw clenched tightly. "She's safe, and therefore you've nothing for which to reproach yourself, eh?"

Andrea looked across the table at him, her hazel eyes widening with injured innocence. "Cousin Tris, you're not *angry* with me, are you?"

"Angry is scarcely the word," he said in disgust.

"But I don't see why. It wasn't my fault that her brother didn't come, was it?"

"*Really*, Andrea!" her mother chided, upset by this new evidence of her daughter's selfishness.

"But it *wasn't* my fault. Besides, if nothing happened—"

Tris expelled an impatient breath. "I said she was now safe. I did *not* say that nothing happened. The fact is that she was left to stand in the cold and sleet for almost an hour, that she was assaulted by a drunken ruffian—"

"Oh, no!" cried Lady Clement.

"My word!" muttered her husband.

"—a drunken ruffian who, if she hadn't had the presence of mind to clout with a jar of jam, might have done God-knows-what dreadful harm to her person, and that she may yet fall ill from exposure or the upset to her nerves."

"Oh, *Tris*!" Lady Rowcliffe breathed, horrified.

"Good God!" Toby's mouth hung open and his knife fell from his hand and clattered on the plate. "It's all *my* fault. I should *never* have—"

"No, you shouldn't," Tris said sternly. "It's inconceivable to me that a young man of sense, as you appear to be, could have been so utterly thoughtless—"

"It w-was *I*!" Andrea confessed, beginning to cry. "I told Toby not to wait. I was *certain* that Robbie would b-be right along."

"And you were too eager to buy your gloves and laces to wait and make sure." Tris, glowering, rose to his feet. "I don't see how you can call yourself her friend and yet have treated her with such callous lack of consideration. It seems to me that you treat your blasted *lap dog* with more solicitude."

"Tris," his mother hissed in a cautionary undervoice, "sit down! We *are* at your aunt's table, you know, not on board the *Providential*. You might at least restrain your 'blasted's."

Tris glanced down at her, momentarily arrested. Then he turned to face his aunt at the foot of the table. "Forgive me for making this scene at your dinner table, Aunt. It was unpardonable of me . . . and also high-handed to have taken it upon myself to upbraid my cousin *in loco parentis*. As my mother reminds me, this is your dining room, not my ship. I'm sorry this came up right in the middle of your excellent dinner, but I can't be sorry for what I said. However, I shall say no more on the subject. If you don't mind, Aunt Sally, I'd like you to excuse me. I find I've lost my appetite." With that, he gave his aunt a formal, frowning bow, nodded brusquely to his uncle and strode out of the room.

Some time later, his mother found him in the library, slouched in an easy chair staring into the fire. "Ah, so this is where the awesome Captain Allenby has hidden himself," she said, coming in and closing the door behind her. "You've shaken the household to the foundations, you cawker. Andrea has gone crying to her room; her father, who wanted to follow and console her, was given a scold by Sally for his indulgence of the girl (as if she doesn't indulge her shamefully herself), and now *they* aren't speaking; and Toby has slunk away to *his* room in abject shame. And all this because my son wants to run the world as he does his ship. I hope you're satisfied."

He gave her a rueful grin. "Is it as bad as that? Shall we have to leave in disgrace, do you suppose?"

She shook her head, made a little moue at him and took a chair. "No, it's merely a passing tempest. It will all blow over by morning. But I must say, Tris, that I cannot like watching you ride roughshod over everyone, even if you *did* have provocation. Is the habit of command so strong in you that you forget the limits of your authority?"

"I hope not," he said, abashed. "Forgive me, Mama. I shall do my best not to overstep again. But I find myself out-of-reason vexed by the manner in which everyone ignores Jenny. Her welfare seems to be of only secondary concern to people who should be putting her first—people like her own family and friends."

"Yes, I noticed that, too. Her mother's largely at fault, I believe. The woman seems to have fallen into the habit of cutting her daughter down. It is very odd."

"Perhaps not so odd. She has a son, you see. Mothers who have sons and daughters all seem to favor their sons."

"That's not true at all. I'm sure that if I'd had a daughter, I should have loved her above *both* my sons. So there!"

"That's only because your elder son in a misanthropic recluse and your younger an overbearing make-bait who's far out to sea when you want him near and insufferably arrogant when he's at hand." He threw her a sympathetic smile. "You haven't had much luck with your offpsring, have you, poor dear?"

She grinned back at him affectionately. "I've done well enough. But I shall do even better when you've given me a daughter-in-law. Am I right in surmising that you've made some progress in that direction today?"

"I'm not sure. I've learned that I want her more than ever. Some small part of her wants me, too. But the other part—"

"The other part still rejects you?" Her brow knit worriedly. "Have you learned why?"

"No. I've only had a glimmering. Something about me frightens her." He ran his fingers through his hair in a gesture of helplessness. "Mama, I know you've found me overweening and top-lofty from time to time—behaving as if the world were the deck of the *Providential*, as you put it—but would you call me vindictive?"

"*Vindictive*? What a very strange question. Of course not! I don't find you top-lofty very often, either. Not nearly enough to cause anyone to be *afraid* of you."

He sighed. "I suppose I should feel comforted by those words. But you *are* my mother. I can hardly expect an impartial judgment from you."

"I may be your mother, but I'm not *besotted*." She jumped up, pulled herself to her full height and glared down at him. "In all your thirty-five years, you've never shown yourself to be vengeful or to hold a grudge. No one with sense would call *my son* vindictive."

"All right, Mama, all right. You needn't gird yourself for battle over this."

"I can't help it. If Jenny Garvin finds you vindictive, she hasn't the intellect with which I credited her." She shook her head and sank into her chair. "I think you must have misunderstood the signs."

"Perhaps. But, Mama, let me pose a hypothetical situation.

Suppose you were being attacked by a lecher and managed successfully to subdue him. And then I came along, evaluated the situation, picked up the wretch by the scruff of his neck and landed him a facer. Would you be horrified by my behavior? Horrified to the core?"

"No, I don't think so," she answered after considering the question carefully.

"Even if, since you were already safe, my blow was no longer necessary for your protection?"

"Ah! I begin to see. The blow in that case was more retributive than useful, is that what you mean?"

"Vindictive, yes."

"But the wretch would have *deserved* the blow, wouldn't he?"

"*I* thought he would."

"But Jenny did not?" She fixed her sharp, knowing eyes on her son's face. "Jenny had subdued her attacker with a jar of jam—that's what you said at the table. And she felt that *that* was sufficient punishment. She didn't approve of your subjecting the fellow to additional battering. Have I come to the heart of it?"

"Yes, more or less."

"But the incident occurred *today*. It doesn't explain her earlier aversion."

"When we met at Portsmouth, she disagreed with my desire to see the thieves who'd stolen her brother's baggage put in prison. Perhaps she found me vindictive even then."

"Vindictive? For merely wishing to see that thieves are given just punishment?" She shook her head in disapproval. "I begin to believe, Tris, that your Jenny has too-delicate sensibilities."

"Perhaps so. Or perhaps your son is too brutal," he murmured thoughtfully.

"*Brutal*! What nonsense! I won't listen to any more of this foolish self-castigation." She rose from her chair once more and went to the door. "I liked your Jenny very much, my love, when I met her. Very much indeed. But if she succeeds in convincing you that you're anything less than a man of the finest character and highest ideals, I shall rue the day you ever set eyes on her. Brutal, indeed! I never heard such rubbish in all my life!"

She slammed the door behind her, but her vehemence only

made Tris smile. She'd sprung to his defense like a tiger with her cub . . . and with as much foolish ardor as Lady Garvin would have exhibited in defending her "Robbie." The judgments of mothers, even his own, were not to be trusted.

But by his *own* standards of judgment he didn't find himself a brute. If the lovely, seemingly sensible Jenny found him so, which of them was right?

On the other hand, did it really matter? He loved her. Even if he was brutal and vindictive to the rest of the world, he would never be so with her. She would always find him the kindest, gentlest, most forgiving of mortals—he'd have to convince her of that. His mother might disapprove of his willingness to accept Jenny's assessment of him. His mother might well rue the day he first set eyes on her. But he couldn't rue that day . . . not as long as he lived.

Chapter Fifteen

The winter-bright sun shone into the sitting-room window at Willowrise with a hazy innocence, as if it knew nothing about having deserted the landscape so devastatingly the day before. Except for some patches of white on the lawn and a number of dripping icicles clinging to the eaves of the outbuildings, the tree branches and the frame of the window, Jenny could see no sign of yesterday's sleet.

"I wish you'd hold your head still," Toby said crossly from the other side of the room where he sat, sketch pad propped up on his knee, working earnestly on a drawing of Jenny with the sunlight on her hair. He'd already thought of a name for it —*Girl in the Window, with Icicles*. If only she'd sit still, he was convinced the sketch would turn out to be his finest piece of work.

"Sorry. But it's taking you such a long while to finish. Am I so difficult a subject?"

"On the contrary, this is going very well. *So* well that I won't have you spoiling it by moving about. Tilt your chin just the slightest bit. Now to the left . . . ah! Yes, just like that."

"Can we speak while you work, Toby? I'd like to hear more about what happened last night. Is Andrea really coming over here to *apologize*?"

"Yes, she is. After luncheon, I expect. Lady Clement made us both promise."

"I think it's quite ridiculous. That business at the crossroad came about through my own decision. No one else should be blamed."

"No, you're out there," Toby said, keeping his eyes on his work. "As the man of the party, I should have been firm, no matter what you and Andrea said. The captain made me see that quite clearly. He made me realize that I've much to learn before I can call myself a man."

"Did he say that? It wasn't kind. He can sometimes be quite cruel, I believe."

"Don't move your head, Jenny, *please*! Cruel? Not at all. Only honest. And he was harder on Andrea than on me, you know."

"On Andrea? But why?"

"I don't know. He said she treats Lumpkin with more attention than she does you."

"Did he? I wish he hadn't. He knows nothing of my relationship with Andrea. Don't you think it was a bit presumptious of him?"

"*Jenny,* you're putting up your chin! Can't you sit still a few moments more? If you ask me, the captain was quite right. Much as I care for Andrea (and you know that for years now I've been asking her to have me) I must admit that she sometimes behaves like the Queen of All the Britons. It worries me more than I care to admit."

"Really? Why? It's only her 'air,' you know. She's quite good-hearted underneath."

"Yes, but how would such an air suit the wife of an impecunious son of a country vicar, eh?"

"But you won't always be the impecunious son of the vicar. You'll be Sir Tobias Boyce, portrait painter royal, with commissions from the Regent and all the peerage. Then your wife can wear all the airs she wants."

He laughed, wrapped up his charcoal sticks and gave his sketch one last look of approval. "There, it's finished," he said, wiping his fingers. "Come and look."

Jenny jumped up and ran to look over his shoulder. The sketch was quite different from anything she'd seen him do before. It was suffused with light and shadow. The face, turned more than halfway from the sunlit window, was shadowed except where the sun struck on the curves of lip and cheek. Little tendrils of hair seemed to wave in the sunlight, and a bit of braid could just be discerned at the edge of the neck. The girl in the picture was thoughtful, dreamy and very slightly smiling. Yet there was an air of sadness, too, that was somehow emphasized by the little icicles that edged the window-frame. "Why, *Toby*! It's . . . almost *moving*. Do I really look like that? No, of course not. I can see that it's much idealized."

"Is it? I didn't intend . . ." He looked it over critically. "I think the likeness rather good, myself."

"Let *me* see," came Andrea's voice from the doorway, and she came in without waiting to be asked.

Jenny ran to welcome her. "Let me have your bonnet, love," she said, kissing her friend's cheek. "I didn't expect you until after luncheon."

"Has Toby told you all? You caused the greatest to-do at our house, you widgeon. You'd never credit what a scene there was."

"I'm sorry, love. I never meant—"

"I know. Never mind that now. Let's see Toby's sketch. We can talk of this later."

Without removing her bonnet or shawl, she crossed the room, took the drawing from Toby's hold and turned so that the light fell on the pad. Her eye ran quickly over the sketch as Toby came up behind her. "It's called *Girl With Icicles*," he said proudly. "What do you think?"

Andrea's face seemed to stiffen. "It's . . . lovely. Quite lovely." Her voice revealed a hint of restraint. "He's made you look beautiful, Jenny."

"Idealized, I think," Jenny said.

Andrea thrust the sketch pad back into Toby's hand. "How is it you never sketched *me* that way?" she demanded. "With the light so . . . so . . . misty?"

He threw her a quick look and flipped the cover of the pad closed. "I don't know. It was a new idea." Andrea was jealous . . . he could see the signs. But he was in no mood to fend off one of her tantrums. "I'll do one of you in this style if you like," he said, packing up his things, "as soon as we can find the time. Meanwhile, I'd best be off. I haven't yet been home."

Andrea remained standing in the window, staring out at the garden, while Jenny went to see Toby out. She turned when Jenny reentered and pulled off her bonnet with an impatient abruptness. "You've been quite the center of attention of late, haven't you?" she accused. "The Damsel in Distress yesterday and the Girl with Icicles today."

Jenny giggled. "Yes, I suppose I have. Here, let me take your things."

"Don't bother. I can't stay long."

Jenny looked at her friend closely. Andrea's face still had a tight, wary look. "You're not going to be jealous, are you, you noddy? You've held the center of attention for so long that you can't really begrudge me a shall share." She gave Andrea a wide grin. "After all, you've shared attention with Lumpkin, so why not with me?"

Andrea gave a reluctant laugh. "So Toby's told you what Cousin Tris said to me. I'm a selfish beast, I know." She tossed her bonnet on a chair and wandered abjectly to the sofa. "And if I didn't know, a houseful of people back at the Hall are ready and willing to tell me so."

"Come now, love, you can't mean it," Jenny said soothingly, drawing her friend down beside her on the sofa. "I'm sure that not one of them has called you a selfish beast."

"Not in so many words, perhaps. But it's true. I'm dreadfully sorry about yesterday, Jenny. Did you have a very frightful time?"

"For a while it was rather nightmarish." Her smile faded, and she gave a little shudder. "Did Captain Allenby tell you about the . . . the man?"

Andrea nodded. "It must have been horrid. I'm so sorry, Jenny."

Jenny shrugged. "It wasn't your fault. *I* was the one who told you to go on to Cheltenham without waiting."

"No, you are being kind. I should have waited no matter what you said. Please tell me that you forgive me. I shan't be able to face myself if you don't."

"Of course I forgive you, you goose," Jenny assured her with a hug. "And after all, no real harm was done."

"No thanks to me, however," Andrea admitted, breaking from Jenny's embrace and twisting her hands in her lap in shame. "Did the man really *molest* you?" she asked, awed.

"I think he meant to. Thank goodness I remembered Gammer Boyce's jam in my muff. All the fellow managed was a kiss."

"A kiss? Ugh! Poor Jenny! How can you bear remembering it?"

"I don't refine on it, you know. Captain Allenby said that a kiss has no real significance."

"Did he? How very interesting." Her apology made, her spirit was beginning to recover its usual self-confidence. She leaned back against the sofa cushions and stretched her arms out along the back. "I wonder if he'd say that about *my* kisses."

"Yours?" Jenny's eyes opened wide. "*Have* you ever—?"

"Kissed my cousin Tris? Not yet. But I mean to."

Jenny felt herself color up, and she turned away awkwardly. "You don't . . . have *designs* on him, do you, Andrea?" she asked, her heart beginning to jump about in her breast quite disturbingly. *So I'm as subject to attacks of jealousy as Andrea is,* she thought in self-disgust.

"Designs on him? Yes, I do. Mama says he's an excellent catch, even if he is a second son. She puts his income at five thousand a year *at least*, and since his brother is unmarried, he may yet inherit the title and the Rowcliffe fortune. I know you don't like him, Jenny, because of all the things Robbie wrote (and even *I* had a taste of his tyrannical side last night) but even so I find him fascinating."

Jenny, painfully aware of the dissipation of her happy mood, turned slowly back to her friend. "I don't dislike him, Andrea," she admitted. "Not any more."

Andrea smiled and squeezed her hand. "I *am* glad. I shouldn't wish us to become estranged because of my attachment to him."

"*Attachment*?" Jenny almost gasped. "Surely matters between you and Captain Allenby haven't reached the stage where you can call it an attachment, have they?"

"Perhaps not yet," Andrea said complacently, rising gracefully to her feet, "but I think, at the ball tomorrow night, I shall permit him to kiss me." She smiled dreamily as she picked up her hat and sauntered to the door. "And then we shall see what we shall see."

After Andrea had gone, Jenny returned to the sitting room window and sat gazing out on the wintry landscape. The glow that had sustained her through last night and this morning was now gone, and the reason for her despond was as clear as the window glass. She'd fallen in love with Captain Tristram Allenby.

Perhaps she'd tumbled at their very first meeting. The possibility was very likely, for she'd been aware of an unaccustomed depression ever since. Even Robbie's letters had upset her more than they would have if she'd had no personal interest in the captain he was so vehemently disparaging.

Every clue he'd revealed about his captain's brutishness had cut her like a knife. She must have cared a great deal even then.

But the moment when she'd actually tumbled into love was not important. What counted was that she loved him now . . . and that she could see nothing ahead but painful consequences. In the first place, there was no sign (except for a kiss which he himself indicated might not be significant) that he returned her feeling. All his kindnesses to her might be nothing more than social grace and superficial charm. In the second place, Andrea wanted him, and Andrea, past experience had proved, had never had the least difficulty winning any man she'd set her heart on. And in the third place, the Tristram Allenby who had charmed her was also the tyrannical captain who brought miscreants to heel by cruel and inhuman punishment. Even if her other doubts were swept away, that last one threatened the future with implacable doom. *How could she love a man whose character she despised?*

The only sensible solution for her would be to keep away from Captain Allenby until he left Wyndham. In time, she supposed, her feeling for him would wither away, especially when he was too far away for his magnetism to affect her. But before she could cut him out of her life, she had one last obligation to him. She'd promised him two dances and a private interview. *I want an opportunity to talk to you . . . and alone,* he'd said. *I have your word? Whatever happens?* She'd given that word, and it would not be right to renege.

She would go to the ball. She would dance with him and talk to him. And when it was over, she would never see him again. She would bury herself in her music, her family's interests and her normal daily life, and one day she'd get over him. Just one more day, and she would be done with him forever. Let Andrea have him.

Chapter Sixteen

The chandelier that ornamented the center of the large ball-room of Clement Hall shed twinkling darts on the one hundred and fifty guests who milled about below. It was a decoration that one might travel miles to admire; a "fire-lustre" of English leaded crystal, it was three tiers high, the brass branches completely covered with diamond-cut, pear-shaped crystal drops. The first tier alone held six hundred and twenty-five candles (there were over a thousand, all told), and Lord Clement was fond of bragging that the thing weighed a quarter of a ton. It glittered and gleamed like a multifaceted jewel belonging to a God of Olympus and shed a shimmering glow over the entire assemblage.

Nine musicians occupied the galleried platform at the far end of the room, and directly before them an area had been marked off for the dancing. Some thirty couples were thus occupied, while the rest strolled about the room, talking, laughing and drinking champagne. The party had been in progress only about an hour, but already everyone agreed that it was the finest ball that Wyndham had ever seen—and they'd not yet even sampled the elegancies which awaited them at the supper to be served at midnight.

On the dance floor, Tris was circling his partner uneasily. Jenny had readily acquiesced to his solicitation for her hand for the dance, but there was something in her manner which gave him pause. Her mouth was tight, her eyes wary, and her answers to his remarks monosyllabic. She'd made a retreat from her position of friendly openness which had marked her manner when he'd left her the night before last. What on earth had made the girl withdraw again?

For Jenny the dance was a difficult ordeal. Her decision to

make this evening the very last time she would see him was, in itself, painful enough, but when she'd taken her first glimpse of him her heart had sunk. He was in full uniform tonight, and the blue coat and gold braid made him the most splendid-looking man in the room. Every eye was on them, she knew, for he'd not attempted to dance at all until this dance with her, in spite of the very obvious lures that the marriageable girls and their parents had sent out to him. She could see the heads turn as he'd led her on the floor. Even Andrea, on the arm of Geoffrey Vesey, had turned and stared.

"Your dress is very becoming," the captain remarked during the promenade. "What is that wine-colored hue called?"

"Your description is quite apt, Captain. It's called burgundy."

"*Captain*, ma'am? I thought we'd agreed to abandon all this unnecessary formality. Once a couple has kissed, you know—"

She felt herself succumb to her annoying habit of blushing. That tendency to redden at the least suggestion of embarrassment did not make the situation any easier. "And *I* thought we'd agreed to forget about that incident," she reminded him.

"No, my dear, you're mistaken. I never made such an agreement. I knew it would be impossible to carry out."

But it was time to turn to opposite corners of the set, and she couldn't reply. By the time they came together again it seemed foolish to bring up the subject. The dance passed with only commonplace exchanges, and she sighed in relief when the music ceased. As they walked off the floor, he took her arm. "May I claim the other part of my reward now, ma'am? If we stroll just a little way down the hall, I think we may find the library unoccupied."

"N-Now?" She felt her pulse flutter alarmingly.

"I'm afraid to wait any longer. It seems that the longer I keep myself away from you, the cooler you grow toward me. Please, Jenny. If you knew how impatiently I've been wishing away the hours . . ."

It would, she felt, be utterly heartless not to grant his request. She nodded, let him take her arm and lead her out of the ballroom. She knew that almost everyone had noted their departure, but the captain seemed completely oblivious to the murmurings and surreptitious glances that followed in their wake. She supposed that her reputation would be permanently ruined, but it didn't seem to matter.

The library was, as he surmised, unoccupied. He couldn't in good conscience close the door, but he led her to a sofa against the furthest wall in the hope that there they would be safe from prying eyes. "Please sit down, Jenny. And don't gaze up at me so beguilingly with that look of bewilderment or I shall find it impossible to speak. Don't you know what I want to say to you?"

"No, I haven't the slightest idea. If it had anything to do with Robbie, I don't believe you'd be so ill-at-ease."

He gave a snorting laugh. "You are charmingly frank, ma'am. But why did you suppose I'd want to speak to you about your brother?"

"Only because he sails under you. I thought that perhaps you had some complaint about him and didn't wish to discuss it with Mama."

He couldn't help smiling at her. "If I *had* such a complaint, you goose, I'd not discuss it with his family. He's in the Navy, not a boy's school, and I'm his captain, not a headmaster. No term reports are sent out to a seaman's parents. His conduct on shipboard, my dear, has nothing whatever to do with you."

"I see. Excuse me for sounding so foolish. But if you didn't wish to discuss Robbie, then what—?"

"You truly have no idea, do you?" He shook his head in dismay and took a turn across the room. "You're not making this at all easy for me," he said from the fireplace and then walked back and stood looking down at her. "I've been brooding for the past two days about how to say what I must say to you, and I still don't know how to begin. I don't feel comfortable about starting by telling you that I love you, for I fear I haven't properly prepared you for it; but if I start by asking you what you meant when you said that you wished you could dislike me, you would be quite justified in telling me it was none of my business. So I've been going round in circles in my mind without finding a solution to the dilemma."

She stared up at him, her face quite pale. "I don't think I . . . I could have . . . heard you properly," she managed.

"Damnation!" he muttered, sitting down beside her and taking one of her hands in his. "I *knew* you weren't prepared for this. I've had no experience in this sort of thing, you know, and I'm sure to make a botch of it. But, Jenny, the truth is that

I do love you . . . and have from that first afternoon at Portsmouth. I thought of nothing else all during the voyage —never took so little interest in ship's business in all my days. I couldn't wait to come back and see you again. But when I did, it was plain you wanted nothing to do with me. Yet there was a moment, the other afternoon in the sleet, when I thought . . . Dash it all, Jenny, I'm adrift in a dinghy without compass or oar! Tell me what to do!"

Her eyes were wide with shock, and she could barely speak. "Oh, *Tris*—!" she breathed.

The same impulse that had gripped him in the curricle two days before took hold of him now. Words seemed suddenly quite unnecessary. He gathered her in his arms and kissed her with all the passion that six months of dreaming had built up in him.

At the doorway, Andrea Clement stood frozen to the spot. Her cousin Tris and *Jenny*! She couldn't believe her eyes. She'd seen them leave the ballroom together, but even then she'd not been able to believe that the fascinating Tris Allenby could be taken with mousy little Jenny. Never, in all the years of their friendship, had Jenny been able to win a beau away from her. Why, *everyone* said that Andrea Clement was the most beautiful girl in Wyndham. Why was Cousin Tris unable to see it?

A knot of jealous fury solidified in her breast, and she tore her eyes from the still-embracing couple and turned away. She couldn't let herself cry, or shout, or even show by the slightest twitch of her lips her inner agitation. There were a hundred and fifty guests in the ballroom; none of them must know the extent of her humiliation.

She put her head up and strode back down the hall in the direction of the music. There were at least four young men waiting for a chance to dance with her. She would dance the night away. There was time, tomorrow, to think about what to do about Jenny and her cousin Tris.

Just before reaching her destination, she spied Lady Garvin approaching her from the ballroom. Jenny's mother's head was lowered, and she was rubbing the bridge of her nose with her fingertips. "Lady Garvin," Andrea said, her voice artificially bright, "what are you doing out here? Are you unwell?"

Lady Garvin had not been enjoying herself. She'd looked forward to the occasion with eagerness, but the affair had been a disappointment from the start. For one thing, her gown was too tight at the waist and made her uncomfortable when she sat down. As a result, she'd spent too much time standing about, and now her feet pinched. Then, too, Lady Rowcliffe had, for the second time, indicated a lack of interest in her company. Lady Garvin, considered by everyone in Wyndham to be a woman of enormous charm, was unaccustomed to being rebuffed. It spoiled all her pleasure in the proceedings. Lastly, she'd foolishly indulged in two glasses of champagne, hoping the French potation would elevate her spirit, but her sensitive stomach would not stand for it. She was now suffering from a most unpleasant aftereffect and wanted nothing more than to return home to her bed. "Yes, Andrea, my dear, I'm afraid my delicate constitution is giving me difficulty. Have you by chance seen Jenny?"

Andrea's eyes flickered away from Lady Garvin's face. "Yes, I think I have. If I'm not mistaken, I saw her go down the hall in that direction. Perhaps you'll find her in the library."

"I don't know what the girl would be doing *there*," Lady Garvin muttered in irritation, "but thank you, Andrea, my love. I'll go along and see if I can find her."

Why can't the chit be on the dance floor like the other girls? Lady Garvin thought as she hurried down the hall. She had been too engrossed in her own concerns to have noticed what almost every other mother in the room had observed: that Jenny had snared the finest catch of the season and left the room with him. But Lady Garvin's mind did not dwell long on the problem of her reticent daughter. She was feeling too ill. Getting home was her prime goal.

In the library, Jenny was trying to gather her wits. She'd been shaken as much by Tris's words as by the shattering embrace from which she'd just been released. Breathless and on the verge of tears, she tried to hold him off. "Tris, don't—! I can't—"

"There you are, my dear," came her mother's voice from the doorway. "I find I'm not feeling at all the thing. I've ordered the carriage. Will you ask the butler to find our cloaks? I'd like to leave right—"

All at once the import of Jenny's situation burst upon her consciousness. Her daughter was sitting on the sofa with Captain Allenby, and he had his hands on her arms! From the expressions on both their faces, it was plain that she'd interrupted a scene of high emotion. There was no question at all that her daughter and Allenby were in some manner *involved*.

She felt her heart leap. Captain Allenby might be a brute as a captain, but there was not one mother of a marriageable girl in that ballroom who wouldn't wish for him as a son-in-law. She, more than any of the others, wished for it, for Robbie's future would be affected, too. The thought had crossed her mind the other day that there was something between Jenny and the captain, but she'd dismissed it as impossible. But now . . .

Jenny had jumped to her feet, and the captain, looking utterly chagrined, had followed suit. "I'm sorry, Mama," Jenny said, starting toward her. "I'll come at once."

Lady Garvin would have liked to cut her tongue out. She wasn't as sick as all *that*. "Oh . . . well, my dear, I'm not in a *great* hurry. If you wish to finish your conversation with Captain Allenby, I—"

"No, it isn't . . . I mean, we're quite . . . finished. I'm ready to leave," Jenny assured her.

Lady Garvin almost stamped her foot in frustration. Jenny hadn't an ounce of cunning in her. Couldn't she have read her mother's signal? Couldn't she have grasped at the pretext her mother offered and remained long enough to conclude her *tête-à-tête*? *This* way, she'd *never* win herself a suitor. No girl could possibly succeed in winning a proper husband if she didn't have a trace of guile.

But Captain Allenby didn't give up easily. "If you must go, Jenny," he said, detaining her by keeping hold of one of her hands, "may we continue this conversation tomorrow? May I call on you?"

"I . . . don't think there's anything to be gained . . ." She tried to wriggle her fingers out of his hold. "There's no use in pursuing the subject further, Captain. I don't have . . . anything to say."

"But you must at least explain—" he begged, quietly urgent.

"Of *course* you may call, Captain," Lady Garvin interjected, smiling at him broadly. If her daughter was too idiotic to play the game, she'd take matters into her own hands. "Will eleven suit you? Jenny is always available to callers at that hour, *aren't* you, my dear?"

Jenny looked from her mother's face (with its expression that clearly ordered her daughter to acquiesce or face her wrath) to Tris's entreating eyes. *Very well,* she thought, surrendering to the inevitable, *I'll see him one more time*. Once more could not make the situation more painful to her than it was already. She nodded meekly. "Yes, I *am* available at that hour, Captain, if it's convenient for you."

He bowed over the hand he still held captive in his own. "Eleven, then. I look forward to it."

"Good night, sir," she said in her low, shy voice.

His eyes locked on hers until hers fell. Then he released her hand with a sigh. "Until tomorrow," he said as he watched her go.

Chapter Seventeen

The next morning Sally Clement came downstairs in her dressing gown, a solecism she would not have permitted herself if she expected anyone else to be up and about. But the ball the night before had lasted until two, and she was certain that nobody in the household but the servants would stir before noon. She padded into the breakfast room on her slippered feet, eager for a cup of her morning coffee, and found to her surprise that Tris was already there, wide awake and fully clothed. She paused on the threshold, pink with embarrassment. "Oh, Tris! Down so early? I didn't dream . . . that is, I was certain everyone would stay abed 'til noon. Here I've come down so informally attired, while you are dressed up to the nines. I should at least have dressed my hair."

Tris laughed and held a chair for her. "Nevertheless your appearance is a delight, Aunt Sally. I've come down early because I've a call to make this morning. I was afraid I'd be forced to breakfast alone. Do sit down and join me."

But they were not destined to remain a twosome. A few minutes later Lady Rowcliffe floated in, dressed in a filmy morning gown, her grey locks still plaited in their nighttime style and falling in two short ropes over her shoulders. "Heavens, what early birds," she exclaimed. "I was convinced I'd have the breakfast room all to myself. If I'd known, I would have dressed my hair."

Her remark brought a burst of laughter from her son and sister-in-law, and she sat down at the table amid much merriment. Tris, in a mood of bouyant optimism about the forthcoming interview with his beloved, teased the ladies about their *dishabille* quite unmercifully, causing Lady Clement to giggle and blush and his mother to slap him playfully on the wrist for his sauciness. But she couldn't help throwing him a glowing look at the same time, for she hadn't seen him looking so content since the day they'd arrived.

Tris winked at his mother in acknowledgment of her questioning glance. He was indeed much happier than he'd been in days. His optimism, he realized, was based more on conjecture than on actuality, but he'd convinced himself that he had good reason for high spirits. It had taken him half the night to come to that conclusion, for when Jenny had left the ball last evening, his frustration at the interruption of their talk had been overwhelming. But he'd lain awake for hours, reviewing the circumstances of their entire relationship, and he'd concluded that he had no reason to despair. While her *words* to him had been reticent and unencouraging, her *behavior* had been quite the opposite. There was no doubt the girl was drawn to him. There was a feeling between them—and he couldn't be mistaken!—of being able to understand each other without mere words, a strong awareness of the other's presence in a crowd, and a physical attraction so powerful that their embraces had seemed almost inevitable. He knew she felt those things as much as he. Some sort of artificial impediment existed in her mind which kept her from opening up to him, but this morning he would make her face that impediment and they would overcome it. He had no doubt of imminent success. She was, at heart, a straightforward, honest, clear-thinking young woman. All he had to do was help her to see the truth.

When Sally left the table to help herself to a dish of kippers and eggs from the buffet, Lady Rowcliffe snatched at the opportunity to ask her son the reason for his high spirits.

"I'm off to see Jenny," he confided in an undervoice. "With any luck at all, I shall have good news for you by afternoon."

Sally rejoined them before anything more could be said. "Cullum has set out a bowl of the loveliest-looking oranges," she reported, "and Cook has dressed them with little decorations of sugared nuts and raisins. It would be a shame not to eat some. Shall I peel one for you, Tris?"

He looked at her with a twinkle. "What a topsy-turvy household this is, Aunt Sally," he teased, "where the oranges are dressed and the ladied aren't."

The "undressed" ladies burst into guffaws, but the gaiety was abruptly stilled by the appearance of Andrea in the doorway. The girl looked like a thundercloud. Her brow was furrowed, her eyes red and darkly circled (as if she hadn't slept at all), and her expression was glowering. She, like the other women, hadn't dressed her hair, and her satin dressing gown was so carelessly tied that her wrinkled nightdress could be seen peeping through the gap. "Why all the merriment?" she inquired crossly, coming into the room without a word of apology for her appearance and surveying the breakfast fare spread out on the buffet with an expression of revulsion.

The trio at the table exchanged questioning looks. "Good morning, love," her mother said quickly, trying to maintain the cheerful atmosphere that had filled the room before her daughter's appearance. "Shall I peel a fruit for you?"

"No, thank you, Mama. I shall only take coffee." She sat down at the table and surveyed the company, her eyes stopping on Tris's face. "You are looking very fine, Cousin. Are you going somewhere?"

"I have a call to make, yes," he answered, taking her cup and pouring for her.

She took the cup from him, keeping her eyes fixed on his face. "A call on Jenny Garvin, I've no doubt."

Something in her tone and the rudeness of her comment made her mother wince. Andrea's mood was one she recognized and could not like. The portents were not favorable. Her daughter, when crossed in any way, was as likely as not to do something destructive. "Andrea!" she muttered warningly.

But Tris's mood was unaffected by his cousin's sulky manner. "As a matter of fact, that *is* where I'm going," he answered cheerfully. "How did you guess?"

"It wasn't difficult. You danced only once last night, and that once was with Jenny. I merely put two-and-two together."

Lady Rowcliffe was studying her niece shrewdly. "My son is sometimes deficient in the social graces, I'm afraid, Andrea. He should certainly have been on the dance floor more than once, and he *certainly* should have stood up with his cousin. You're a clod, Tristram."

"But my cousin danced every dance, Mama, I assure you," Tris said, giving his cousin an admiring wink. "The eligibles were lined up six deep for a chance with her. I'm sure she didn't want her elderly cousin to get in the way."

"Elderly, indeed," Sally twittered. "But I must agree, Andrea, dearest, that you were much sought-after. She was the belle of the evening, wasn't she, Dulcie? But then she always is."

"You needn't pour the butter sauce over me, Mama," Andrea said in irritation. "There were at least three other girls who danced as much as I. And it was Jenny who won the biggest prize of the evening, *didn't* she, Cousin Tris?"

No one could miss the heavy sarcasm of her question. Tris, his expression stiffening, raised his eyebrows coldly. "I don't know what you mean, Cousin Andrea."

"I think you do. When all the girls in the room were hoping for a chance to dance with you, you gave the chance only to Jenny. It was quite a feather in her cap, you know."

Lady Rowcliffe leaned back in her chair. "How nice," she said smoothly, "that Tris was able to do that for the girl. It's time that Wyndham took proper notice of your friend, don't you agree, Andrea, my dear?"

Tris threw his mother a look of admiration. Her remark showed the sophistication of the true diplomat. Without the least strain or hint of criticism, she'd appealed to her niece's better nature and, ignoring the girl's obvious jealousy, reminded her that loyalty to one's friends was a praiseworthy quality.

But Andrea had spent a sleepless night and was in no mood to take the hint. In her view, a ballroom was an *arena* where she and the other unmarried girls competed like gladiators for the acclaim of the onlookers and, in the end, the richest matrimonial prize. In that arena she'd never been bested. Since the age of twelve, when her form had first begun to take on the shape of slim womanhood, she'd been able to turn her wide, hazel eyes on any man she chose and win his immediate admiration. She'd been the undisputed belle of the town ever since, and she had no intention of surrendering first place to anyone—at least not yet. Not until she was an elderly thirty-year-old, safely married to the finest "catch" that Wyndham society offered her. She sometimes wondered, during rare moments of failing self-esteem, if she would do as well in the arena of London society, but certainly here in Wyndham it was *unthinkable* that Andrea Clement could fall into second place before she was even betrothed!

Jenny's unexpected success had left her astounded, confused and enraged. Her response to these unaccustomed emotions was a determination for revenge. "But it's so strange,

Aunt Dulcie," she said, her mouth stretching into a malicious smile, "that my cousin should have singled out *Jenny* for his attentions."

"Why strange?" Dulcie asked. "Jenny is a lovely girl."

"Yes, but after all the things she's been saying about Tris—"

Sally, blinking at her daughter in confusion, suddenly froze. Her daughter's ugly intention broke upon her consciousness like an exploding bomb. "Good God! *Andrea*!" she gasped, horror-stricken.

The girl reached for a slice of toast and began to spread jam on it with deliberate casualness. "It's funny that Tris should have been so kind as to single out the *one person* in Wyndham who has consistently maligned him," she said, ignoring her mother's strangulated breathing. "It strikes me as amusingly paradoxical."

"*Maligned* him?" Lady Rowcliffe asked, throwing Tris a look of dismay.

"Oh, yes. For months now. Ever since Robbie began to report—"

"*Andrea Clement*, what's come *over* you?" her mother demanded, white-faced. "I can't believe that a daughter of mine would so wantonly reveal . . . I mean, wantonly repeat . . . I mean, it's gossip of the most—"

"It's not gossip, Mama," Andrea said, proceeding heedlessly with her destructive strategem. "Gossip is rumor—unsubstantiated rumor. But I'm talking about things Jenny told me *directly*."

Sally was on the verge of tears. That her own daughter, on whom she'd lavished all her love and every advantage that money and position could provide, could so viciously hurt the family that had been their intimates for a lifetime was devastating. Couldn't the girl see that, by cutting down Jenny and the rest of the Garvins, she was also hurting herself? Her cousin and her aunt would never respect her again. Was she so lost to reason, so vindictive over Jenny's small triumph, that she would destroy her own reputation in order to punish her friend? "Andrea," she ordered, her voice shaking, *"leave this room at once!"*

"No, Sally, let her be," Dulcie said with soft-voiced authority. "I want to know how Jenny Garvin has maligned my son."

"Mama, *must* we—?" Tris began, wishing only to escape from the table, the room and the house.

His mother gave him a level look. "Yes, I think we must, my dear. It will be good for you to learn the truth."

He shrugged and pushed himself from the table. With a gesture that indicated she could do as she liked, he got up and went to stand at the window, where he stared out at the lawn. The landscape sparkled in brilliant sunshine which, earlier that morning, had struck him as pleasingly appropriate to his mood. Now it shone with an agonizing, ironical incongruity.

"Go ahead, Andrea," Dulcie commanded. "We're listening."

Andrea looked from Tris's straight back to her mother's anguished face and knew she'd gone too far. But her aunt's expression was steely as she waited, erect and motionless, for Andrea's revelations, and the girl realized that there was no turning back. She'd taken the plunge from a precipice called betrayal, and there was nothing left to do but fall. "She said he's a petty tyrant," she began, lowering her eyes to the coffee cup before her, "who abuses the men who sail under him."

Dulcie lifted an eyebrow. "Did she indeed? And is that all?"

"No, it's not all," Andrea said defensively, lifting her chin and plunging on. "She described him as cold and inhuman. She said that he's incapable of kindness or forgiveness. That he exacts cruel retribution for minor offenses and even has his men whipped until they bleed. In sum, that he's a monstrous brute. So there!"

In the long silence that ensued, no one moved. The words seemed to hang in the air as tangible as the motes of dust that were visible in the morning sunlight. It was Tris whose voice finally broke through the charged atmosphere. "That was very well done, Cousin Andrea," he said with icy sarcasm, turning to face her. "Your recital was a revelation. It's given me a completely new concept of the meaning of friendship."

Andrea stared up at him, her lips beginning to tremble. Then, with a choked little cry, she rose from her chair and ran from the room.

Sally pressed her hands to her mouth. "I'm . . . so sorry. I don't know what to—"

"Don't trouble yourself, Aunt," Tris said in a flat, contained voice. "There's no real harm done. Now, if you'll excuse me, I have an appointment to keep."

His mother started from her chair. "Tris? Do you think you should?"

"Yes, I do, Mama. I promised."

"But if the girl's so foolish as to think of you as a *monster*—"

"Nevertheless, I'm expected at eleven. I shall be there on the dot." He smiled at his mother grimly. "It should be a most interesting interview."

At Willowrise, the scene at the breakfast table was equally tense. Robbie had breakfasted early and had gone out to ride, so Jenny and her mother were alone. Lady Garvin had been berating the girl for more than an hour. Jenny sat huddled over her teacup while her mother stood over her haranguing her mercilessly. "I don't see why you can't give me your word!" she nagged. "This matter is too important to be left to chance and whim."

The argument had been going on for so long that Jenny was benumbed. "But Mama," she pleaded for the dozenth time, "we don't even know that he's coming to make an offer. How can I make a decision when I don't even know his intentions?"

"His intentions are quite obvious. What other reason could he have? His conduct last night left room for no other interpretation, unless it would be to offer you a *carte blanche*."

"Oh, now, Mama! *Really*! You can't believe—"

"Of course I don't believe it. I only said it to prove my point. A man like that, with wealth and position in society, doesn't seek an innocent and gently reared country girl as a mistress. He can choose from among the most expensive and beautiful pets of the fancy. But when he chooses a *wife* . . . a mother for his children . . . a woman to run his home and entertain his friends . . . well, then, he looks for something else entirely. You will suit him very well."

"Mama, *please*! I don't want to talk about it any more."

"But we must. This is not a matter to be left to chance, as I've said."

Jenny put her fingers to her forehead and rubbed it despairingly. "Must I make a decision on the matter now? I don't know how I feel. I need more time—"

"But there isn't any time, don't you see? If you don't snatch your chances when they are offered to you, you may lose them forever. If you put him off, he may turn to Andrea, or to some

London creature whom his mother will dredge up for him. A man like that is like mercury. He'll slip through your fingers before you've managed to get a good grasp on him!"

"Oh, Mama," Jenny sighed miserably, "you make it all sound so . . . so . . . avaricious."

"But you must be a bit avaricious, my love." Her mother, exhausted, sank down on the chair beside her daughter. "I know it sounds dreadful to young, romantic sensibilities, but a mother in my position, with two children whose futures are not in any way secure, cannot afford to indulge in romance. I must make you see how important this meeting will be in our lives. You have, by some miraculous quirk of fate, won the eye of a man who can give you everything a girl could want. *Everything*. But even more wonderful, it will make your *brother's* future every bit as bright as yours. Doesn't that mean anything to you?"

"Yes, of course it does, Mama. I care about Robbie's future as much as you do. But it doesn't seem proper to make a . . . marital arrangement on that basis. Besides, didn't you say, just the other evening, that Captain Allenby was a beast?"

"Yes, I did. But I didn't mean it. Besides, even if he is a bit brutal to his crew, he would never be so to you."

"No, I don't suppose he would. He had always shown me the greatest kindness."

"There! You *see*?" She leaned forward with a hopeful smile. "I knew you're too clever a puss not to understand. So you *will* accept him, won't you?"

Jenny could feel her throat tighten with unshed tears. She was too confused to make such a decision on the basis of her mother's harangue. She needed time to think, to sort out her feelings, to try to understand the nature of the man who'd already won her heart but not her mind. But there was no time.

She lowered her head to her hands and forced herself to remember what had made her come to the decision, just a short while ago, to put Tristram Allenby out of her life. There had been three reasons. The first had been her doubt that such a fascinating, sought-after gentleman could actually have fallen in love with *her*. That reason had, since last night, completely lost its validity. He'd *told* her he loved her—and with such fervor that she couldn't doubt his sincerity. The second reason had been that Andrea wanted him. But she, Jenny, had not done anything to steal Tris's affection away from Andrea. He'd told her that he'd loved her since the day at Portsmouth. So Andrea would not be justified in accusing Jenny of beau-snatching. That left only the third reason: Tris's reputed tyrannies as a sea captain. That was the only stumbling block in the whole situation. And for that, Jenny could find no solution.

She glanced up at her mother who, with hands clenched at her breast and eyes eager with hope, sat waiting impatiently for her daughter's answer. It was almost time. A mere fifteen minutes remained before Tris was expected. Jenny's innards were trembling like a pile of nervous leaves shimmering in the wind. She needed to calm herself. She yearned for a few minutes at the piano to steady her mind, to find some semblance of serenity before facing Tris again. If she told her mother that she didn't yet know her mind, she was certain the nagging would be resumed. One more moment of her mother's importunities would completely shatter her control.

She lifted her head and met her mother's eyes. "All right, Mama," she said wearily, "I'll do it. I'll accept him . . . if he's foolish enough to ask me."

Chapter Eighteen

He paused before knocking. The sound of a piano, coming to him faintly from somewhere within, stilled his hand. There was something soothing in the sound. She was playing Bach, and the intricate regularity of the rhythm, the mathematical precision of the interlocking harmonies, seemed to create an antidote for the unruly trumoil in his head. He would have liked to stand there listening until the music ceased, but she played on and on as if driven, and he realized that he would be accused of tardiness if he procrastinated any longer. He lifted the knocker and hammered it firmly.

The music stopped abruptly. "I'll get it, Cullum," he heard Lady Garvin call from within. She opened the door and ushered him in with babblings of eager welcome. Her effusions sickened him. She couldn't have made it more clear if she'd said in so many words that she expected him to make her daughter an offer.

"Jenny's in the music room," she said with a conspiratorial twinkle. "It's just down the hall, opposite the drawing room. You can find your own way, can't you, Captain? I'm . . . er . . . needed in the kitchen, so I'll have to leave you and Jenny to your own devices for a while." She gave a shrill, high-strung laugh. "I suspect you won't mind."

Before he could reply, she scurried off. He looked after her in chagrin. In her excitement she hadn't even taken his hat. Perhaps his mother had been right—he shouldn't have come. He could have written a note . . . made some excuse. What was the point of coming here now?

Nevertheless he walked down the carpeted hall in the direction Lady Garvin had indicated. He found the music room without difficulty, for its large double doors were open and he could see the piano at once. It stood in the far corner of the room, brightly lit by the sunshine filtering in through two tall windows on the adjacent wall. Jenny still sat on the piano bench, her eyes lowered and her hands folded in her lap. She had evidently not heard his approach. "Good morning, ma'am," he said from the doorway.

She gave a little start and jumped up. "Capt—Tris!" she said, with a quick, nervous smile. "Come in. I was expecting Cullum to announce you. Goodness, where *is* he? Why hasn't he taken your hat?"

"Your mother admitted me," he explained, feeling a sharp sting of pain at the sight of her face—the sweetness of her expression, the innocent glow in her eyes, the slight flush of embarrassment creeping into her cheeks.

"Mama is sometimes a bit . . . overzealous. She shouldn't have . . . but never mind. Let me take your hat."

"It doesn't matter. I'll just leave it here." He deposited the headpiece on the nearest chair and looked down at her, feeling miserably awkward and boyish. "Is it permissible to close the doors, Jenny?"

"I don't know if it's permissible or not," she said frankly, "but I wish you would. My affairs have been receiving more attention from my family than I can bear, and I'd welcome a little privacy. You take that door and I'll take this."

As the doors met in the center, his hand brushed hers, and the touch sent a tremor right up his arm. To make matters worse, she looked up at him with a completely unexpected grin. "There!" she said mischievously as the latch clicked shut. "I feel better already."

He couldn't manage an answering smile. *Damnation,* he thought, *if she's going to be charming, I'll have the devil's own time of it. I should never have come.*

She led him to the love seat which was set between the two windows and sat down. He stood uncertainly before her, reluctant to take a seat so close to her. He was a fool to have come. He didn't even know what to say to her.

She peeped up at him shyly. "Are you going to sit here beside me, sir, or will you be more comfortable pacing about? You may do anything you like, of course, so long as you don't continue to stand there and glower at me. You're putting me quite out of countenance, you know."

"Was I glowering?" A small smile appeared at the corners of

his mouth. "I'm sorry." He took the seat beside her. "I think sitting will be less nerve-wracking than pacing, don't you?"

"Infinitely less."

She took a quick look at his face. For the first time, she noticed a tightness around his mouth and a wary, strained look in his eyes. But even though she felt a tiny suspicion that something was amiss, she was aware of how pleasant it was to be sitting beside him. Whenever he was near her, it was hard to remember that he was Robbie's tyrant. She relished sitting close to him like this.

His eyes were on her face with an enigmatic, searching look, and her eyes fell away. "Did you enjoy the ball last night after we left?" she asked, not being able to fathom his silence. "I expect that the supper was a veritable feast."

"Yes, the supper was gargantuan, ma'am," he said drily, "and, yes, the weather is a delightful change from what it was a few days ago. Are there any other irrelevancies of which you wish to speak?"

She giggled. "I suppose I *was* babbling. I'm not accustomed to . . . er . . . interviews of this sort."

"Neither am I."

She glanced up at him from the corner of her eye. "But I'm quite willing to speak about whatever you wish. Choose your subject, sir."

"You know the subject. I'd like an answer to the question I put to you last night. Have you given it any thought?"

"To be honest, I've had nothing on my mind *but* last night," she admitted with a sigh. "But the goings-on in my head can't possibly be described as thinking."

A reluctant laugh was wrung out of him. "Yes, I know what you mean. I've been in a fog of confusion myself."

"*Have* you? I should never have guessed. You always seem so remarkably logical and in control of your thoughts."

"It's only a veneer. Ever since I met you, I've been anything but 'logical and in control,' " he said with a touch of bitterness.

She was quick to catch the tone. His manner began to puzzle her. He was not the same as last night. The importunate lover was quite gone. She didn't know what to make of it. "I didn't know I had so disturbing an effect on you," she ventured timidly.

"Then you know it now. And you'll understand, therefore,

why I'm impatient to settle matters between us so that I can return to the more stable mentality of my former self."

There was no question that something in him had changed, and her instinct warned her that the change was not in her favor. A little seed of dismay took root in her chest and began to grow. "What matters are there to settle?" she asked shakily.

"Are you playing female games with me, Jenny? It's not like you to be coy and evasive. Last night I said certain things to you which you must surely recollect—"

"Yes." She lowered her head and bravely plunged into the heart of the matter. "You said you . . . l-loved me."

"Yes, I did. And one can't go about making such a statement . . . or receiving it . . . and then try to pretend that it never happened. Such a declaration must be in some way faced . . . acknowledged . . . dealt with."

"I don't wish to be coy and evasive, Tris," she said softly, unable to decipher his mood or his intentions, "but I'm not sure what it is you wish me to say."

"Say whatever your instincts tell you to."

Her fingers twisted nervously. "My instincts are too confused. Besides, you said earlier that you wanted me to answer a question. A declaration of love is not exactly a question, you know."

He gave a sneering laugh. "Ah, my dear, you *are* adept at female games after all, I see. I hadn't thought it of you. What you're saying, with typical feminine circumlocution, is that I must first make you an offer of marriage before you can respond to my declaration, isn't that it?"

His tone chilled her to the marrow. What had turned him so bitter? Now that she was willing to accept him, had he changed his mind? She turned to him, her eyes searching his face for a clue. "I've been taught to believe that such was the usual procedure," she admitted. "Am I wrong?"

"I don't know. I had always imagined that when I was ready to propose marriage, I would have reached a level of intimacy with the lady which would negate the necessity for following proscribed procedures."

"So had I, Tris."

"Then why are we playing this game? Why can't you say what's on your mind without my making the ritual marriage proposal?"

"Because," she said, turning away, "I suddenly have the

distinct impression that you don't . . . wish to marry me at all."

He stared down at her bent head. This conversation was becoming unbearable to him. *Why did I come?* he asked himself again. *Did I imagine I would find satisfaction in taking a paltry revenge on the girl by making her miserable? If so, perhaps I* am *a vindictive beast, as she suspects!* But it was not so. He had no wish to give her pain. He put a hand on her arm. "Jenny, I—"

But she turned around, her eyes wide with a sudden shock of apprehension. "*Oh*! You don't mean . . . you *can't* mean . . ."

"Mean what, Jenny?" he asked, nonplussed.

"Can it be that . . . that instead of marriage you've come to offer me a *carte blanche*?"

"*What*?" He gaped at her, completely taken aback.

"I'm being shockingly blunt, I know, but you said you didn't want female evasiveness. I'm trying to understand what's in your mind. You said you love me, but if you don't wish to marry me, what else can you have in mind but a *carte blanche*?"

He stared at her in utter amazement. "A *carte blanche*?" He seized her arms, wanting to shake her until her teeth rattled. "You shatterbrained little innocent, I'd wager you don't even know what those words mean!"

"Then you would most certainly lose," she declared, putting up her chin. "I know *exactly* what they mean."

He felt a laugh welling up inside him. "If you do, my dear, I must admit to a feeling of admiration for your ability to speak of it so frankly."

She colored. "You're laughing at me, aren't you? I don't blame you. I'm sorry to have suspected . . . it was very foolish of me. Mama says that I'm not the sort that a . . . a man of parts would choose for a mistress, especially someone like you, who can choose from among the most beautiful and expensive—"

"Your mother, my girl, doesn't know the first thing about the desires of a 'man of parts,' " he muttered, fighting with all his might against a desire to gather her in his arms.

Her eyebrows rose in astonishment. "Does that mean that you *do*—?"

It was too much for him. With a guffaw that was closer to

hysteria than laughter, he pulled her to him. "Oh, my sweet, *sweet* Jenny," he murmured into her hair, "you can't really believe that, loving you as I do, I would ever demean you in such a way?"

She sagged against him, relief flowing through her like a cleansing breeze. "I didn't *seriously* think that to be your intention," she whispered, burying her burning face in his shoulder.

They clung to each other for a long while, each one finding solace in the closeness of the other. Then, without a conscious realization of what he was doing, he lifted her chin, turned her face up to his and kissed her. It was so instinctive and natural that, for a moment, he forgot the bitter anger that had been tormenting him. This sweet, vulnerable girl in his arms had been so devalued by her mother that she didn't know what a prize she was. He wanted nothing more than to protect her, to prove to her what a gem she was.

But when he let her go, Andrea's revelations came flooding back into his mind. Staring up at him, Jenny could see his eyes darken. "Tris, what *is* it?" she asked, putting a hand to his cheek.

"Blast it, Jenny," he muttered, thrusting her hand away and jumping to his feet, "I should never have done that!" He turned and strode to the window, keeping his back to her and his hands clenched. He had to find a way to extricate himself from this entanglement with the least possible pain to her and to himself. *What insane impulse,* he wondered again, *made me come here today?*

In numbing bewilderment, she got up and followed him. Placing a light hand on his arm, she asked quietly, "Can't you explain all this to me, Tris? If you love me as you say, why is it you don't want to . . . to offer for me?"

He wheeled about and grasped her by the shoulders. "Do you *want* me to offer for you, Jenny? Deep down in the secret recesses of your soul? No, don't look away from me! I want the truth at last."

She could feel her face pale. It was as if he could peer inside her and read all her secret fears and doubts. She wanted to be honest with him. But how could she answer when she wasn't sure of the truth herself? "I . . . I *think* it's what I want."

"Is that the truth? Or is it your *mother's* wish coming from your mouth?"

"My mother wishes it, yes . . . but I would not bend to her desires if they were not also my own."

His eyes narrowed. "Do you really expect me to believe that you are willing to accept me because you love me?"

To Jenny, the answer was so obvious that she couldn't believe it needed saying. "No, you cawker," she said with a tremulous little laugh, "it's because I want Robbie to be an admiral."

He seemed to freeze on the spot. Without releasing her, without moving a muscle, his whole visage hardened. "So *that's* it," he said in a flat, dull voice.

She felt her chest constrict in fear. Putting out a hand toward him as far as she could (for his grasp on her shoulders was like iron), she cried out, "Tris! I was *joking*!"

"Joking?" His face was disfigured with an icy sneer. "But they say, don't they, that many a truth is spoken in jest? And it is like you, I think, to be willing to sacrifice yourself for your brother."

"You *can't* believe that!"

"I can believe it more readily than I can believe you've fallen in love with a man you consider a petty tyrant."

"A p-petty tyrant?"

"Don't look up at me so innocently, ma'am! You *do* believe that I'm a tyrant, don't you? That I abuse the men under me, isn't that so?"

She seemed to wilt in his hold. How had he guessed her secret agony? "Well, I—"

He shook her furiously. "Let's have it out! It's *true*, is it not?"

She stared up at him miserably, her cheeks like chalk. "Yes," she said in a whisper.

"That I'm incapable of kindness or forgiveness?"

"Y-Yes . . ."

"And that I'm vindictive and 'exact cruel retribution' even for minor offenses?"

Two tears welled up in her eyes. "Yes."

He thrust her from him. "And that is the 'monstrous brute' whom you wish me to believe is the man you want for a husband? You'll pardon me, ma'am, if I say that I find the premise incredible."

"Tris, you d-don't understand," she said, the tears spilling over.

"I think I finally do understand. From the first you've shown signs of revulsion . . . an antipathy to what you still believe is my true character. But your mother has convinced you, for your brother's sake, to overcome your antipathy and accept an offer from me. I can't make that offer, Jenny. I love you—I can't seem to change that. I probably will love you all my life. But I don't want a wife who believes, for whatever reason, that I'm so flawed a man. I want a wife who'll come to me with love—not fear or loathing."

He turned and walked swiftly to the chair on which he'd deposited his hat. He picked it up, paused, and, turning the brim in his hand absently, he said, "Goodbye, Jenny. I'm sorry if my attentions set up expectations in your mind—or in your mother's—which cannot be fulfilled. If the failure of those expectations causes any pain, I hope it will be of some comfort to you to know that it cannot be any greater than my own."

He closed the door quietly behind him. She stared at it numbly, only a small corner of her mind aware that her one hope of happiness was disappearing down the hall. In the front of her mind, a little voice was saying, *He can't believe I loathe him . . . He can't!* She loved him. Whatever came of it, it was only right that he know it! Before he left the house forever, she had to catch him and tell him.

She dashed the tears from her cheeks and ran to the door and down the hall. "*Tris*—!"

His hand was already on the knob of the outer door. He turned round, his mouth stiff and his eyes guarded. But at least he paused. She took a deep breath and, with eyes fixed on his face, tried to calm herself before speaking. But a voice from the stairway broke upon them like a thunderclap. "Captain Allenby," Lady Garvin cried, "you're not *going*?"

He looked to the stairway, made a quick bow and threw open the door without a word. Before Jenny's mind could recover from the effect of the untimely interruption, he was gone. She stared at the door in a kind of dazed trance. She felt as though everything inside her had drained away, leaving only a quivering emptiness—like the feeling when the mind knows one has received a terrible wound but the body is too shocked to send out the expected waves of pain.

Lady Garvin gaped at her daughter. "Jenny, what *happened*?" she asked, a look of consternation coming into her face. "You didn't *refuse* him, did you? You *promised*—!"

The outer door swung open, and they both whirled round, their faces lighting with hope. But it was Robbie, returning from his ride. The boy looked chagrined, and he threw his riding crop and hat on a side table with unmistakable annoyance. "I just met Captain Allenby," he said, perturbed, "and he looked as cross as nine highways. He didn't even answer my greeting."

Receiving no response, he looked from his mother's dismayed face to Jenny's benumbed one, and his eyebrows rose in sudden anger. "What did you *say* to him, Jenny," he asked furiously, "to get him into such a state?"

"What?" Jenny asked, trying to force her mind to function on the small realities around her.

"I asked what you *said* to him to make him ignore me!"

"What did *I*—?" she sputtered, beginning to tremble. A completely unfamiliar feeling of rage surged up in her chest. "*I*?"

"Yes, you! If you've angered him, Jenny Garvin, I'll . . . I'll never *speak* to you again!"

She stared at her brother as if she'd never seen him before. Her heart lay cracked within her breast—and at least partly because his interests had been placed before hers—and yet he had the temerity to speak to her in that way! For the first time in her life she realized how little her brother—and her mother, too—concerned themselves with what happened to her. How indifferent they were to her feelings! And how minuscule was their interest in the tribulations of her life. Robbie, the little brother she'd always adored, cared only for himself . . . for how his captain's displeasure might reflect on his own career. He cared not a whit for what might have happened to his sister. The boy was a self-centered *brat*.

"Well," he demanded again, "what you *say* to him?"

Shaking with pain and rage, Jenny did something she'd never done to any human being in her life—she slapped him, hard, right on the face.

Her mother screamed. Robbie's hand flew to his reddened cheek. "*Jenny*—!" he gasped, stunned.

With a choking sound, she clapped her hands to her mouth and ran to the stairs.

"Jenny, have you lost your senses?" her mother cried, reaching for her arm as the girl sped by. "What on earth's come *over* you?"

But Jenny shook off her hand and, sobbing, ran up the stairs and down the corridor to her room.

They saw no more of her that day. She refused to answer when they knocked on her door, and she didn't come down for meals. The next day she appeared at breakfast, dry-eyed, self-contained, tight-lipped and pale. There was something so withdrawn, so frighteningly cold about her demeanor that neither brother nor mother dared ask her any questions. Nor did they make any attempt to bridge the rift that they dimly perceived had damaged their relationship but couldn't quite understand.

At the end of the day, Lady Garvin sat down at her writing table and, with many agitated sighs, penned a letter to the one person she surmised could help her—her brother-in-law. *Dear Alistair,* she wrote, *we have fallen into the most Dire Straits, and all because of You. Your insistence on a Naval Career for Robert has brought Disaster upon the Entire family. You Must find a way to remove my Robbie from his Commitment to the Navy, or his life will be Utterly Destroyed. Jenny's is, I fear, already Ruined Beyond Repair. I am in the Greatest Affliction and fear for my Health and Sanity. Come at Once! Your unhappy sister, Margaret Garvin.*

Chapter Nineteen

The next morning, Toby came to Clement Hall to make amends. Aware that he'd displeased Andrea by sketching Jenny, he planned to make a drawing of Andrea in the same penumbral style. Although she seemed remote and withdrawn, Andrea nevertheless agreed to pose for him, and he placed her in a chair along the west wall of the sitting room where the sun, shining in from the south-facing windows, could make a golden glory of her hair. Behind her, on the wall, hung a still life featuring a bowl of apples. Toby cleverly placed a similar bowl of fruit into Andrea's lap. "I'll call it *Girl With Apples*," he said and set to work.

He had barely begun when the sitting-room door opened and Lady Rowcliffe poked her head in. "Am I interrupting, Andrea?" she asked. "I have a message to deliver to you."

"Come in, Aunt Dulcie," the girl said, jumping up. After her ugly display of the day before, she was pathetically eager to win back a place in the family's good graces. "A message, you say?"

"Yes. From your cousin Tris. He had to leave very early this morning and asked—"

"Leave? You don't mean for *good*, do you?" She felt a sinking sensation in her chest.

"Yes, I'm afraid so. He has to oversee the work on his ship, you see, and so he's returned to our London house to be closer to the shipyard. I shall follow him this afternoon."

"Oh, *no*!"

"I'm disappointed, too, my dear, but it can't be helped. I feared from the first that a month in the country would be too long a stay for him. And as for me, I don't like to leave him alone in the London house. You can understand, I'm sure, that

I treasure the days when he's not at sea and can't bear to be far from him when he's on leave."

"Yes," her niece muttered disconsolately. "Yes, of course." She would never win back a place in their affections now.

"In any case, Tris has ordered me to say his goodbyes for him. He is sorry that he had to leave before you rose this morning. He thanks you for your many kind offices during his stay and asks you to accept this small token of his regard." And she handed a carved wooden box to her niece.

Andrea opened the box with unsteady fingers. Inside, on a lining of green velvet, lay a beautiful ivory fan. "It's . . . lovely . . ." she said, her teeth chewing on her lower lip in agitation. "Lovely."

"Yes. He brought it back from the Indies, you know. I'm so glad you like it."

But Andrea didn't like it. It was a correct and tasteful gift, but it was clearly impersonal. There was no note, no card, no sign of any wish to express affection for her. Although there hadn't been anything in his attitude toward her throughout his stay to indicate the particular interest she desired, she had continued to expect (and even after yesterday's scene, the hope remained) a change in his attentions. But this polite gift was a tangible sign of his indifference, and now that he was gone, her hopes evaporated. "Thank you, Aunt Dulcie. And . . . thank Cousin Tris for me, too. If you'll excuse me, I'll take this up to my room."

"But can't that wait, Andrea?" Toby objected. "I want to finish my sketch before the light changes."

"No, I don't want to pose any more." She walked swiftly from the room without giving Toby a second glance.

He glared after her, shaking his head. Then he shrugged and began to wrap up his charcoals. Lady Rowcliffe, however, crossed the room to look at what he'd done. "This is very promising, Mr. Boyce," she remarked. "Are you an artist?"

"No, not really. I like to sketch, but I've had only the most rudimentary instruction. There aren't any teachers here from whom I could learn proper technique."

"You must go to London, then."

He threw a smoldering glance at the door. "If I had a grain of sense, that's just what I'd do."

She studied the drawing more closely. "What were you going to do in this shaded part, here?"

"Well, you see, if I highlight only this small part of the face and leave the rest in shadows, one becomes more aware of the play of the light. It's rather hard to explain. But if you look at this *other* sketch of mine—" He ruffled through his sketch pad and showed her the drawing. "Here, you see? The light only touches the lip and cheek line, but your imagination fills in the rest—"

"Why . . . it's Jenny!"

"Yes. I did it the other morning. Do you like it?"

She peered at it with intense interest. In her anger at the chit for what she'd done to her son, she'd forgotten what a sweet-natured girl Jenny was. But the charcoal portrait reminded her . . . and showed something more. Jenny was suffering, too. "This is *marvelous*," she said to the young artist. "I think you've caught . . . something more than a mere likeness."

He beamed at her. "Thank you, Lady Rowcliffe. It's very kind of you to say so."

"Is this . . ." She hesitated for a long moment. Then, cocking her head, birdlike, she peeped up at him. "Is it for sale?"

He laughed. "I've never sold a sketch in my life. Please take it as a gift."

She shook her head. "My dear boy, if you are to be an artist, you must learn at once that your work is not to be given away. I know a bit of the world, and I'll tell you one indisputable fact about dealing with patrons of the arts: the more you demand for your work, the greater will be your reputation among them. Now, when I ask you again if this drawing is for sale, you will say, 'For you, ma'am, because you so admire it, one hundred pounds.' "

Toby gawked. *"One hundred—?"*

"Done!" She grinned up at him. "I shall have my man send you a note as soon as I return to London. Do you suppose you might let me take the sketch with me?"

"With the greatest pleasure, my lady," Toby assured her, overwhelmed. He ripped the sheet from the pad and handed it to her. "You've given me the feeling that I may yet make something of my life."

"I shouldn't be at all surprised," Lady Rowcliffe said, studying the drawing with a smile. "If you *do* come to London, young man, be sure to call on me. I shall show this to Henry

Fuseli, who, though he is an eccentric and rather dreadful old man, is a fine artist and an acquaintance of mine. If he sees promise in this—and I suspect he will—he may take you on as a pupil."

She remained staring at the portrait after Toby Boyce had taken his leave. The girl the young artist had caught with his charcoals was too special to put aside. She had badly misjudged her son, but Lady Rowcliffe was not as unlike Admiral Nelson as her son supposed. She would not give up the battle either. She held the picture up to the light and smiled at it. The girl was still young. There was time for her to learn . . .

So the famous visitors departed, and several of the inhabitants of Wyndham were left battered in their wake. At both Clement Hall and Willowrise, the devastation was complete. Both houses were as quiet as if in mourning. No visits were exchanged, no outings were arranged and no messages passed between them.

At the vicarage, Toby was basking in the unfamiliar light of parental approbation. Ever since he'd told his parents about the sale of his drawing for one hundred pounds, they'd gaped at their son with new-born respect. *"One hundred pounds?"* his mother asked over and over. "Amazin'! And for a drawin' that took less than four hours to complete. It's the most astoundin' pass ever t' befall this house."

"Told you I could draw," Toby bragged shamelessly.

"So you did," the vicar said, shaking his head bewilderedly. "I had no idea that a drawing could command such a sum as that."

"We ought t' send the lad t' London for study, just as he's always asked us t' do," his mother murmured as she sat posed before the fire while her son sketched her face, having been given permission to do her likeness for the first time in his life.

"Mmmm," the father mused, watching over his son's shoulder as his wife's features began to be recognizable on the paper. "Perhaps we should."

Toby looked from one to the other in pleased surprise, but soon his expression changed to a thoughtful frown. "But no . . . I couldn't. Wouldn't wish to leave Andrea, you know."

"Don't be a mooncalf, boy," his mother said, not changing

her position or her "portrait" face. "She'll never have you. She's nothin' but a boy's dream, y' know."

"Is that what you think?" Toby asked, startled.

"Yes, I do. And so does yer father, though he's not the man t' say so. An' I think somethin' else as well."

"What's that?"

"Be still, woman," the vicar cut in, turning away from his fascinated study of the drawing and going to the fire to light his pipe. "It's not a matter for us to discuss so freely."

"Why not?" his wife demanded, turning her head to glare at him. "We don't have t' discuss scriptures all the time. He's our son, ain't he? Why can't we talk freely to him?"

"Yes, Papa, why not? What is it, Mama, that you think about Andrea and me?"

Before responding, Mrs. Boyce threw her husband a look of arch rebellion and resumed her pose. "I think," she said, not letting her thoughts affect the stiff, upturned tilt of her head, "that your feelin' for her comes more from habit than from honest emotions, that's what I think."

Toby stopped sketching in surprise. "*Habit*?"

The vicar puffed at his pipe and nodded. "That's just what it is," he agreed. "And, may God forgive me for speaking so bluntly, you have more important things to do with your life than to sit about here waiting for a smile from the likes of Andrea Clement."

Toby stayed awake all that night reviewing what his parents had said, and by morning he felt in complete agreement with their opinion. Once that momentous realization had been made, it took no time at all for him to decide to go to London at once. The one hundred pound note which arrived from Lady Rowcliffe did much to make the parting easier for the Boyces to bear. With one hundred pounds a young man, if he were frugal, could live in London for a year!

On the day that Toby Boyce's phaeton trundled off for London, a crested but shabby equippage drew up the drive to Willowrise. The Earl of Wetherbrooke alighted, tired and disgruntled. "Send the whole family to me at once!" he ordered the butler as soon as he was admitted. "I shall await them in the library."

Lady Garvin came in first. "Thank *goodness* you've come!" she cried, falling on his neck and beginning to sniffle. "You don't know how I've been suffering these past few days!"

The earl disentangled her arms from about his neck and led her to a chair. "Stop the waterworks, ma'am," he demanded. "I need a coherent account of what's happened. Your letter didn't make a jot o' sense."

Robbie entered next, still buttoning himself into his coat to make a proper appearance before his uncle. "How good to see you, Uncle Alistair," he said with real feeling, pumping his uncle's hand. "I've been wishing for a chance to tell you my adventures. You won't believe some of the scrapes and squeezes—"

The earl's brow cleared. "Well! *You* don't look destroyed, at any rate. In fact you're lookin' very fit. Grown a few inches, I shouldn't wonder. So what's wrong with you, laddie?"

"Wrong with me? Who said there was anything—?"

But Jenny entered at that moment. Neat, trim and composed, with every hair in place, she nevertheless seemed to him to be the one person in the family who'd altered for the worse. He scrutinized her carefully while she greeted him and kissed his cheek affectionately. "What's this, girl?" he asked bluntly. "Been sick?"

"Of course she hasn't been sick," her mother said impatiently. "Everything would have been fine if you hadn't placed Robbie in the Navy. It's all your fault, Alistair, and you must undo what you've done at once."

"What are you talking about, Mama?" Robbie asked, confused.

"Yes, what?" the earl echoed. "Can you possibly calm yourself sufficiently to tell me what's happened in clear, simple sentences? I ain't no clairvoyant, y' know." He dropped into a chair opposite his sister-in-law and signaled for her to begin.

"What's happened is that your Captain Allenby came to Wyndham for a visit. He, as Robbie will be glad to tell you, is quite monstrous. He completely upset poor Jenny (who, if you notice, is not yet recovered from the experience) and has taken Robbie in such dislike that he will undoubtedly ruin the boy's life if he returns to the ship. So the only thing to do is buy the boy out of the Navy—or whatever it is you must do to win his release—and send him back to school, which, as I've always said, is the place he belongs."

"Mama, what are you *saying*?" Robbie exclaimed. "I don't want to be released from the Navy. I *love* the Navy."

"*What*?" Lady Garvin and Jenny turned to stare at the boy in disbelief.

"Do you, lad?" his uncle asked, a small smile turning up the corners of his mouth. "I thought you would."

"Have you suddenly lost your *wits*?" his mother demanded. "We've heard of nothing but Captain Allenby's cruelty for months and months. And now you say you *love the Navy*?"

"Well, I'm not saying that I love everything about it, of course. The food is revolting, the work is sometimes very hard, and standing watches in bad weather is not a joy. And Captain Allenby does seem to have taken me in dislike. But I've had some grand adventures—wait 'til I tell you about the fight I had with the bully of our berth, Uncle Alistair; it quite made my reputation among the other middies—and I've made lots of friends. I wouldn't dream of doing anything else."

"I think he *has* lost his wits," Jenny murmured, dropping into a chair.

"And so do I! Grand adventures, indeed. And how, may I ask, are you to progress in your career if you've stirred up the enmity of the captain?" his mother demanded furiously.

The boy blinked at her bewilderedly. "I don't see why you're making so great a to-do over this. I don't think Captain Allenby is my enemy. I'm not important enough. It's a big ship, Mama, with over six hundred men. There are fifteen middies besides me. The captain doesn't even concern himself with us."

"But those things you wrote in your letters . . . the time he invited you to dinner and then scolded you . . . and all the other times when you felt he'd taken unfair notice—"

"I never said he was unfair. Captain Allenby is one of the fairest captains in the fleet. Everyone says so, don't they, Uncle?"

"So I've heard," the earl said, leaning back in his chair and surveying the scene with detached interest.

"Uncle Alistair," Jenny said in a voice that surprised him by its low-pitched intensity, "is that *true*?"

"Of course it's true," Robbie insisted. "Don't you think we middies know about such things? We talk about them all the time. Collinson's the kindest, Fothergill's the cruelest, Allenby's the fairest. Everyone knows it."

"The boy's right," Alistair said to Jenny. "I hear he never has to impress to get his full complement of men, because even the common seamen know they'll get a fair shake from Allenby."

The girl pressed her fingers to her temples as if she'd been struck with a splitting headache. "The *fairest*—!" she murmured, shaking her head in amazement.

"This is the most confusing conversation I've ever endured," Lady Garvin said. "Didn't you tell us, Robbie, in your very own letters, that he was cold, aloof, cruel and beastly?"

"And that he'd punish men for the most minor infractions?" Jenny added.

"And that he was vindictive and infected the lieutenants with his prejudice against you?" Lady Garvin reminded him.

"Well, boy?" the earl asked, looking up at him curiously.

Robbie turned from one questioning face to the other, suddenly feeling very uncomfortable. Was this fuss in which he was so surprisingly embroiled something of his own making? "I suppose I *did* say all those things," he admitted, running a hand through his dark hair embarrassedly, "but I didn't intend to upset you with them. It was only a way of . . . of easing the strain. When things seemed difficult or depressing—like the time I was sick and had to stand watch anyway—it was a bit of a relief to write my complaints to you. Once I'd written them, things didn't seem so bad, you see."

"But the complaints were *true*, weren't they?" Jenny asked.

"Yes, but not in the way you're describing them now. When I was scolded or punished, it was because I wasn't doing exactly as I ought. No infractions are minor on a ship, you see. Everything must be done just so. And things are exaggerated out of all proportion when you're out at sea. Everything seems much worse when it's happening so far from home and from everything one is used to. Now that I look back on it . . . on what I wrote . . . on all my complaints . . . I seem to have been a . . . a bit of a crybaby."

"Oh, *Robbie*!" Jenny murmured, dropping her head in her hands.

"But even if the voyage was not as bad as you painted it," his mother insisted, "you still have to face the captain when you return. And he dislikes you—you've admitted that. So your future is *still* doomed, is it not?"

"No, it isn't, Mama. When I heard that Captain Allenby was coming here, I suppose I hoped to gain a special advantage by trying to get close to him. It was wrong of me. But even if the captain dislikes me personally, it won't affect my promotions if I do a good job. He's fair, as I said. And I have very little to do with him on shipboard. If the lieutenant under whom I serve finds me capable, I should get ahead well enough. And I shall do better this time, you know. I know better what's expected."

"Good for you, boy," his uncle said. "So you'll return to your ship just as expected, eh?"

"That was always my intention, Uncle."

Lady Garvin threw her hands in the air in disgust. "I don't think I shall ever understand you, Robbie. Not as long as I live. But if you're sure that is what you wish—"

"I'm sure, Mama. And don't look so unhappy about it. I won't be such a crybaby this time."

Jenny, who was thoroughly shaken by these revelations, got up from her chair. "If I'm not needed any more, Uncle Alistair, I'd like to go up to my room. You're staying for dinner, aren't you? I shall see you then."

She walked unsteadily out of the room. Her uncle watched her go, his brow furrowing again. Without excusing himself, he got up and went quickly after her, closing the door behind him. She was already on the stairs. "Jenny," he asked with unaccustomed tenderness, "do you wish to tell me what passed between you and Allenby?"

She paused and looked down at him with a pathetic attempt at a smile. "Don't trouble yourself about it, Uncle. It was not a matter of great moment."

"From the look of you, lass, I'd say it was."

She shook her head. "Spilt milk, you know. It does no good to dwell on it." But she turned and came down toward him. "However, there is one thing I'd like to ask you . . ."

"Yes?" He came to the bottom step and clumsily sat down upon it, motioning for her to join him. "What is it?"

"There's something Robbie wrote which I . . . I can't get out of my mind." She sat down beside him and hugged her knees. "Be honest with me, Uncle Alistair. If a captain orders a man to be whipped . . . whipped so badly that his back is sore and bleeding . . . wouldn't you call that cruel and bestial?"

"You're speakin' of floggin'. It's common practice in the Navy, lass. Standard punishment for infractions. All captains have to do it, you see, or there'd be no discipline."

"All captains? Good God! Is there no other way?" she asked incredulously.

"Oh. there are other ways, all right. Gaggin', floggin'-round-the-fleet, runnin' the gauntlet—lots o' ways, all worse. A daily, formal floggin' is considered the best disciplinary—"

"Daily? Did you say *daily*?"

"Yes, on most ships it's as regular as mess call."

"But . . . but Robbie only wrote about it *once*! After he'd been aboard ship for a couple of *weeks*!"

"Yes, but Allenby runs a tight ship, y' see. He doesn't have pressed men and quota men that give the others all the trouble. He has a good, loyal crew and doesn't have to have floggin's very often."

Jenny's eyes, wide and brimming with tears, were fixed on her uncle's face. "Oh, Uncle Alistair, what a f-fool I've been!"

He put an arm about her and patted her soothingly. "I don't know what foolish thing you've done, girl, but it's never too late to—"

"I'm afraid it is," she said, struggling to regain her composure. She leaned against her uncle's comforting arm and gave a deep sigh. "If only I'd spoken to you about this long before. What a very different state I'd be in now!"

Chapter Twenty

In the middle of January, Robbie received his orders to return to his ship. As he packed his sea chest, he thought about the difference between this departure and the last one. There had been many changes since last spring, and not all of them to the good. This time neither his mother nor his sister offered to travel south with him to see him off. This didn't trouble him—he preferred the independence of traveling alone. He'd be happier traveling without his mother's supervision; he was old enough and brave enough now to manage on his own without unease. That much was to the good.

But he would miss his sister's company. The change in their relationship was not to the good. He was still not sure what specific act of his had caused the rift between them, but he was sensible enough to know that it had come about because of his heedlessness. He had never before troubled himself about her feelings, her cares, her woes. It was a new experience to force himself to consider the concerns of anyone but himself. Now that he'd done it, however, he felt more adult. Perhaps this rift had done him some good at that. When he next came home, he would see what he could do to mend it.

His new awareness of his family's needs led to one final resolve. As he closed the sea chest and snapped the locks, he made up his mind to put on a brave front in his future letters home. He had to begin to behave like a man, and it was not manly to worry his family with every discomfort and misery he suffered. They had troubles of their own, and from now on he could at least protect them from suffering over *his*. He would handle his own difficulties.

He bid them goodbye with cheerful optimism and set off by stage to Portsmouth. It was only when he found himself on the dock that he remembered what troubles still awaited him. Was Captain Allenby really his enemy? He'd made light of it to his mother, but what new troubles would he now have to face aboard the *Providential*?

Back at Wyndham, Jenny did what she could to pick up the pieces of her life. It was puzzling that Andrea was avoiding her. She'd made several attempts to see her friend, but she was invariably greeted with some excuse. One day, however, the reason was made clear. Lady Garvin announced to her daughter over tea that she'd just received a tearful apology from Sally Clement. "You'll never credit it, Jenny, but it was *Andrea* who caused your troubles with Captain Allenby."

"Nonsense, Mama. Whatever passed between Captain Allenby and myself was of our own making. Andrea had nothing to do with it," the girl said flatly, not looking up from her teacup.

"You're quite wrong. Sally told me that the day before the captain took his departure (which, you remember, was the very day he paid the call on you), Andrea had one of her tantrums and told him that you regarded him as a monstrous beast. Sally is horribly ashamed of the whole incident."

Jenny was startled. It had never occurred to her to wonder how Tris had been able to read her mind that day. She had simply supposed that love had made them transparent to each other. But it had been *Andrea*! So *that* was why Andrea was avoiding her now.

After the initial shock, Jenny was able to understand her friend's betrayal. Andrea had wanted Tris for herself. To her it had been a ploy in the game of love, where all was fair. Well, there was no longer any point in dwelling upon it, or in indulging in resentment. She didn't wish, either, for Andrea to wallow in guilt. Neither of them had won in this affair. The best course for them both would be to forget it.

With that in mind, Jenny wrote an affectionate note to Andrea, suggesting that they leave the past behind. Andrea gratefully accepted the suggestion, paid a call that very day, and the relationship was resumed. But Jenny could see that things between them were no longer the same. She was no longer the lighthearted young girl she'd been, and Andrea, too, had suffered a change. Some of her "air" had disappeared.

The extent of the disintegration of their friendship was not made clear, however, until they each received a letter from Lady Rowcliffe. The letters were almost identical. *Now that I am alone again,* Lady Rowcliffe wrote, *it has occurred to me that it would be very pleasant to have a couple of young people about the house. If you and your friend could endure the chaperonage of an old lady, I would like so much to have you both pay me a visit. There is so much in town that I would love to show you—the Elgin Marbles, the Pantheon Bazaar, the Opera House at Covent Garden, and a dozen other delights. Your friend, Toby Boyce, who dines with me from time to time, will be overjoyed to see you both, and we have already made plans for a welcoming dinner in your honor. Though the season has not yet begun, there are a good number of "eligibles" already in town, all eager for the social whirl to begin. Please let me know if and when I can expect you on my doorstep.*

Jenny read the letter over and over with mounting excitement. The prospect of a visit to Lady Rowcliffe seemed to her an unexpected but timely blessing. Her life had been excessively painful during the past few weeks. Not only had her everyday amusements begun to seem empty and meaningless, and her friendship with Andrea more nostalgic than real, but her relationship with her mother was almost unendurable. Since the day that Tris had walked out of her life, she'd been unable to ignore the gap that existed between her mother and herself. Unlike Robbie, Margaret Garvin had no comprehension of her indifference to her daughter's feelings. She believed that she was a perfect mother. With complacent self-centeredness, she went about her daily rounds without troubling herself about Jenny's obvious unhappiness. Whatever troubled the girl would pass, she convinced herself. Not once did she offer solace or affection. It never occurred to her to question the adequacy of her feelings for her daughter.

On the other hand, Jenny remembered with the fondest pleasure the kind attention which Lady Rowcliffe had showered on her. It was Lady Rowcliffe, not her mother, who'd found her beautiful. It was Lady Rowcliffe, not her mother, who'd enjoyed her music. How soothing it would be to live for a while with someone who really *liked* her.

She had been thinking, before the letter from Lady Rowcliffe arrived, of asking her Uncle Alistair if she could go to Yorkshire and stay with him for a time. She needed a change of scene. But she'd not asked him. She knew that her uncle liked her, but he was fond of his solitude—she hadn't felt comfortable about asking him to inconvenience himself on her behalf. But now she had an invitation—a sincere, eager, warm invitation—from Lady Rowcliffe herself. It was a prospect that filled her with excitement. It was an opportunity to expose herself to a different sort of life, to new surroundings, new people and new experiences. And Andrea would be with her. Perhaps in the stimulation of London's atmosphere, their friendship could be mended and enlarged. Eagerly, with Lady Rowcliffe's letter clutched in her hand, she threw on a cloak and ran down the road all the way to the Hall. She and Andrea had plans to make.

Andrea received her in the sitting room. Jenny could see at once that something was wrong. "Didn't you get Lady Rowcliffe's note?" Jenny asked as she threw her cloak over a chair, her chest constricting with a cold clutch of foreboding.

"Yes. This morning." Andrea walked to the fireplace and stood staring into the flames. "It was very kind of Aunt Dulcie to invite us both."

"Is something the matter, Andrea? Aren't you overjoyed? You've always talked about wishing to go to London . . . to the shops, the theaters, the parties—"

"Yes, I know. But . . ."

Jenny carefully lowered herself on the chair, her eyes on her friend. "But—?"

"I'm not going."

"What? I don't believe it!" It was incredible that Andrea would refuse such a rare, desirable opportunity. "Why not?"

"What does it matter?" the girl muttered. "I'm not going, that's all."

"But it matters very much." Jenny rose, went to her friend and put a gentle hand on her arm. "We've always *dreamed* of such an opportunity. To be able to go to *London* . . . and together! It's almost too good to be true. I can't believe you'd let such a chance pass us by."

Andrea threw her friend an enigmatic look. "It won't pass *us* by. *You* still can go."

"Without you? I couldn't!"

"Of course you could."

"No. I don't think Lady Rowcliffe would wish for that."

"Yes, she would." Andrea turned slowly and faced Jenny eye-to-eye. "It's you she wants. She only asked me because she thought it might be said that she'd invited a total stranger and ignored her own niece."

Jenny gaped at her. "Wherever did you get wind of such *humbug*?" she asked in disbelief.

"You may call it humbug if you wish, but even Mama agrees with me."

"I don't understand. Why would you and your mother take it into your heads that Lady Rowcliffe wants me and not you?"

"Because my Aunt Dulcie doesn't even *like* me," Andrea admitted, turning back to contemplate the flames.

"Rubbish! Of course she likes you. Just because she once said some kind things about *me* doesn't mean—"

"Oh, I'm not blaming you in any way, Jenny. Not at all. It's my own fault, I don't deny that. I behaved very badly in front of my aunt, you know, so it's not surprising—"

"Andrea, you're being foolish. I thought we'd agreed to forget all about that. I'm sure Lady Rowcliffe has."

"No, she hasn't. She couldn't. You weren't here, Jenny, so you don't know how dreadful I was."

"I think you're being too hard on yourself. She *asked* you to come, didn't she? She wouldn't have done it if she didn't want you."

"Perhaps." Andrea sighed and walked away, dropping down on a large wing chair. "I've thought about this all day, Jenny. My mind is made up. I . . . I wouldn't be happy at my aunt's."

"How could you *not* be happy there?" Jenny demanded, following her and perching on a nearby ottoman. "We would be in London! Together! Just as we always dreamed."

Andrea's eyes fell. "Not as *I've* dreamed, my dear. I don't think you really know me, Jenny. I'm . . . not like you. I'm not kind, or giving . . . or self-effacing, as you are. You see, you're the one Aunt Dulcie wants, and you would be *first* with her. I couldn't *bear* that, don't you see?"

Jenny winced as if from a blow. For a moment she tried not to face the implications of Andrea's words. She gazed up at her friend's face, hoping to see a sign that she'd misunderstood . . . that she hadn't heard the words clearly. But after a while, the emptiness in the pit of her stomach told her that the words must be faced. She looked down at her hands and said quietly, "If what you say about your aunt is true—and I don't for a moment believe it—then you're telling me that you can't, even *temporarily*, take second place to me. *But I've taken it with you for all these years.*" She looked up and met her friend's eyes. "Why should second place be acceptable for *me* but not for *you*?"

Andrea couldn't meet Jenny's direct gaze. "I don't know," she answered slowly. "I suppose it's because I'm . . . just not used to it."

"And you can't endure it even for a *while*?"

"No, I don't think I can."

They sat in silence for a few minutes while Jenny gathered herself together. Then she got up, picked up her cloak and went silently to the door.

Andrea lifted her bent head. "Will you be . . . going anyway?"

Jenny looked back at her erstwhile friend sadly. "Yes, I think I shall. And I think, in spite of everything, that I shall have a . . . a l-lovely time."

Chapter Twenty-one

Robbie received the bad news before he even boarded the ship. It was customary for the ship's officers to take up lodgings in the inn nearest the harbor while the first lieutenant organized the ship's quarters for the warrant officers and staff who were the vessel's central core. Only after this basic core of the ship's crew had been installed did the officers take their places aboard ship to receive the main crew. Meanwhile, they gathered at the inn, checked in with their immediate supervisors and awaited further orders. It was at the inn that Mr. Meachin, a sub-lieutenant under whom Robbie had served on the last voyage, told him the news. He was to be transferred.

Robbie was dumbfounded. "Are you sure? How do you know?"

"I saw the papers. Mr. Parslow had them on his desk when I checked in."

Robbie bit his underlip so that Mr. Meachin should not see it tremble. "Is this your doing, Mr. Meachin?" he asked bluntly. "Were you not satisfied with my performance?"

"Nay, laddie," the young officer assured him sympathetically. "I gave a good report of ye." He threw a grin at the agonized boy. "Didn't say a word about yer bein' a lazy lout."

Robbie was too devastated to laugh. "Then why do you suppose—?"

Mr. Meachin shrugged. "I thought ye'd asked fer it yerself."

"No, never! Why should I have?"

The lieutenant shook his head. "I was as surprised as you are."

Robbie felt desperate. "Is there anything I can do about it?" he asked, appalled.

"I dunno. Ye might talk to the first officer. But ye know how busy he'll be until we're under way . . ." He looked at the boy's distraught face and sighed. "I'll see if I can get him to spare ye a minute or two."

Robbie had to wait until the following day before he was granted an interivew. Mr. Parslow, the first officer, sat in his undersized room at the inn behind a table littered with papers, maps, plans, letters and lists. He had no time in which to waste words. "Sorry, Midshipman Garvin," he said at once. "Here are the transfer papers. There hasn't been time yet for your reassignment, but you should hear from the Admiralty in a few weeks. Meanwhile, I suppose, you may consider yourself on leave."

"But, sir, I don't wish for a transfer. Is there no way—?"

"Mr. Meachin told me you don't wish for it. This is most unusual, I admit, considering your satisfactory performance. But the papers were given to me by the captain himself. I don't see how anything can be done now."

"Could I . . . see the captain, then?"

Mr. Parslow's eyebrows rose. "See the *captain*? Oh, I don't think so, Mr. Garvin. He doesn't have time to involve himself with the personal concerns of the middies, you know."

"But, sir, could you at least *ask* him—?"

"No, I couldn't. You know what it's like the week before a sailing. He'd have my head if I pestered him with trifles. Sorry, Garvin."

Robbie had been dismissed. He turned, disconsolate, to the door. "Mr. Parslow, sir," he asked in a desperate last try, "don't I deserve at least an *explanation*? You said yourself that the transfer is unusual. Couldn't you ask the captain to see me on that basis?"

Mr. Parslow was clearly annoyed, but a quick look at the midshipman's disturbed face touched him. "The captain's not due for two days," he said gruffly, "but if you're willing to wait around on the chance—and it's a very slim one—I'll see what I can do."

Captain Allenby came aboard after the entire ship's company had been installed, and Mr. Parslow accompanied him on a full inspection. In spite of the captain's approval of the repairs and the manner in which the first officer had handled the preliminary organization, Mr. Parslow noticed that the captain seemed unusually brusque. Nevertheless, on the morning after the captain's arrival, after they'd gone over all the other matters on the morning's schedule, Mr. Parslow broached the subject of Midshipman Garvin. "He's requested permission to see you, sir. About the matter of having received a transfer without putting in for one."

"I ordered the transfer myself," Allenby replied, turning his attention to his charts. "Tell him to go home and await orders from the Admiralty."

"I already have, sir. But the boy is clearly upset. He's been waiting for almost a week for an opportunity to have a word with you. It might make the blow easier for him to bear if you—"

The captain cut him off with a wave of the hand. "All right, Parslow, all right. Send him in."

The first officer opened the cabin door and admitted the young midshipman. The lad was attired in full dress blues, with his hat tucked under his left arm. He saluted smartly.

"Well, Garvin, what is it?" the captain asked curtly, not turning from the table where he stood, in shirt-sleeves, studying the charts.

"It's about these transfer papers, sir. I was wondering, since I didn't put in a request for them, why I—"

"I issued them myself," the captain told him. "Am I to take it that you object?"

"Well . . . yes, I *do*."

Mr. Parslow did not at all approve of the boy's tone. "He means, sir," he interrupted smoothly, throwing Robbie a reproving look, "that he's been very happy in his brief service on the *Providential*."

"Has he indeed?" the captain muttered drily.

"Aye, sir, I have," Robbie said earnestly.

The captain turned from the table on which his charts were spread and strolled to his desk. "Mr. Parslow, you may go about your duties. Midshipman Garvin and I can discuss this matter without you."

"Aye, aye, sir," the first lieutenant said, saluting briskly. Then, with a last warning glance at Robbie, he went quickly from the cabin.

The captain sat down behind his desk. "You may stand at ease, Garvin. This is not a court martial. There's no need to make yourself blue-deviled over this matter. There's nothing punitive in the transfer, you know. I've said nothing in my report to damage your swift progress to Admiral of the Fleet."

Robbie reddened. "Did I give you the impression that I'm over-eager for promotion, sir? Is that the reason for—?"

"No, no, of course not."

"Then I don't see why—"

Tris frowned at him. "Come now, fellow, you know the reason. Let's hear no more rubbish about how 'happy' you are to be on board this ship. I think we both know how far that is from the truth."

"But it *is* the truth, sir, I assure you! If my mother and sister made you think otherwise—"

"Dash it, boy, I don't wish to involve myself in a personal discussion of this matter. I simply wish to assure you that this is not a matter to cause you or your family the slightest grief. In a short while you'll be asigned to another ship—one, I'm sure, with equal or better opportunities for—"

"But I don't *want* another ship!" the boy burst out. "Do you think I don't know how desirable it is to win a berth on this ship? All the middies know that they get the best navigational training, the finest strategical experience, the fairest—"

"That's *enough*, Garvin." Tris was becoming uncomfortable. He had not expected the boy to object to the transfer. Quite the reverse, in fact. He hadn't counted on being pressed for an explanation. "It won't do you any good to go on in this vein. My mind is made up. Take it in stride. In a few months, it won't matter a jot. Good luck to you."

He turned his attention to the log book on his desk. Robbie, crushed, turned to go. "It's because you came to Wyndham, isn't it?" he muttered under his breath.

"What?" the captain asked, his head coming up angrily. *"What's* that you said?"

"Don't think you can deny it!" Robbie accused, turning around facing the captain bravely. "If you hadn't come to Wyndham and met my mother and sister, this would never have happened."

Tris glowered at him. "I don't bring my personal business on board this ship!"

"Well, you did this time!" Robbie shot back. "If you didn't know anything about my personal life, you'd never even have *noticed* me."

"Mr. Garvin," Tris snapped, using his authority in place of his reason, "I don't like your tone."

"I know," the boy muttered, close to tears, "but what have I to lose now? Everyone always says how f-fair you are. Do you think it's fair to take it out on m-me just because . . . because . . ." He put up his chin belligerently. ". . . just because you had some sort of quarrel with my sister?"

Tris slammed his hand down on the desk furiously, making the poor boy jump. But he was angrier with himself than with Robbie. How had he made such a mull of this affair? "Your sister has nothing to do with this," he said, keeping his anger under tight restraint. "It's just because I don't like personal involvement with my staff that I took this action."

"But if the personal involvement is between you and Jenny —?" Robbie ventured.

"Damnation, Robbie," Tris burst out, "I thought you'd be overjoyed! Why this sudden about-face now?"

"It's not an about-face. I never wanted to leave this ship."

"That's not the impression I received from . . . ." He looked at the boy with considerable chagrin. "But never mind all that. Just take my word for it that the transfer is for the best. Now get out of here and let me get back to work."

"But—"

"Did you *hear* me, Mr. Garvin? *Out*!"

Robbie choked back a rush of tears. "Aye, aye, sir," he managed to utter and turned away. "I *knew*, when Jenny slapped me that day, that I'd find myself in trouble," he mumbled to himself as he shuffled to the door.

Tris lifted his head abruptly. "What was that you said?"

"Nothing, sir. Only aye, aye, sir."

"No. After that."

"Oh. Sorry, sir, it was . . . only grumbling."

The captain got up and came around his desk. "It was something about Jenny."

"Oh, yes. She slapped me that day, you see. I knew right off it would mean trouble."

"She *slapped* you?"

"Yes, sir. Never did such a thing before in her life."

Tris looked at the boy sharply. "But . . . why?"

"I don't really know. It was the day you paid us a visit . . . right after you left. I've never seen her in such a state, so I knew right off you'd quarreled."

"You mean she just slapped you without provocation?"

Robbie had no idea why the captain was studying him so intently. "Well, I had only asked . . ." He hesitated.

"Go on. You had only asked what?"

"I'd only asked what she'd done to anger you."

"And then she slapped you?"

Robbie blinked up at him. Why was the captain so interested? "Well, I may have asked her the question once or twice more before she did it."

"But you said nothing else?"

"No, sir. Nothing."

Tris turned back to his desk, his mind whirling. Had he been wrong in accusing Jenny of wishing to wed him for Robbie's sake? If that had been her goal, and she'd been angered by his failure to come up to scratch, she certainly wouldn't have slapped *Robbie* for it. This scrap of information opened up a host of new possibilities. He dropped down on his chair, staring ahead of him thoughtfully.

"Am I dismissed, sir?" Robbie asked from the door.

His eyes focussed on the boy's face. "If I let you stay on this ship, Mr. Garvin—"

The boy's eyes lit. "*Sir?*"

"—will you be able to forget the existence of any personal ties that may connect us?"

"Oh, *yes, sir*! I mean, aye, sir!"

"And you'll never come to me for special consideration, favors or promotions?"

"No, sir!"

"And you're aware, I trust, that life will henceforth be much harder on you than the others, not easier. My knowing you will give you no privileges at all. On the contrary, I'll be all the more likely to keep a critical eye on you. You'll have to watch yourself every minute, get up earlier, work harder and do better than all the other middies put together. Knowing all that, do you still wish me to rescind that transfer?"

"Aye, sir," the boy said, grinning, "I do!"

"Very well, let me have those papers. Report to Mr. Parslow and tell him I've changed my mind. He'll reassign you."

"Aye, aye, sir. *Thank* you, sir!"

Tris waved him away and turned his attention to his log. Robbie ran eagerly to the door, but there he paused. He turned and walked with trepidation back to the captain's desk. "Captain?"

Tris didn't look up. "Yes?"

"I just want to say . . . you won't be sorry. I promise."

The captain looked up at him with a frown, but Robbie was almost certain he could detect a gleam of amusement in the back of his eyes. "Midshipman Garvin," he said with gruff authority, "I have work to do, and so do you. Take yourself out of my sight!"

Chapter Twenty-two

As soon as Lady Rowcliffe received Jenny's tentatively worded response to her invitation, she sent her carriage to Wyndham to pick up the girl. Jenny could scarcely believe, as the carriage rumbled over the cobbled city streets, that it wasn't a dream. Everything had happened so quickly. Her mother had made no objection to her leaving (in fact she'd reminded Jenny that she'd tried for years to convince her to go to London to stay with her old friend Millicent Hopgood, but Jenny had refused. "Now," she'd said, "you may at last have an opportunity to arrange an eligible match for yourself. After the last debacle, I was almost on the point on giving up hope."), Sally Clement had given her the gift of a fur tippet to wear in town, Uncle Alistair had sent his blessing and three hundred pounds to cover her expenses, she'd packed one undersized portmanteau, and here she was!

From the moment she arrived, Jenny realized that Andrea had been right—it *was* Jenny whom Lady Rowcliffe wished to see. Not only was her ladyship's welcome sincerely warm and affectionate, but she showed, in a dozen small ways, how delighted she was to have Jenny's company. She'd prepared her bedroom with brand-new bed-hangings and draperies, filled the wardrobe with gowns and clothes that fit Jenny to perfection, provided her with her own abigail, kept fresh flowers by her bedside and inquired, daily, before making any plans, just what it was that Jenny would prefer to do. Never before had Jenny been made so much of.

But the moment that most touched her heart was her first glimpse of Lady Rowcliffe's private sitting room. There, hanging in a gilt frame over her ladyship's little Sheraton writing table, was Toby's sketch. "Why, that's . . . that's *me*!" she exclaimed in amazement.

"Yes, it is," Lady Rowcliffe said, smiling. "I had it framed as soon as I returned from Wyndham. I love to look at it, you know. Whenever I sit down to do my accounts, I find myself gazing up at it. It never fails to give ma a lift."

The two women got on famously. It was a delight to learn, as they visited the theaters, opera houses, museums, libraries and shops, that they both had similar tastes. They discovered that they liked the same sorts of plays, that they both preferred orchestral music to opera and that, when possible, each would rather walk to a destination than call for the carriage. It was not surprising, therefore, that they soon became comfortably intimate and that, one rainy evening, Jenny revealed to her new friend the whole story of her association with Lady Rowcliffe's son.

Lady Rowcliffe listened to the tearful recital with rapt attention. The irritation she'd felt toward Jenny for misjudging her son's character was soon forgotten in her sympathy for the girl's pain. When Jenny's account was concluded, Lady Rowcliffe said very little. Even though she'd learned enough to realize that only a minor misunderstanding now stood between her son and this girl who was already like a daughter to her, she did not intend to interfere. It would be more satisfying, she decided, for the lovers to find their own way into each other's arms than for her to push them. Tris would be back in a few months—not too late for them to rediscover each other and settle their differences.

It was clear to Lady Rowcliffe that Jenny was suffering, and she determined to do everything she could to ease the girl's pain. She took her to the theater, the shops and the exhibits. She held three small dinners at home and invited Toby Boyce to insure that the shy girl would have one familiar companion to talk to besides herself. And she took Jenny with her to two parties, where she watched with interest as various young men tried to make an impression on the reserved but interesting new female who Lady Rowcliffe had taken up. She was relieved to see that Jenny showed no more than a polite interest in any of the gentlemen who came her way. Lady Rowcliffe would not be serving her son a good turn if she were the instrument through which Jenny found herself another man to love.

For Jenny, the London visit was a strange mixture of joy and pain. Bereft of both a lover and a friend, Jenny could not be happy. And although Lady Rowcliffe's devoted attentions did wonders for her self-esteem, Jenny found that living in the house that was Tris Allenby's home was a constant reminder of the wound in her heart. There was a painting of a young Tris standing with his mother in a garden which hung over the fireplace in the drawing room. Though the boy in the painting was only eight, the features were instantly recognizable, and the painting drew her eye like a magnet whenever she was in the room. His bedroom was just down the hall from hers, and every time she passed it she felt a little spasm of pain. On a shelf in the dining room was a model of his first ship, and the stairway wall was covered with pictures and mementos of his voyages and battles.

But the ache of these constant reminders was a small price to pay for what she received from Lady Rowcliffe. Their association was a revelation to Jenny. Every remark she made was appreciated, every mood acknowledged, and every wish respected. Jenny could tell even from the attitudes of the servants that in this household she was of first importance.

Lady Rowcliffe encouraged Jenny to play the piano as much as she wished. The music room was situated in the back of the house, and Jenny went there every morning after breakfast to play. Lady Rowcliffe often sat and listened, working on her embroidery or merely leaning back in her chair with eyes closed and lips smiling in pleasure. It was a favorite time of day for them both, for her ladyship loved having her house filled with music, while, for Jenny, it was the one time of day when the pain that always pressed upon her chest would momentarily recede. Her playing required her utmost concentration. When her mind was engaged in the challenges of harmony and counterpoint, she couldn't think of other things.

One morning, about a week after Jenny's arrival in London, the two ladies sat lingering over their breakfast coffees. Although almost eleven, they seemed unable to shake themselves from a rather pleasant lethargy. The rain was pattering upon the windows, which made the warmth of the breakfast room even more inviting than usual, and neither of them wished to unsettle the cozy atmosphere. But at last, Lady Rowcliffe roused herself. "I ought to do some work on my household accounts this morning, my love," she said with a sigh. "Why don't you spend the time going through the contents of the chest in the music room? My late husband was very fond of playing the pianoforte (though he was not as talented as you are), and he collected a great number of piano compositions. I refer to the chest under the far window. Perhaps you'll find some pleasant surprises among the collection. I think Rowcliffe's taste, if not his technique, was very good."

Jenny went off with an eager step, as if to explore a treasure. Lady Rowcliffe smiled as she watched the girl disappear down the hall, and then she turned in the other direction to the stairs. She had mounted the fourth step when she heard a key rattle in the lock of the front door. She stood still, transfixed in surprise. Only Tris had a key to her door, and, as far as she knew, he was far out to sea.

But it *was* Tris who opened the door. He was disheveled, spattered with rain and breathless. "Mama, there you are. Good! I have only a moment, and I must see you."

"Tris! Good God, is anything amiss? Why haven't you sailed?"

"We don't sail until tomorrow." He pulled out the key, closed the door and came to the stairs. "You'll think I've taken leave of my senses," he said sheepishly, looking up at her. "In fact, I'm not sure I haven't."

"You've left the ship?" she asked incredulously.

"Yes. I put the first lieutenant in charge. Naturally, this is the worst time to take French leave. I feel like a fourth form schoolboy cutting class."

"But what's happened?"

"Nothing, really. A change of heart, perhaps. I don't know. I had a talk with Robbie Garvin yesterday, and something he said . . . Do you think, Mama, that I'm unhinged to wish to make one more attempt to talk to Jenny?"

"You want to talk to Jenny? *Today*? But you're *sailing* tomorrow."

"Yes, but somehow I couldn't face waiting three months or more before . . . ! Dash it all, you *do* think I'm unhinged."

"I don't know if I'd go so far as to call you unhinged, love, but you're certainly not very coherent. Are you intending to ride all the way to Wyndham in one day?"

"And return to the ship tonight, yes. Unless you convince me that I've lost my mind. You see, Robbie told me that she slapped him that day . . . right after we had our talk. I don't know why I find that fact so significant, but it seems to me—"

From down the hall came the unmistakable sound of the piano being played. The notes were faint at first, and somewhat hesitant, but they soon became more firm and sure. The music itself was unfamiliar to Tris, but the style of the playing . . .

He stared up at his mother, his face growing pale. "Mama, *who*—?"

She looked down at him and shrugged, her lips curving in the very slightest smile. He stared at her for one more moment in frozen astonishment, and then, with a gasp, ran down the hall.

Lady Rowcliffe pattered down the stairs and peered after him, her heart pounding in excitement. Then, with a youthful skip, she went to the bell-pull near the door and rang for the butler. He came running up from below to find his mistress prancing about the hallway in a delighted dance. "Ah, Lockhurst," she said in a sort of whisper, gliding to a stop and taking a more dignified stance, "do you remember those bottles of Montrachet that I hid away for a special occasion?"

"Yes, my lady, I do," he answered, whispering in return.

"Well, then, I'd like you to get them out at once. How quickly do you think you can have them chilled? In half-an-hour, do you think?"

If the butler was puzzled by the whispering, he made no sign. With a bow, he turned to do her bidding, but the door knocker sounded at that moment. Lockhurst opened the door to Toby Boyce. "Good Morning, Mr. Boyce," he whispered, putting a finger to his lips.

"Good morning," Toby answered, lowering his voice obediently. "Ah, good day, your ladyship," he greeted her cheerfully. "Why are we whispering?"

"Can't you hear? Jenny is playing," Lady Rowcliffe murmured. She seemed to be listening avidly. "I wonder why she's still . . ." She frowned worriedly and shook her head. Then, looking up at Toby as if she found it difficult to concentrate on his presence, she asked, "What are you doing here at this hour? Shouldn't you be working? Is no one in the world where he's supposed to be this morning?"

Toby handed his hat to Lockhurst, who took it and went off. "Mr. Fuseli is in one of his pets today, having had a terrible argument with someone at the Academy last night. And after cursing and ranting for an hour, he threw me out for the day. I was wondering if you and Jenny would like to go with me to—"

The music ceased abruptly. Lady Rowcliffe's breath seemed to catch in her throat. "Hush, Toby dear, hush," she hissed excitedly. "I don't want them to hear us. We mustn't do anything to disturb them."

"Them?"

"I can't explain yet. You'll learn all about it in due course. But I'm much too nervous to discuss anything now." She took a few steps toward the stairs on tiptoe and peered down the hallway. Satisfied at what she saw, she tiptoed back to him. "I don't want to do anything but sit here on the stairs and wait. You may sit with me if you wish, but you must promise not to make a sound for—let me see . . . what would be a reasonable time?—for a quarter of an hour. Yes, the passage of a quarter of an hour should give us ample evidence of satisfactory progress. If no one emerges from the music room by that time, Toby, I shall feel confident enough to take a deep breath."

Tris didn't really believe his eyes or ears. He stood motionless in the music-room doorway gazing at the girl playing the piano as if she were a manifestation of the supernatural. But she looked real enough. She was leaning toward her music sheet, her eyes intent on the page while her fingers moved with firm assurance over the keyboard. Her brow was furrowed in concentration and her mouth slightly open. Her hair was braided and twisted into a knot at the back of her head, just as it had been when he'd last laid eyes on her, the grey light from the window behind her accenting the little tendrils which escaped from bondage and made a soft frame around her face. Yes, he realized as his mind recovered from the shock, she was very real indeed.

He couldn't bring himself to interrupt her. Not permitting himself even to take a deep breath, he stood watching her, letting his eyes drink in every detail of her face. He had no sense of the passage of time. The music flowed around him, seeming to encircle them both in a world of their own, in which there was no time, no distance and no possibility of invasion from outside. He felt content, at peace and without any urge to do anything but stay just where he was.

But suddenly, for no apparent reason, she looked up and met

his eye. Her hands froze in the air, and for a moment she remained as motionless as glass, except for the dilation of her eyes. Then she gave a gasping breath. "*Tris*!"

He didn't know that he was moving toward her or that he'd lifted his arms. All he knew was that she rose from the bench and flew into them. Their arms tightened about each other, and, when he could think, he realized that she was sobbing into his shoulder. "Jenny, *don't*," he murmured into her ear. "I'll do whatever you say, be whatever you wish! I'll open the brig, throw the lash overboard, even make your blasted brother an admiral, if only you'll have me!"

She gave a bubbling sort of laugh and tried to speak, but he lifted her face and kissed her with such burning intensity that she gave up the struggle. There would be time later for explanations, apologies, confessions and declarations. There would be time later for all the words. But for now, this closeness, this warmth, this heady joy was quite enough.

After ten minutes, Lady Rowcliffe could bear no more suspense. She jumped up from the stair and tiptoed down the hall, Toby, burning with curiosity, following at her heels. When she reached the open door of the music room, she hid behind the doorpost and cautiously inched her head forward until she could see inside. What she saw caused her to wave an arm trumphantly in the air. When she'd seen enough, she tiptoed away, and Toby took her place. He would have gasped aloud if she hadn't clapped a hand over his mouth.

She took his arm and pulled him away, back down the hall and into the dining room. She carefully closed the door and then gave a loud crow of triumph.

Toby, flabbergasted, fell upon a chair. "Captain Allenby and *Jenny*? I never *dreamed*—"

Lady Rowcliffe chortled. "That's because your artist's eye is not yet fully developed," she said with sublime authority. "*I* could see at *once*—"

But Lockhurst came in at that moment with a tray of glasses and three bottles of wine. "Shall I open one, my lady?" he inquired.

"Yes, of *course*," her ladyship declared.

"But . . . aren't you going to wait for them to come out of

the music room and make an announcement?" Toby asked, still stunned.

"*Wait*? It might take all *day*." She lifted an empty glass from the tray and held it up to the butler with a wide grin. "Lockhurst," she ordered, "pour!"